Communication Tools to Empower You

What you can do to achieve your goals

Zalman Puchkoff MSU, PFA

authorHOUSE®

AuthorHouse™
1663 Liberty Drive, Suite 200
Bloomington, IN 47403
www.authorhouse.com
Phone: 1-800-839-8640

First published by AuthorHouse 5/27/2009

ISBN: 978-1-4389-5368-7 (sc)

Printed in the United States of America
Bloomington, Indiana

This book is printed on acid-free paper.

DEDICATION

Nobody does anything by themselves, and yes we need to help ourselves by getting people to help us. Without the help of my wife Janet, who was an award-winning direct mail writer and creator of many magazine sweepstake packages, this book would have been a jumble of thoughts and misconnected ideas, thrown together and connected by illiterate punctuation, even with using a spellchecker.

She has given me the confidence, and the time, to put down on paper what I have learned, and the way we live together creating our relationship anew, each day.

We celebrate our marriage each year on Sept. 8th, by repeating the marriage vows we said to each other that day, with Janet wearing the same fuchsia colored straw hat she wore at our wedding. We cry, we kiss, and pop open a bottle of champagne! Life is good; we work at it.

Book cover and back design by Perry Sandlewick; perry@upowerit.com

TABLE OF CONTENTS

Dedication iii
Section I
 The Reality Analysis Systems® 1
 Expectation vs Reality 3
 Part I
Introduction 11
Overview 13
Different Types of Upsets 15
CHAPTER I: Belief It or Not 17
CHAPTER II: Consumers & Suppliers 19
CHAPTER III: The 7 Expectation Issues 25
CHAPTER IV: The Upset Analyzers® 32
CHAPTER V: Examples of Upsets And Resolution 34
CHAPTER VI: Disease And Upsets 38
CHAPTER VII: How Good Can You Stand It 41
Section II
 1, Forms 45
 2. Which Analyzer to Use 47
 3. Directions: How to fill out an Analyzer 57
  3a. Consumer Past Analyzer™ 57
  3b. Consumer Future Analyzer™ 59
  3c. Supplier Past Analyzer™ 59
  3d. Supplier Future Analyzer™ 61
 4. Explanation of the 7 Issues 62
  4a. Consumer Past 62
  4b. Consumer Future 64
  4c. Supplier Past 66
  4d. Supplier Future 68
 5. The Meaning of the Connections 70
 6. Plans of Action 72
  6a. Consumer Past & Future – Issue I 72
  6a. Consumer Past & Future – Issue II 74
  6a. Consumer Past & Future – Issue III 76
  6a. Consumer Past & future – Issue IV 78
  6a. Consumer Past & Future – Issue V 80
  6a. Consumer Past & Future – Issue VI 82
  6a. Consumer Past & Future – Issue VII 84
  6b. Supplier Past & Future – Issue I 86
  6b. Supplier Past & Future – Issue II 88
  6b. Supplier Past & Future – Issue III 90
  6b. Supplier Past & Future – Issue IV 92

6b. Supplier Past & Future – Issue V	94
6b. Supplier Past & Future – Issue VI	96
6b. Supplier Past & Future – Issue VII	98
7. Catch 22	100
Section III	
Part II Through Supplier Eyes	105
Part III Through Consumer Eyes	135
Section IV	
Part IV Personal and Business Analyzers	160
1. The Relationship Analyzer™	162
2. The Interview Analyzer™	174
3. The Career Analyzer™	185
4. The House Buyer's Analyzer™	190
5. A Competitive Advantage™	203
Section V	
The Beginning	221

SECTION I
THE REALITY ANALYSIS SYSTEMS®

EXPECTATION VS REALITY

What do you expect to get out of this book?

What magic words will transform your life into what you've wanted ... maybe featuring something that other people have that you don't have?

I'll tell you. There are no magic words! So how do other people succeed and you're always in survival? Their expectations are based upon their intention to succeed. If your intention is to succeed, you will succeed. If you fail, then it was your intention to fail.

Intention always shows up in your universe

If it is your intention to use the tools in this book and create what you want in your life, you will learn how to use the tools and work at it and succeed. Otherwise, this will be just another exercise in self-help that didn't work. The truth believed is a lie!

Self-help is a misnomer. You can't help yourself unless you use tools you already have. You have to get help from somewhere, use other resources, and then use those tools to build.

Think of anything that can be built or made in this world that can be constructed without using a tool of some kind or another.

You can't build anything without using tools. And nothing was ever accomplished by thinking alone. The cognitive word is 'do'. You have to do something to accomplish something.

Tools can be defined as any resource that is used as an adjunct to build or create.

The tools that you'll be learning to use are communication tools - language. They express our thoughts and ideas and attitudes that must be put into motion – by doing. But you can't be objective and effective when you get upset.

During any interaction, you are either a Consumer or a Supplier of information or action. Consumers get things, take things, and Suppliers give things, offer things.

The purpose in life as a Consumer is to get what you want
and not get what you don't want.

3

The purpose in life as a Supplier is to give what you want
and not give what you don't want to give.

You already have the power to create your life the way you want it to be, but perhaps you don't have the tools or forgot how to use the tools you have to accomplish what you want in life. The tools in this book will provide you with the means and/or re-instill the power you already have to use new tools – communication tools -- to help you build what you've always wanted to build.

I'm a businessman and among other things that I've done, I was a professional magician. When performing, I would tell my audience:

"First, I'm going to tell you what I'm going to do
then I'll show you what I'm going to do
and then I'll do it – so you won't ask me to do it again."

I entertained them and they almost always asked me to do it again. My answer, "I wish my wife would say that." They also said, "Show me how to do it." And I would answer "Sure, how many weeks or months do you have to learn?" They didn't believe me.

I'm not going to entertain you. I will show you how to use communication tools, but you have to do all the practicing. (That's how you get to Carnegie Hall). It's up to you to figure out first what you want to build as it's your life!

Give a man a fish and he'll eat for a day
Teach him how to fish and he'll sit in the boat
And drink beer all day.

The Reality Analysis Systems® of tools used in this book arises out of a methodology that allows you to see the difference between what you expect and the reality of the situation. The six different analyzer programs deal with different types of relationships, personally and in business.

You will learn how to use contextual tools which are the six analyzer programs. You will see – on paper – graphically, when you fill out an analyzer, your expectations as compared to the reality of the situation. In addition, you will learn how to use conceptual tools, which are the language tools that in time you will internalize, like learning a whole new language.

Imagine that you've come to the end of this book, and you've read it from cover to cover and you've filled out every analyzer in the Reality Analysis Systems™ series. You've made copious notes in the margins and underlined everything that had some impact on you. You probably have lots of questions and possibly doubts about what you've read.

What are you supposed to do with all this information?

If you are a little overwhelmed, you should be. You've been given TMI, Too Much Information at one time. Building anything requires the ability to learn how to use new tools. But you can't learn how to use more than one tool at a time. It's not about multi-tasking. It's about practicing one thing until you become an expert at it.

But you have to know what to build, and that's the first step. You must clearly define a plan, much as an architect needs a blueprint; what do you want to build?

If all you have is a hammer, every problem looks like a nail

If you don't know what you want to build, how do you know which tools to use to build it?

The first tool you need to learn how to use deals with understanding Consumer and Supplier roles, which are in program #1, The Emotional Toolbox™, the companion guide to the Upset Analyzers™. This program allows you to resolve your upsets with other people and to prevent yourself from getting upset in the future.

Using The Emotional Toolbox™, you will learn:

> How to stop getting upset with other people
> How to stop taking it out on your body
> How to prevent yourself from getting upset
> How to tell when you're being conned
> Why people get upset
> …and more

When you have completed your first analyzer, you will then have the tools to read, "Through Supplier Eyes", and "Through Consumer Eyes" which are conceptual tools. They allow you to make changes in your life based upon choices you now have, that you didn't think you had.

You then have the opportunity to choose any one or more of the five analyzer programs to fill out.

Before you fill out an analyzer, you must ask yourself: WHAT AM I BUILDING? If you can clearly define your goal you will know which tools you will need to help you build what you want. If you don't want to build anything, you don't have to pick up any tools.

Isn't this simple when you put it on paper?

I will empower you, teach you how to use new tools so you can build whatever you want. That is my intention. It can be how to feel like a kid again and catch fish with a pole and worms in a lake or create a new political party called, the 'Empowerment Party.'

Accept the fact that there are things that you don't know and that you are capable of learning how to use new tools – at your own pace – on your own time schedule. Be prepared to follow the directions for filling out the analyzer forms.

Life works when you follow the directions!

We will start with the Emotional Toolbox™ program. Everyone gets upset at one time or another, so this is a good place to start. The 7 Reality Analysis Systems® chapters discuss Consumer and Supplier roles around which, all of the analyzers were created and explain the core technology of why people get upset.

If you glossed over reading this part, when you get to the end you would have read the whole book without knowing what to do next! You're rushing through life ... to where?

Become an expert on a particular situation, so when it comes up with the same or a different person you'll be ready to solve it. Keep on practicing and fill out the analyzer again and again until it becomes second nature to you, then move on to the next program and set of tools. If you solve the first problem, consider it an accident, but if you succeed the second time, you're now an expert.

I'm not the one who's doing the magic now. I've told you what to do, how to do it, and I'm giving you the communication tools in this book for you to take over. Now you're the magician ...transform your life into whatever you want it to be for yourself.

After filling out The Upset Analyzers™ ask yourself, what did you learn? What were your expectations and what was the outcome, the reality?

The Reality Analysis Systems® series are structured for you to see objectively what options are available to you when you have a problem, and offer you choices and plans of action to solve your problem. The analyzers don't care about what you feel or what you think.

Let's look at the choices that you are given when your expectation doesn't match the reality of the situation:

1. You can change your expectation
2. You can change the reality
   if you can't do either,
3. You can leave the relationship

If you choose to do nothing, you will continue to remain upset.

If you don't like the choices offered to you, you're not paying attention to the ruthless rules of reality, the 3 R's. These are the only choices you have! Not to be significant, here are just a few of them, and I'm sure you have a few of your own, based upon your own life experiences.

- Never cook bacon while you're naked
- Never look through the rear view mirror to see where you're driving
- Never pack your car keys in your airline luggage

Did you play on the monkey bars in the playground as a child? I did. I had lots of fun swinging through and making believe I was a snake slithering through them on the different levels. I even stood up on the top rung and straddled two bars and I also did chin-ups. It didn't occur to me that I could get hurt.

Monkey bars don't care how you feel!

The world doesn't care either, only you do, so it's up to you to make choices that work for you. Notice I didn't say right choices or wrong choices. If you create a situation that you don't like, the question to ask is, 'who owns the problem?' If it's you, do something about it and clean it up.

How do you do that? Go into the hall closet, put on the raincoat, rain hat, galoshes, gloves, and don't forget the shovel, because you've got a lot of shit to clean up and just wade through! When you're finished, make sure you've hosed down everything nice and clean and hang everything back in the closet and take a shower. Now you have to remember what you have to go through the next time you make dirty!

I digressed from the three choices:

1. To change your expectation means that you realize that the other person will never change, never see your side of the story, and you have to do the changing in your approach and attitude. Don't tell me that person does change on occasions, and you're opting to hold out until they do change, otherwise you'll feel disloyal.

Mice are smarter than humans. After 3 attempts to find the food at the end of the maze after it's taken away, they'll give up – humans never do!

Don't expect the situation to change or the other person to change. They won't. You have to change your expectation and see the other person for who he or she is and respond accordingly.

2. To change the reality means to do something, change something, so that you don't have to keep on accepting the same situation; you are doing something differently. The other person will fight you on this and to improve the relationship, you have to be more aggressive and positive, and stick to your guns.

3. To leave the relationship means that you cannot change either your expectation or the reality of the situation, so you are walking away from it, leaving it. There is nothing to change! This is not a sign of weakness.

Read the meaning and plans of action on any issue to help you keep grounded and on-track. It takes about two to three weeks to establish new patterns of behavior. And don't worry. Your personality isn't going to change; it's just that your approach to problem solving can now be objective, not subjective.

For those readers who are interested in understanding and seeing the thread that links the seven Chakras through the interpersonal upset analyzer issues with business issues and cognitive therapy issues, on into Consumer and Supplier issues, the mapping is charted below. You'll see that issues and relationships are not confined to just a single area in one's life. It permeates throughout.

Inter-person issues are those that concern relationships with other people and the analyzers address these issues. Intra-person issues are those that deal with relationships and problems with oneself or with a deity, which are not discussed in this book.

Reality Analysis Systems® Methodology
Issues Relationships

Chakra	Upset Issue	Business Issue	Expectation	Cognitive therapy	Key Issue	Consumer Upset Issue	Supplier Upset Issue
Wisdom	VII	Make-to-order or Supply from stock	Surprise	Achievement	What to give or get?	New vs old response	Giving old or new response
Perception	VI	Recall defects?	Agreements	Perfectionism	Tell or know About changes	Changes to agreements	Changing agreements
Communication	V	Negotiate or Stipulate	Alternatives	Entitlement	"Who" negotiates?	Alternatives or not	Giving alternatives
Heart	IV	Profile for Future buying	Understanding	Love	'Who' is the Consumer?	Being understood	Giving understanding
Power	III	Rent or Sell	Blame	Omnipotence	Consumers feelings	Blame for feelings	Taking blame or not
Pleasure	II	Deliver now or In the future	Priorities	Autonomy	When to give or get response	Setting others Priorities	Setting own priorities
Security	I	Bill customer or Take cash	Feedback	Approval	Giving or getting (dis)approval	Giving or not giving feedback	Getting feedback

Part I.

INTRODUCTION

The Emotional Toolbox® contains communication tools designed to give you insight about your own beliefs and expectations. They provide opportunities to get rid of any emotional baggage that no longer serves you, and to re-discover what you may have forgotten about yourself:

You hold the power over your own life!

You don't need special training or background to use The Emotional Toolbox®. It is non-judgmental and non-confrontive and is not intended to replace psychological therapy.

This Emotional Toolbox™ booklet is the companion guide to the Upset Analyzers®, which lets you see graphically, on paper:

- Why you got upset
- Which of the seven expectation issues upset you
- What you can do to resolve it
- How to prevent yourself from getting upset in the future

After testing the technology with people from all walks of life who have experienced different upsetting situations, I find that it has one fundamental characteristic:

It works!

Zalman Puchkoff

OVERVIEW

The Emotional Toolbox™ lets you look at upsetting situations in a new way, so you can see the difference between what you expected to happen and what actually did happen.

Some of the underlying principles of the methodology:

- Upsetting situations constantly occur in life
- Upsets affect our ability to be clear about how to achieve goals
- Upsets affect physical well being
- Unresolved upsets get in the way of developing relationships
- Unresolved upsets stunt intellectual and emotional development

The practical communication tools include:

1. CONSUMER AND SUPPLIER ROLES
This is the "power" tool. During any interaction, you are either a Consumer or a Supplier of information or action. Knowing which role you were in when you got upset helps you choose which role you need to be in to resolve it.

2. CHOICES
This is the "strategy" tool that helps you define and formulate a plan of action to resolve your upsets.

3. THE 7 EXPECTATION ISSUES
This is the "reasoning" tool that helps you identify which area, or areas, of relationship -- there are 7 of them -- caused you to become upset. As you learn which areas are problematic for you, you will be able to stop a potentially upsetting situation from turning into an upset.

4. THE UPSET ANALYZERS®
These "identification" tools provide a graphic X-ray of the situation that's upsetting you. There are four Upset Analyzers® -- Consumer Past, Supplier Past, Consumer Future, Supplier Future -- in the program. You fill out a Past Upset Analyzer® about something that already happened, and then use the Future Upset Analyzer® when you have devised a plan of action to see if you have resolved your upset. The Upset Analyzers® will help you identify and understand your unmet expectations, which are the glue that holds all upsets together.

As you use the Upset Analyzers® to resolve individual upsets, there's a good chance you'll begin to see a pattern, running like a thread through your life. You will be able to spot which one of the seven issues is your "hot spot", the area of upset over which you have no control and keeps repeating itself. You will see that to resolve one conflict is to approach solving related conflicts.

The Future Upset Analyzer® is also used as a "testing tool" to help you resolve an upsetting situation that you think will happen in the future. Deciding on a plan of action beforehand will help you to be objective and to establish realistic, achievable goals. As an example, if you're upset now because you don't think the boss will give you the raise you want when you ask him next week, the Future Upset Analyzer® will 'coach' you. You cannot be upset in the future. You can only be upset now about an event that you think will happen in the future.

DIFFERENT TYPES OF UPSETS

1. INTERPERSONAL UPSETS
This type of upset deals with situations that occur between you and another person. To use the Upset Analyzers® effectively, you have to be specific about the incident. Fill in the space provided, "I am upset because you_____(you fill in the blanks with your specific upset).

2. INTRAPERSONAL UPSETS
This type of upset deals with situations that involve only you. For instance, you get a flat tire, find that the spare tire is missing from the trunk and know that it was you who took it out and forgot to put it back!

3. THIRD PARTY UPSETS
This type of upset deals with situations that do not involve you directly, i.e. you think someone did or did not do something to someone else. Use the "someone else" as the person with whom you are really upset. That person probably didn't do something you wanted him or her to do ... or perhaps didn't take your advice.

This program can help you learn:

> • when and why you get upset
> • what to do when you get upset
> • the difference between expectation and reality
> • what the seven issues are that cause upsets
> • why most people get upset for the wrong reason
> • how and what to listen for when others speak

You can gain more knowledge about your physical health by learning:

> • where you hold upsets in your body
> • how your body lets you know what's upsetting you
> • the relationship between dis-ease and upsets

You can impact your emotional life by learning:

> • how to improve relationships with your spouse, boss, employees, friends and family members
> • which of your beliefs are serving you and which ones are holding you back

- how to create a win for both parties
- how to stop blaming other people for how you feel
- how to forgive yourself and others
- how to deal with your anger, hurt, fear, and other emotions in a constructive way
- how to ask for what you want without feeling afraid
- how to stop being the victim
- how to recognize mixed messages

Using the tools in the Emotional Toolbox™ and the Upset Analyzers®, you can learn how to reduce your upsets and be more effective -- with anyone, anytime, anyplace!

CHAPTER I: BELIEF IT OR NOT

This chapter is intended to help you detect when your beliefs are serving you and when they are not.

> We communicate beliefs when we use the words "should" and "shouldn't" and "ought to" in our conversation and in our thinking.

> We get upset when we think our beliefs are being challenged.

Beliefs may come from parents, friends and relatives, the environment, or the cultural and religious background in which we live. We hold on to beliefs when we think they work for us, and change them when they don't. For example, as adults we may believe that parents should control their children. But as children we believed that parents should leave us alone.

Others become habitual:

- like saying "please", "thank you" and showing good manners
- always keeping your promises to others
- never trusting anyone you don't know
- defining what a real friend would or wouldn't do for us
- staying in love forever.

Some of our "shoulds" or beliefs protect us while others create problems. If we insist upon holding onto a belief and continue to act in ways that are in conflict with it we will get upset, and if left to continue may lead to long term stress.

In order to see an upsetting situation, we have to separate our actions from our feelings. Then we can match our expectation with the reality of the situation.

We even have little voices in the back of our head that tell us from time to time what we "should" and "shouldn't" do, say, and think! We may express it as, "If I were you, I would... " or, "What you should do is ..."

The Upset Analyzer® compares expectations or beliefs with the reality of a situation. It lets you see whether you need to change either your beliefs to be consistent with your actions, or change your actions to be consistent with your beliefs.

As an example: One woman believed that she "should always be nice", and if she said what was on her mind she was a "bad person." She often found herself ineffective in solving her problems.

In filling out the Upset Analyzer®, she became aware of her internal conflict and realized what she needed to do. She chose to change her behavior, and speak her mind. She gave herself permission to protect her health instead of protecting the other person's feelings. She realized that she could only be responsible for her own feelings, and not those of someone else.

The circumstances could be different and still have a recurring theme. A case in point: A woman's father died. She was extremely upset over the loss of her father for a long time. In filling out a Consumer Upset Analyzer® she saw that she was upset because her father "left her."

When asked to project the same or similar upsetting situation into the future she said, "How could this happen again, I only have one father!" However she also saw in filling out the Consumer Future Upset Analyzer®, that she became upset when anybody "left her," that is, any friend or relative, or whenever a relationship was terminated. She got to see that things change and loved ones do leave.

The Upset Analyzer® allows you to see where your expectations and your reality are mis-matched. The rest is up to you … to decide if holding onto your belief is useful or not.

It takes only as long to change a belief
as it did to adopt one in the first place!

And remember…

DON'T "SHOULD" ON YOURSELF!

While you're filling out the expectation side of the Upset Analyzers®, picture the upsetting situation with the other person in your mind. Listen to the conversation going on in your head. Do you hear yourself using the word "should" or "shouldn't"? If so, your beliefs are showing!

If I have to explain it further, then you don't understand.
Understanding is the booby-prize in life, so accept what is!

CHAPTER II: CONSUMERS & SUPPLIERS

The same terms that are usually used in business, Consumer and Supplier, are used in the Emotional Toolbox™ to explain people's relationships with one another. Consumers are people who use things, buy things, accept things. Suppliers are people who give things, offer things, and provide things.

Your expectation … and the reality of a situation are dependent upon your role as either a Supplier or a Consumer -- how you perceive what is going on at any given time.

Each of the six Reality Analysis systems® programs that follow measure your alignment or misalignment of your expectations with the reality of a situation in both personal and business areas, as Supplier or as a Consumer.

More than 85% of the time people feel that they are Consumers, and upset Consumers, so the Consumer role will be explained first.

THE CONSUMER ROLE

If you are the listener in a conversation and the other person tells you something, gives you something, does something for you, or if you ask for something, you are the Consumer.

The role of the Consumer is to make a request, and to receive a response.

The key words to listen for are:
- Give me	- I need	- I want
- I got	- Will you please	- I don't want

These words identify you as a Consumer. There is power in being a Consumer -- it is the Consumer who initiates all requests for action. If you don't ask for anything, no one will supply it to you.

Have you ever been afraid to ask for something because you thought you wouldn't get it? If so, which upset you more...not asking, or the fear of not getting?

It's easy to switch roles to handle "gives" and "takes" almost simultaneously, however …

> *… You cannot be in both roles at the same time!*

In a conversation with someone, listen carefully to the words that you speak and to the words of the other person.

If you find yourself asking, requesting, wanting, needing, desiring, you are the Consumer.
If you find yourself giving, offering, answering, fulfilling requests, you are the Supplier.

Here are some examples of Consumer roles:

- Child asking mother for an ice cream cone
- Student getting his report card from the teacher
- Teacher receiving an answer to a question
- Employer requesting an employee to work late
- Lover getting a kiss
- Actor taking applause from the audience

As a Consumer, your objective is to get something you want and to not get something you don't want.

You become an upset Consumer when you get something you don't want, or you don't get something you do want.

You may ask someone for something and not get it; or you may get unsolicited advice and be told something that you don't want to hear. Let's look at a potentially upsetting situation.

Keith sends his 22 year-old son Ron a birthday card with a $50 check in it. He expects a thank you note or phone call from his son.

Ron has always received a present of one kind or another from his father on his birthday. He expects his father to know that he appreciates a present without having to tell him.

Who is the Consumer, who is the Supplier? Keith is the Supplier because he gave something to his son. Ron is the Consumer because he received something from his father.

An upset may occur because the father wants to be a Consumer. He wants his son to be a Supplier and acknowledge him with a thank you. Ron does not wish to be a Supplier. He doesn't feel he has to acknowledge his father for the gift. Both want the other person to be in a different role than each really is! Looking at it this way, it's a lot easier to understand how and why our upsets get activated.

To prevent an upset from occurring, each person must communicate to the other in which role he or she wishes to be treated. If not, the other person will treat you as they always have or as they want to. If this is not acceptable to you, you must tell the other person. No one is a mind reader.

Let's look at another potentially upsetting situation.

Jim comes home from work and wants to eat dinner and plunk down in front of the TV. He expects his wife, Joan, to have dinner ready for him.

Joan spent the day cleaning the house, taking care of the children and coaxing the repairman to come to the house and fix the TV which went blank. She would like to be taken out to dinner and a movie.

Who is the Consumer and who is the Supplier?

Jim and Joan are both Consumers. They both want something to be given to them, and they both want the other to supply it. An upset may occur if they both continue to expect to get what each want without coming to some understanding as to who will be the Consumer and who will be the Supplier.

Another example:

> Barbara lives alone on a 33 acre farm, posted with 'no trespassing or hunting' signs. She saw hunters cross her property and told them to leave. One of them said, "Yea, what are you gonna do about it."
>
> Barbara got upset, went into the house and called the sheriff's office. The deputy said he couldn't come out every time someone complained about poachers. Barbara said, "Oh, I don't want you to do anything, I just called to tell you that I'm going to shoot them."

The sheriff was at her house in 3 minutes flat! What had Barbara done? She changed roles from being an upset Consumer to being a Supplier. She supplied the sheriff with information about her intention.

To resolve your upset, you must change roles.

You cannot resolve your upset in the same role in which you got upset. To remain in the same role is to continue to be upset.

THE SUPPLIER ROLE

If you are the speaker in a conversation or you provide or offer something to the other person, you are the Supplier.

The role of the Supplier is to give something and fulfill requests.

The key words to listen for are:

- Do you want...?	- I will	- Can I get you...?
- I won't	- I can	- I am not able to

These words identify you as a Supplier. There is power in being a Supplier -- it is the Supplier who takes action. If you don't act upon the requests, nothing gets accomplished.

Have you ever been afraid to offer something because you thought it wouldn't be accepted? If so, which upset you more ... not offering, or the fear of being rejected? As soon as you stop giving and ask for something, you become the Consumer.

Listen carefully to the words that you speak and to the words of the other person. If you find yourself giving, offering, answering, and fulfilling, or providing, sending, doing -- you are the Supplier.

If you find yourself asking, requesting, wanting, needing, desiring, you are the Consumer.

Here are some examples of Supplier roles:

- Good Humor man giving a child an ice cream cone
- Teacher giving student a report card
- Student offering teacher an answer to a question
- Employee telling his boss that he will stay late
- Lover giving a kiss
- Audience clapping for the performance

As a Supplier, your objective is to give something you want to give and to not give something you don't want to give.

**You become an upset Supplier when you can't give something
you want to give, or you give something you don't want to give.**

When you give someone unsolicited advice and it is not taken (that is, you can't give something you want to give), you may become upset. Other times you may be asked to give something you don't want to give and become upset. These are supplier upsets. Here's a look at a potentially upsetting situation.

Your spouse asks you to go out for the evening with another couple and you think the man is a bore. You may get upset if you say yes because you don't want to give something, that is, your presence for the evening.

You would use the Supplier Past Upset Analyzer® and Supplier Future Upset Analyzer® to resolve the problem.

Not all upsetting situations are the same. Another example: Jane is an experienced real estate broker. Her brother Phil had never been in real estate and she set him up in his own business. Her expectation: Phil would appreciate what she did and listen to her advice about running the business. Phil is the older brother, and at 6' 2" he towers over Jane, who is 5' 4". He literally considered Jane his "little sister" and thought he knew more than she did. His expectation: He didn't need her advice; he can run the business without her interference and show her how smart he is.

Jane will be an upset Supplier if Phil won't take her advice. Phil will be an upset Consumer if Jane won't stop offering what he doesn't want.

You may get upset when you expect the other person to be
in one role and they want to be in the same role as you are!

When two people are Suppliers, there is no communication and possible cause for an upset. When two people are Consumers, there is no communication, and possible cause for an upset. Sometimes a person may appear to be the Supplier and give you something, yet secretly want to be a Consumer and get something from you. This is a "mixed message!" Sound familiar?

On the other hand, a person may appear to be the Consumer and ask you for something, yet secretly want to be a Supplier and give you something (like verbally letting you have it). This is another "mixed message." Is there someone in your life giving you mixed messages?

For effective communication between two people, each person in the interaction must be in a different role. One person must be the Supplier and the other person must be the Consumer. Using the terms Consumer and Supplier to identify the roles takes the charge off potentially upsetting situations and allows you to be clear about what you expected.

When two people talk to each other at the same time, they are both supplying. No communication takes place. Usually they both gradually raise their voices, attempting to shout down the other -- an upset in the making.

When two people "hold it in" and don't talk to one another, no communication takes place. They are both consuming -- an upset in the making.

Try an experiment. Begin talking with someone on any topic, i.e., what you did on your last vacation. Continue talking and do the following:

1. Increase your volume
2. Keep repeating yourself
3. Add gestures, e.g., shake your finger at the other person
4. Tell the other person to shut up and listen to you

These are tactics to emphasize your role as a Supplier. How far does it get you? Now try:

1. Keeping quiet
2. Listening to the other person
3. Asking for more information and clarification on what the person is saying

These are tactics to emphasize your role as a Consumer. What happens to the conversation and to your feelings as a Consumer, and as a Supplier?

Your upset is determined by the role you were in at the time you got upset. In order to resolve your upset, you must change roles -- from being a Consumer to being a Supplier, or vice versa.

Now that you know the function and use of the Supplier and the Consumer roles, as you fill out each analyzer consciously chose the role you are in as you answer each question. In time, you will be able to internalize roles without having to read their description and definition.

CHAPTER III: THE 7 EXPECTATION ISSUES

The more you understand the underlying principles of each issue and how they affect your behavior, the greater the opportunity to resolve your upsets. You will also gain insight on how to prevent a potentially upsetting situation from bothering you!

1. THE RESPONSE EXPECTATION: "How can you say that?"

Response expectation is just what the name implies ... one person has an expectation of how the other person will respond to a statement or an action.

When we anticipate one type of response and get another, we may become upset.

As a Consumer, we get upset when we want something new or different from the Supplier, and don't get it. Or when we want a familiar response and get a surprise.

As a Supplier, we get upset when we give one type of response and the Consumer wants a different one. Or if we're called upon to give something we don't want to give.

When you greet someone with, "How are you?", are you anticipating the habitual response, "Fine, how are you?"...or do you want a new and unusual response, i.e., really hear how the person is?

Sometimes our responses are habitual, because it takes less energy and thought than to create a response "in the moment." If the Consumer expects the Supplier to respond favorably to a request and the Supplier responds negatively or with a cliche, that may cause an upset because it's not what the Consumer wanted or expected.

If you ask for something as a Consumer, are you prepared to take "no" for an answer? If "no" is not acceptable, you may become upset. On the other hand, if you don't ask for what you want, you will not get it -- unless, of course, the other person can read your mind!

If you want to give something to someone as a Supplier, can you accept a refusal of your offer? If not, you may get upset.

2. CHANGES TO AGREEMENTS: "You broke your promise!"

This issue has probably caused more upsets than any other. As a child we remember when the phrase "a promise is a promise" was sacred. Upsets may occur when agreements or promises are broken.

Agreements can be: (1)one sided, where only one person thinks that both parties have agreed to some stipulation (2)two sided, where both parties agree verbally or in writing or (3)third party, where two people agree based upon something from a third person or institution.

Once an agreement is made, we assume it will remain in force until it is changed or broken.

If a new secretary makes coffee for the boss during the first week of work, the boss may assume he or she will always make the coffee. As long as the secretary continues, that's okay. However the boss may get upset when he or she stops making coffee.

An agreement is considered broken by the Consumer when he or she doesn't agree with changes made by the Supplier. If the secretary tells the boss that making coffee takes time away from getting the work out, the boss can accept that answer as a changed agreement.

When you receive news of a changed or broken agreement, you become the Consumer, and make the decision to become upset or not. As an example:

When a husband left to go to work, he promised to take his wife out to dinner. He then called near quitting time to say he had to work late. If the wife thinks he broke his promise, she will get upset. If she thinks there's a valid reason, she may consider it a changed agreement and not get upset. If the wife demands that the husband "repent" or somehow atone for the wrongdoing, then she wants him to get rid of the upset. That is impossible.

The person who breaks an agreement can do nothing to repair the break. Even a sincere apology cannot alter the situation and resolve an upset. The upset is now in the past and nothing either party may do or say can change that fact.

Only the upset party can do the forgiving

Relationships are built on trust, the fiber that binds them. Every broken agreement is a break in that trust. Break enough fibers and the relationship falls apart. The Consumer, the one whose trust was broken, is the only one who can reweave the fibers of the relationship!

If you recognize that some type of agreement controls interactions and relationships and that all agreements can change, you create an important shift in your outlook. As the Supplier, you can stop taking every request for change as a command, or as the Consumer every change as a rejection.

Rigidity about changing an agreement may occur in the absence of favorable options. As the Supplier, provide options and choices to the Consumer when you have to make changes. If you promised to have merchandise delivered to your customer on Wednesday by ground transportation and you couldn't ship it out on time, offer to ship it by air at your expense. Or ask the customer if he would accept delivery on Thursday, and explain what happened.

> TIP: If the other person both attacks and defends with explanations of the reasons why he or she broke the agreement, you can bet you are being conned!

The husband who berates his wife when he broke his promise to take her out to dinner by responding that he's working hard to support her is trying to put the "blame" on her. He's not taking responsibility for his actions.

In business, a customer will give you an order and before you can fill it you need to know the specifications. You promise delivery based upon the information the customer gives you.

When the customer changes the order request or does not tell you everything you need to know about that order, and you can't ship as promised, the customer will say, "you broke your promise." Your evaluation of that customer is that he lied to you. He didn't tell you all the facts to begin with or he changed the agreement after he gave you the order. You have to remember that this customer will continue to make changes to other orders he gives you.

Suppliers track lies
Consumers track broken promises

When you apply Consumer and Supplier roles to your relationships with others, you will see that the role you are in at any given time determines how you view that relationship.

You must accept the fact that people will make promises that they cannot keep, so do you. You need to provide a built-in safety net so that when a promise is made or given that may affect your physical, financial, or emotional well being, you will have alternative means at your disposal.

Never let anyone get between you and your goal!

Do you know someone who consistently breaks promises? Why are you keeping that relationship?

3. EXPLORING ALTERNATIVES: "We do it my way or not at all!"

Upsets occur when one party wants to explore alternatives and the other party does not. When one party gives orders or has decided that "this is the way it will be done," and the other party has other ideas, they may both get upset.

Negotiation is the tool that reduces the heat of a confrontation. The key to successful negotiation is the willingness of both parties to examine alternatives -- without being emotional -- so that both can win. Nobody wins when one or both parties are upset.

Suppose you want to go to the movies and your boyfriend wants to stay at home and watch TV. Does one of you have to win and the other have to lose? Negotiation allows you to be in control of your feelings. You might suggest the following alternatives:

1. Agree to watch TV that night if he agrees to go to the movies on the next date.
2. Agree to go to the movies and watch TV the next date.
3. Each does his or her thing and don't spend the evening together.
4. Break up because you both can't agree.

Which alternative would you choose?

Another example: Two sisters each wanted a bag of oranges and fought over who should have it. What they never bothered to disclose was why each wanted it. One sister wanted the oranges to make a fruit salad, and the other wanted the skins to make an orange flavored cake. They both could have won!

> TIP: Find out what the other person wants and doesn't want before you express your own wants. You'll have a better chance to negotiate and get to WIN/WIN.

Breaking promises and providing alternatives go hand-in-hand. When you cannot keep your promise – for any reason, provide alternatives to show the Consumer that you are willing to make amends and continue the relationship. The Consumer can consider the change as a "broken promise" or simply a change in your agreement. That is the choice that the Consumer makes regarding your motives.

You have no control over the Consumer's feelings

4. BEING UNDERSTOOD: "You don't understand me!"

Successful communication in a relationship requires each party to understand the other, regardless of how trivial or weighty the subject matter. Each must be able to identify with the feelings, thoughts or attitudes of the other, which is sometimes expressed as, "put yourself in someone else's shoes."

When we meet new people, we may want to be comfortable about "who they are" and use an old set of standards about how to treat them ... as a parent, teacher, boss, employee, husband, wife or lover. These kinds of stereotype roles are often hard to change.

When another person treats us in a way that is inconsistent with the role we want to be in, we may get upset. A wife resents being treated like a maid. An adolescent does not like to be treated like a child. An employee does not like to be treated as if he or she were owned.

The best way to be treated and understood as you wish to be, is by clearly telling the other person. If you feel you are being lectured to or the other person is talking down to you, you can say, "You have something I'd like to hear but you're talking at me, not to me. Please change your tone of voice."

If someone gets upset with you because you didn't understand his or her needs, it could well be because those needs weren't clearly communicated to you ... or that you didn't want to hear them.

As the Supplier, if you will not or cannot listen to the other party because you see the other person in a stereotype role, you may not understand what the other person wants to communicate to you. You may need to get your own prejudices out of the way and just listen without judging.

Feed back what the other person said to you to insure that you got the right message. Rephrase it with, "As I understand it, you are saying," or, "As I see it..."

As the Consumer, if the other person does not or will not listen to you, perhaps the way you are saying it is feeding into his or her stereotypes.

Getting our stereotype roles and prejudices out of the way is the first step in creating mutual understanding and acceptance.

5. OWNERSHIP OF FEELINGS: "You made me so mad!"

In the same way that a material possession can be owned, so can a feeling; it can also be denied.

> "That dog destroyed your flowerbed? No, that's not my dog." "Hostility towards you? I'm not aware of any bad feelings between you and me."

Statements like these are ways of hiding our feelings, whether we're aware of it or not. Awareness is the beginning of learning to own feelings and also a giant step towards resolving conflict and upsets.

When we say, "you made me angry," or, "you upset me" we're blaming the other person for our upset and expecting that person to fix it.

As the Consumer, you will remain upset and powerless as long as you wait for the other person to act! Fortunately or unfortunately, no one else can take away YOUR upset.

If you take responsibility for your feelings, you won't blame the other person. This puts you in the driver's seat. In other words, you "own" your feelings, and you deal with them. Also, this process does not necessarily have to involve the other person.

The basic issue here is one of POWER. If you believe that the other person controls your feelings and reactions to his or her behavior, he or she is in control of you and the relationship. You may not like being controlled, and that can cause an upset.

When you blame someone else, you're giving that person your power, and the control over how you feel. Think about that for a minute.

> *Is there someone in your life whom you're allowing to push your "hot button" and then blame because you are upset?*

The Consumer gets upset and blames the Supplier for trying to control. The Supplier gets upset and blames the Consumer for not allowing him or her to control.

6. SETTING OF PRIORITIES: "I never told you when I'd do it!"

Timing and priority go hand in hand in the development of an upset. What may be appropriate at one time may be inappropriate at another time.

Upset occurs when the Consumer initiates a request and the Supplier may not be willing or able to respond at that time. An upset may also occur when the Consumer may not want what the Supplier is offering at the time. There is cause for an upset when both the Consumer and the Supplier want to make the decision and they each think the other "should." "When do you want to...?" "I don't know. When do you want to...?" "I don't know, when...?" Sound familiar?

If you think that the timing or appropriateness of a discussion or action with someone may not be advisable, you can soften the exchange with a qualifier such as, "I know you hate to make major decisions in the morning, but are you willing to make an exception?" Or, "I may have gotten you at a bad time, do you have a moment?" A qualifier lets the other person know that you are considerate of his or her feelings.

Another aspect of timing is the setting of priorities, i.e., what is to be done and when. If you let someone else set priorities for you or determine when a task will be done, you give up some of your power. If this happens frequently, it will lead to resentment and an upset.

An open verbal agreement to share the deciding of who will do what and when, can avoid this conflict. Is there someone you know who is always telling you what to do and when to do it? Does it upset you?

7. GIVING AND GETTING FEEDBACK: "I want to tell you how I feel about it."

This last of the seven upset issues is difficult for many people. The first issue, response, is the answer given by the other person to your communication or action. This issue, feedback, is about your reply to the other person. Giving and receiving praise is an art that is many times awkwardly performed and easily misinterpreted, and therefore often neglected altogether.

Feedback is essential to good human relations. As a Consumer, you can get upset if you want to express how you feel and don't, because you are afraid that the other person won't like what you say or how you say it. When you are upset, you may accuse or attack the other person. "You always...", and point a finger, make a negative gesture or facial expression. The alternative is to own your feelings and tell the other person how the incident affected you.

An upset can occur when the Consumer states his or her feelings and the Supplier isn't interested, or when the Supplier expects feedback and doesn't get it.

> "I asked you to clean up your room because it's embarrassing to me to have people see it the way it is."

> "You don't mow the lawn well enough so I'm hiring a professional lawn care company."

If you are a Supplier expecting positive feedback and you get a negative reply, you may become an upset Consumer: you got something you didn't want.

Feedback can be verbal or non-verbal. A person may make a face, turn away from you, or simply refuse to reply to you. If you don't get feedback, it is impossible to know how you are doing. You may make assumptions that you are doing well or poorly, but you don't really know where you stand. When this happens, stop and ask for feedback! You may need to look at what you're afraid of. Do you consider feedback as a criticism of you personally, rather than of your performance or behavior?

CHAPTER IV: THE UPSET ANALYZERS®

There are four Upset Analyzers® in the toolbox: Consumer Past, Consumer Future, Supplier Past, and Supplier Future. Each contains seven pairs of precisely developed statements that are based on characteristics common to every upsetting situation affecting human beings.

Consumer upsets deal with situations involving getting or not getting something you want. Supplier upsets deal with situations involving giving or not giving something.

"Which Analyzer to Use?" will guide you in selecting the most appropriate analyzer to fill out.

The Consumer Past and the Supplier Past Upset Analyzer® are filled out when you are upset about a past event. You start off by being as specific about the event as you can, i.e. "I am upset because you"_____(:did not mail our tax return on time).

After you complete an Upset Analyzer®, you will connect your responses with a line drawn between your expectation and the reality side in each issue. The pattern of connecting parallel or diagonal lines will reveal a diagram or X-ray of your upset.

> **Diagonal lines show that you are upset.**
> **Parallel lines show that you are not.**

The more diagonal lines you have, the more you are upset. Diagonal lines also show you which issues upset you. If you show more than one diagonal line, you are upset in more than one area. You will choose the one issue that really upset you more than any other one and circle that Roman numeral.

You have three strategies from which to choose:

> **Change your expectation**
> **Change the reality of the situation**
> **Leave the relationship.**

After you have chosen a strategy, you will choose a plan of action based upon the Roman numeral you circled. Plans of action to choose for each of the Upset Analyzers® will help you to resolve your upset. You will be referring to them every time you fill out one of the analyzers.

You then decide what you're going to do if the same or a similar upsetting situation happens again. How many times have you said, if that ever happens again, I'm going to . . .

Here's your chance! You next fill out a Future Upset Analyzer®. You cast your upset into the future using the same words of your upset, except say, 'I am upset because you will or won't, [do or say]... and finish the sentence.

These instructions will be repeated when you're ready to fill out your first analyzer.

CHAPTER V: EXAMPLES OF UPSETS AND RESOLUTION

The examples in this chapter have all been taken from real life situations.

The events, the actual strategies used and the plans of action came from people who filled out Upset Analyzers® in Reality Analysis® workshops. Only the names of the participants have been changed.

The reader is cautioned to use the examples for comparison purposes only. A particular strategy or plan of action that works for one person may not work for another. What is important is for you to see that communication tools are available, and they work. If you are open to using new tools, you can get what you want out of your relationships.

UPSETS AND THE FAMILY

Joyce has a husband, three children, and a full time job. She was upset because no one in her family helped her do chores. In filling out the Consumer Past Upset Analyzer® she saw that she was not getting agreement.

She told her family that she no longer was going to do chores for them and they had to devise their own plan to get them accomplished. She agreed to continue to feed the dog, but she shopped, did her own laundry, and cooked only for herself.

After two weeks, she said her son started doing his own laundry and her husband tried to enlist their teen-age daughter to take over mom's jobs, to no avail. The family had still not agreed on a plan of action for the housekeeping. Joyce doesn't care how long it takes. She's sticking to her guns.

Another example...

Phyllis's sister-in-law Nancy frequently asked her to baby-sit for her two children, Kevin 6, and Suzy 12.

Phyllis said that she couldn't say no because she was afraid it would hurt Nancy's feelings. In filling out the Supplier Past Upset Analyzer®, Phyllis saw that she did not have to baby sit just because she was asked to. The next time Nancy called, Phyllis told her, "No, I won't baby sit. I have other things to do. The first 34 years of my life were for everybody else, the next 34 years are for me." Nancy found another baby-sitter.

Another example...

Joanne, a psychologist, filled out the Consumer Past Upset Analyzer® recalling an incident with her husband. When her first child was born, she asked him to bring nuts to her in the hospital. He brought her a bag of nuts and she was furious and never said a word.

She really wanted her husband to bring her a fancy basket of nuts and fruit as an acknowledgement of their love. She got to see that her husband wasn't a mind reader. How was he to know what she wanted when she didn't really ask? She was able to forgive him and resolve an upset that she was holding on to for 18 years!
Another example...

Faye, a nurse, was divorced for seven years. She thought she gave her ex-husband everything, especially in sex. She was still angry at him for leaving her and blamed him because she was having problems having an orgasm.

In filling out the Consumer Past Upset Analyzer®, she saw that she was overly concerned with taking care of her partner, not in being the Consumer in sex. She didn't think herself worthy enough of receiving. Her strategy was to change her expectation and recognize that she was entitled as a human being to take from her partner and still give. In a short while, Faye's sexual problem disappeared.

Another example...

Herbert constantly fought with his wife, even after going through a triple by-pass heart operation and being told to stay away from stress. In filling out the Consumer Past Upset Analyzer®, he saw that he was unable to change his expectation about his relationship with his wife or change the reality of the situation. Six months later they divorced.

UPSETS AND FRIENDS

Al had a 40-year friendship with George, dating back to when they both went to summer camp. They lived in different states and occasionally George and his wife would visit Al and his wife and vice versa. The two couples decided to rent a villa together in Jamaica for a week.

After four days, Al was ready to pack it in and go home. He had enough of George. In filling out the Consumer Past Upset Analyzer®, Al saw that he was always playing Supplier to George, and that in the 40 years of their friendship, George never supplied him with what he wanted. He could not change the reality of the situation or his expectation of George.

When Al returned home he ended his relationship with George.

UPSETS AND BUSINESS

David ran a small paper converting business and treated most of his customers as if they were friends. He expected them to pay on time, within his payment terms of 30 days. When they didn't, he would get very upset, but wouldn't send a dunning letter or call to ask for money.

In filling out the Consumer Past Upset Analyzer®, he saw that his customers were really not his friends. Friends would not treat him as they did. He was able to change his expectations and separate his feelings from the business in order to make the necessary calls to collect his money.

Another example...

Alan was upset because a customer did not treat him the way Alan thought he should. In a phone conversation, Alan told the customer to return the merchandise and told his sales department never to accept another order from that customer.

In filling out the Consumer Upset Analyzer®, Alan got to see that he was really upset because he "blew his cool", and left the relationship with the customer. In other words, he lost a customer. His strategy was to change his expectation of a customer who behaved like the one he lost, so as not to lose his business. Alan filled out the Consumer Future Upset Analyzer and saw that he resolved his upset. Alan was upset because he got something he didn't want, and that was, a negative answer from the customer. He could also have been upset because he didn't get something he wanted, and that was cooperation and understanding from the customer. Either way, he was an upset Consumer.

Let's look at it from a different viewpoint. Alan could also have been upset as a Supplier, because he couldn't give something that he wanted to give to the customer, i.e., satisfaction and acceptance of his merchandise. This didn't occur to Alan, although he did resolve his upset.

Another example...

Larry, a lawyer who specializes in probating wills, spends a lot of time sitting in court waiting for judges, who, he said, rarely show up on time. It always makes him angry. He could tell the judges to be on time, he could arrive late too, or do nothing and continue to get upset.

He decided that he couldn't incur a judge's displeasure by saying something, or arrive late for proceedings that might start on time. He couldn't change his expectation that judges will be on time, and he couldn't change the reality of their being on time.

What he did was to bring work that he could do while waiting! He went from being an upset Consumer to being a Supplier to himself.

> The determining factor as to which Upset Analyzer® to use is, which upset you more -- getting or not getting, or giving or not giving?

If you are not sure, fill out both a Consumer and a Supplier Upset Analyzer®. It will soon become apparent which role you were in at the time you got upset. You will feel it.

CHAPTER VI: DIS-EASE AND UPSET

WHAT DO YOU EXPERIENCE WHEN YOU GET UPSET?

You can generally detect an upset by the emotion you feel ... anger, sadness, anxiety, humiliation, grief or disappointment. You may also detect an upset by a physical sensation or a sense of energy drain in your body.

Each of us experiences different body symptoms, ranging from an eye tick or twitching nose to shooting pains in the stomach. Physical symptoms of every type and description can erupt in our bodies, depending upon the severity of the upset and the personality traits of the individual.

> Your hands may get clammy and cold.
> You may start to sweat.
> You may grit your teeth.
> Your body temperature may rise.
> You may throw up.
> Your neck muscles may tense up.
> You may get lower back pain, a headache, or diarrhea.

You may turn the upset inward and hurt yourself by bumping your head or hitting your hands or feet against some object. You may express it outwardly by lashing out at the closest person or object available.

WHAT BODY SYMPTOMS TELL YOU

By listening to your own signs, your body will not only tell you when you are upset, it will also pinpoint where.

Many of us use body language in our conversation or in our thoughts:

> · Get off my back! · I'm pissed off!
> · Have a heart! · You're a pain in the ass!
> · I can't stomach that! · Stop bending my ear!
> · Oh, shit! · He's a pain in the neck
> · You're pulling my leg! · My gut reaction is...

You first need to listen to the signals and recognize which role you are in so you can change it. When you change roles, you are no longer stuck in your position and can get out of the way of the oncoming upset.

It's important to remember: You cannot prevent an upset from occurring or resolve an upset in the same role in which you are getting, or got, upset.

THE BODY MIND RELATIONSHIP

In Kundalini, a division of Tantric, yoga there is the idea that an energy canal runs through the spine from the base of the anus to the top of the head. On either side of the spine there are two energy channels running up the spine that intertwine at seven areas, called Chakras or energy wheels.

These seven Chakras represent seven human characteristics and their related body areas and show a correlation with the seven expectation issues that cause upsets.

RELATIONSHIPS BETWEEN DIS-EASE AND UPSET ISSUES

Expectation	Body area	Disease effects	Chakra
Response	crown, head	headache, nervousness, insomnia, vertigo	Wisdom
Agreements	eyes, nose, ears	allergies, sinus, fainting, eye problems	Perception
Alternatives	mouth, throat	sore throat, colds, hay fever, bursitis	Communication
Understanding	lungs, heart	asthma, coughs, shortness of breath, fever	Love
Blame	stomach, intestines	ulcers, hives, diabetes	Power
Initiate	genitals	colitis, cramps, diarrhea, constipation	Pleasure
Feedback	buttocks, anus	backache, piles, sciatica, pruritus	Security

People have reported that when they fill out an Upset Analyzer®, they experience symptoms in specific areas of their body. In the chart above, note the relationship between the expectation issue, the body area that is affected, and the dis-ease symptom. They may reveal some interesting things to you.

Using the chart, we might be able to say, "Tell me what body symptom you're experiencing and I'll tell you what expectation factor is upsetting you!" Conversely, "tell me what expectation issue is the cause of your upset and I'll tell you where in your body you're having symptoms!"

While you were reading the material in this booklet, did you notice any changes in your body or feel any emotions that you didn't expect? Where? What triggered the changes?

Did an upsetting situation or event come to mind? If so, were you in the role of the Consumer or the Supplier and which issue was it? Look and listen to the clues your body gives you when you get upset.

There is a strong possibility that our upsets are tied to dis-ease in our body. One source of further information on this subject is Body-Mind, by Ken Dychwald, Pantheon Books, New York 1977, available in paperback.

The effects of dis-ease shown on the chart are by no means complete. The list is too long for all of them to be included here. The next time your body gives you a signal or a warning sign, notice where it's coming from. It may give you a clue as to what expectation issue upset you.

Fill out an Upset Analyzer®. Does the body area that's giving you a sign correspond to an upsetting issue? If you get rid of the upset, it may also help you to get rid of the body symptom! Be aware of what you are doing to your body every time you get upset.

CHAPTER VII: HOW GOOD CAN YOU STAND IT?

At the top of a piece of paper write, "How good."

On the left-hand side column of the page, write "Consumer." Then list, one under the other, the things that you want for the current year -- regardless of whether you think you can get them or not.

Take as much time as you need.

Now make a column with the word Supplier on the right-hand side. Next to each want, write down what you are going to do to give yourself what you want.

If you cannot think of a single thing to do, write "nothing."

Take the sheet and stick it on a wall or a mirror where you can look at it every day. When you have gotten what you want, cross it off. If you no longer want an item, cross it off. In the next year, start a new list transferring those items you still want and haven't gotten, adding any new items you discovered you want.

Underneath the old list write down all the things that you did get or accomplish that you didn't put on the list. Acknowledge yourself for achieving them. When you have supplied yourself with each item on your list, the game will be over -- and you'll be the winner!

You now have all of the communication tools in the Emotional Toolbox™ to help you resolve an upset and prevent it from ruling you. If you are willing to make changes in your attitude, actions, and beliefs about the way you see yourself and other people, you will have achieved a major goal in your life.

SECTION II

FORMS

Now that you have an overview and an understanding of the roles of Consumers and Suppliers, it's time to put your knowledge of the communication tools into practice; use them to fill out your first analyzer, the Consumer Past Upset Analyzer™.

You may not have access to a copy machine to fill out the Analyzer forms, so 3 copies of each of the 4 Upset Analyzer™ forms as well as mini-analyzer forms are provided at the back of the book. Cut them out where shown. To help you resolve upsets that occur during the day at work or away from home, the mini-upset analyzers can be filled out anywhere, anytime, when carried in your pocket or purse. The mini Consumer and Supplier past and future analyzers are provided on the same page.

When two people fill out an analyzer independently using the same upsetting situation, and then compare notes as to which issue is the most upsetting to each of them, it takes the heat off the situation and discuss it objectively, using Consumer and Supplier terms. A non-threatening dialogue is the best way to bring down walls very quickly and resolve an upset.

Follow the directions from #2 to #7 in sequence to take you through the process of completing an analyzer and interpreting your answers.

1. The Forms:

       a. The Consumer Past Upset Analyzer® form
       b. The Consumer Future Upset Analyzer® form
       c. The Supplier Past Upset Analyzer® form
       d. The Supplier Future Upset Analyzer® form
       e. The Consumer mini-analyzers
       f. The Supplier mini-analyzers

2. Which Analyzer to Use?

3. Directions: How to fill out an analyzer

       a. The Consumer Past Upset Analyzer®
       b. The Consumer Future Upset Analyzer®
       c. The Supplier Past Upset Analyzer®
       d. The Supplier Future Upset analyzer®

4. Explanation of the 7 issues

5. The meaning of the connections

6. Plans of action for each issue

      a. The Consumer Past & Future Upset Analyzer®
      b. The Supplier Past & Future Upset Analyzer®

7. Catch 22

2. WHICH ANALYZER TO USE?

If you're upset because you got something you didn't want or you didn't get something you wanted … you would be an upset CONSUMER.

So you would fill out the Consumer past Upset Analyzer®.

If you're upset because you gave something you didn't want to give or you couldn't give something you wanted to give … you would be an upset SUPPLIER

So you would fill out the SUPPLIER past Upset Analyzer®.

You can also be upset both as a Consumer and a Supplier! For example:

A woman told her husband that she needed more money to pay the monthly bills. What did the husband, as an upset Consumer get, that he didn't want?

The request for more money.

Using the same example; if the husband couldn't afford to give his wife more money, he would be an upset Supplier because he couldn't give her what she wanted.

> *The deciding factor as to what causes an upset in any situation is the role you were in at the time you got upset*

Are you listening as a Consumer to hear what you're getting or not getting?

or

Are you listening as a Supplier to hear what you can give or not give?

If you listen carefully, your role and the real upset will become apparent to you!

If you fill out a Consumer analyzer and you don't feel 'comfortable' in the role – switch analyzers and fill out a Supplier analyzer or vice versa. Which role best satisfies your feelings?

POSSIBLE CAUSES OF YOUR UPSET

		<u>Use Analyzer:</u>
You got something you didn't want	You didn't get something you wanted	Consumer Past
You couldn't give something you wanted to give	You gave something you didn't want to	Supplier Past
You will get something you don't want to get	You won't get something you want to get	Consumer Future
You won't be able to give something you want to give	You will give something you don't want to give	Supplier Future

1a. CONSUMER PAST UPSET ANALYZER™

I am upset because you_____

I EXPECTED:		IN REALITY I GOT:
Part A		**Part B**

1. Response

| An unusual response | [ ]   [ ] | An unusual response |
| A usual response | [ ]   [ ] | A usual response |

I1. Agreement

| A changed agreement | [ ]   [ ] | A changed agreement |
| The old agreement | [ ]   [ ] | The old agreement |

111. Alternatives

| Alternatives | [ ]   [ ] | Alternatives |
| No alternatives | [ ]   [ ] | No alternatives |

IV. Understanding

| Your understanding | [ ]   [ ] | Your understanding |
| No understanding | [ ]   [ ] | No understanding |

V. Control

| T not blame you | [ ]   [ ] | To not blame you |
| To blame you | [ ]   [ ] | To blame you |

VI. Initiate

| To initiate | [ ]   [ ] | To initiate |
| To not initiate | [ ]   [ ] | To not initiate |

VII. Feedback

| To give feedback | [ ]   [ ] | To give feedback |
| Not to give feedback | [ ]   [ ] | Not to give feedback |

1b. CONSUMER FUTURE UPSET ANALYZER™

I am upset because you_____

I WANT:			I WILL REALLY GET:

Part A   **Part B**

I. Response

| An unusual response | [ ] | [ ] | An unusual response |
| A usual response | [ ] | [ ] | A usual response |

II. Agreements

| A changed agreement | [ ] | [ ] | A changed agreement |
| The old agreement | [ ] | [ ] | The old agreement |

III. Alternatives

| Alternatives | [ ] | [ ] | Alternatives |
| No alternatives | [ ] | [ ] | No alternatives |

IV. Understanding

| Your understanding | [ ] | [ ] | Your understanding |
| No understanding | [ ] | [ ] | No understanding |

V. Control

| To not blame you | [ ] | [ ] | To not blame you |
| To blame you | [ ] | [ ] | To blame you |

VI. Initiate

| To initiate | [ ] | [ ] | To initiate |
| To not initiate | [ ] | [ ] | To not initiate |

VII. Feedback

| To give feedback | [ ] | [ ] | To give feedback |
| Not to give feedback | [ ] | [ ] | Not to give feedback |

1c. SUPPLIER PAST UPSET ANALYZER™

I am upset because you_____

I EXPECTED TO: ## IN REALITY:

Part A   ### Part B

I. Response

Give an unusual response   [ ]   [ ]   You wanted an unusual response
Give my usual response   [ ]   [ ]   You wanted my usual response

II. Agreement

Change our agreement   [ ]   [ ]   You wanted changes
Not change our agreement   [ ]   [ ]   You didn't want changes

III. Alternatives

Explore alternatives   [ ]   [ ]   You wanted alternatives
Not explore alternatives   [ ]   [ ]   You didn't want alternatives

IV. Understanding

Understand your side   [ ]   [ ]   You wanted understanding
Not understand your side   [ ]   [ ]   You didn't want understanding

V. Control

Not control   [ ]   [ ]   I didn't control
Control   [ ]   [ ]   I did control

VI. Initiate

Be the initiator   [ ]   [ ]   I was the initiator
Not be the initiator   [ ]   [ ]   You were the initiator

VII. Feedback

Get feedback   [ ]   [ ]   You gave feedback
Not get feedback   [ ]   [ ]   You didn't give feedback

© **Copyright 2009, Zalman Puchkoff**

1d. SUPPLIER FUTURE UPSET ANALYZER™

I am upset because you_____

I WANT TO: I KNOW YOU WILL:

Part A   Part B

I. Response

Give an unusual response   [ ]   [ ]   Want an unusual response
Give my usual response   [ ]   [ ]   Not want my usual response

II. Agreement

Change our agreement   [ ]   [ ]   Want changes
Not change our agreement   [ ]   [ ]   Not want changes

III. Alternatives

Explore alternatives   [ ]   [ ]   Want alternatives
Not explore alternatives   [ ]   [ ]   Not want alternatives

IV. Understanding

Understand your side   [ ]   [ ]   Want understanding
Not understand your side   [ ]   [ ]   Not want understanding

V. Control

Not control   [ ]   [ ]   Not be controlled
Control   [ ]   [ ]   Be controlled

VI. Initiate

Be the initiator   [ ]   [ ]   Not be the initiator
Not be the initiator   [ ]   [ ]   Be the initiator

VII. Feedback

Get feedback   [ ]   [ ]   Give feedback
Not get feedback   [ ]   [ ]   Not give feedback

3. Directions: How to fill out an Analyzer

3A. Consumer Past Analyzer™ Directions:

Step 1. Think of a specific situation or event between you and another person that upset you. You want to stop feeling upset now, and whenever a similar incident occurs again.

Step 2. Identify that person by name if you can, even visualize that person saying or doing something that concerned you. Choose an upset where:

- you got something you didn't want, or
- you didn't get something that you wanted.

The something could be the other person's response or action toward you. It could have happened anytime in the past – 10 minutes ago or 10 years ago. When you think about it now, it still brings up all of the feelings associated with the past incident.

Step 3. Clarify the words in your mind by saying, "I am upset because you…", and finish the sentence on the Consumer Past Analyzer™.

Step 4. Fold the form in half exposing only Part A., With the words of your upset in mind say, I EXPECTED, and read the two statements in the first issue and put an X in the most appropriate box that applies to your upset.

Step 5. For an explanation of each issue, read the Consumer Past explanation of issues, Part A &B.

Step 6. When you are finished putting X's in each of the seven issues, turn the page over, exposing only Part B, and do the same thing. With your upset in mind say IN REALITY I GOT and read the two statements in the first issue. Put an X in the most appropriate box that applies to your upset.

Step 7. When you are finished putting X's in each of the seven issues, open the page and connect each of the X's from Part A to Part B in each of the seven issues. The pattern of connecting parallel or diagonal lines, including unconnected lines will reveal a diagram or X-ray of your upset.

Diagonal lines show that you are upset
Parallel lines show that you are not upset

The more diagonals you have, the more you are upset. Diagonal lines also show you which issues upset you.

Step 8. There is usually one major issue that is the key to your whole upset, and to resolve this issue is to resolve the upset. Which one of the numbered seven issues is your main upsetting issue, the one that really upset you? Circle that number.

Step 9. Choose a strategy. These are your choices:

Change your expectation
Change the reality
Leave the relationship

If you do nothing, you will continue to be upset.

Decide what you're going to do if the same or a similar upsetting situation happens again.

Step 10. To assist you in resolving your upset, and prevent it from happening again, there are plans of action based on each of the diagonal lines and each issue.

Step 11. Read the plan of action issue number that is applicable to your most upsetting issue and diagonal line, the one you circled.

You will now get a chance to test out your plan of action to see if you have resolved your upset by using the Future Analyzer; it is also used to help you resolve future upsets. However, you cannot be upset in the future. You can only be upset now about events that may take place in the future and you are anticipating an outcome that is upsetting to you.

If you say, "I know what will happen!" you'd be right. That's a self fulfilling prophesy. In filling out a future analyzer, you will gain insight into how to get what you want as opposed to what you think you will get.

By seeing which upset issue(s) triggers your present concern, you can choose a strategy and a plan of action to help you get what you want, without the emotional baggage attached to the anticipation of something that may or may not happen.

Step 12. Fill out the Consumer Future Upset Analyzer™.

3B. Consumer Future Analyzer™ Directions:

Step 1. Change the grammar and cast the same words of your upsetting issue event into the future using the future tense, such as; will, will not, or aren't going to. For example, if you wrote, "I am upset because you didn't give me a raise, you now write "…aren't going to give me a raise." Clarify the words in your mind and fill in the Consumer Future Upset Analyzer® upset.

Step 2. Fold the page exposing Part A and with your plan of action in mind say, I WANT: and mark an X in the top or bottom pair of each of the seven issues

Step 3. Read the definitions of each future issue

Step 4. Turn the page over and now fill in Part B with plan of action in mind and say, I WILL REALLY GET: and mark an X in the top or bottom pair of each of the seven issues.

Step 5. Open the page and connect the X's across the page

If you have a parallel line in your most upsetting issue, you have resolved your upset. Congratulations! You have changed the way you look at situations and upsetting events using communication tools to empower you.

If you still have a diagonal line in your most upsetting issue, you have not been able to resolve the upset. Your strategy and plan of action didn't work. You have some more work to do. Read Catch 22 and apply it to your upset. If you've changed your attitude as a result, redo the Consumer Future Upset Analyzer® choosing a strategy and a plan of action that will now work for you.

If you have diagonal lines in other issues, not your main issue, then perhaps you've uncovered the main issue of your upset, not the issue you thought it to be. Do another future analyzer.

3C. Supplier Past Analyzer™ Directions:

Step 1. Think of a specific situation or event between you and another person that upset you. You want to stop feeling upset now, and whenever a similar incident occurs again.

Step 2. Identify that person by name if you can, even visualize that person saying or doing something that concerned you. Choose an upset where:

- you gave something you didn't want to give, or
- you couldn't give something that you wanted to give

The something could be your response or action toward the other person. It could have happened anytime in the past – 10 minutes ago or 10 years ago. When you think about it now, it stills brings up all of the feelings associated with the past incident.

Step 3. Clarify the words in your mind by saying, "I am upset because you…", and finish the sentence on the Supplier Past Analyzer™.

Step 4. Fold the form in half exposing only Part A., With the words of your upset in mind say, I EXPECTED TO, and read the two statements in the first issue and put an X in the most appropriate box that applies to your upset.

Step 5. For an explanation of each issue, read the Consumer Past explanation of issues, Part A & B.

Step 6. When you are finished putting X's in each of the seven issues, turn the page over, exposing only Part B, and do the same thing. With your upset in mind say, IN REALITY, and read the two statements in the first issue and put an X in the most appropriate box that applies to your upset.

Step 7. When you are finished putting X's in each of the seven issues open the page and connect each of the X's from Part A to Part B in each of the seven issues. The pattern of connecting parallel or diagonal lines including unconnected lines will reveal a diagram or X-ray of your upset.

Diagonal lines show that you are upset
Parallel lines show that you are not upset

The more diagonals you have, the more you are upset. Diagonal lines also show you which issues upset you.

Step 8. There is usually one major issue that is the key to your whole upset, and to resolve this issue is to resolve your upset. Which one of the numbered seven issues is your main upsetting issue, the one that really upset you? Circle that number.

Step 9. Choose a strategy. These are your choices:

Change your expectation
Change the reality
Leave the relationship

If you do nothing, you will continue to be upset.

Decide what you're going to do if the same or a similar upsetting situation happens again.

Step 10. To assist you in resolving your upset and prevent it from happening again, there are plans of action listed based on each of the diagonal lines and each issue.

Step 11. Read the plan of action that is applicable to your most upsetting issue and diagonal line, the one you circled.

You will now get a chance to test out your plan of action to see if you have resolved your upset using the Future analyzer; it is also used to help you resolve future upsets. However, you cannot be upset in the future. You can only be upset now about events that may take place in the future and you are anticipating an outcome that is upsetting to you.

If you say, "I know what will happen!" you'd be right. That's a self fulfilling prophesy. In filling out a future analyzer, you will gain insight into how to get what you want as opposed to what you think you will get.

By seeing which upset issue(s) trigger your present concern, you can choose a strategy and a plan of action to help you get what you want, without the emotional baggage attached to the anticipation of something that may or may not happen.

Step 12. Fill out the Supplier future Upset Analyzer™.

3D. SUPPLIER FUTURE ANALYZER™ DIRECTIONS:

Step 1. Change the grammar and cast the same words of your upsetting issue event into the future using the future tense, such as, will, will not, or aren't going to. For example, if you wrote, "I am upset because you asked me for a raise, you now write "…will ask me for a raise." Clarify the words in your mind and fill in the Supplier Future Upset Analyzer®

Step 2. Fold the page exposing Part A and with your plan of action in mind say, I EXPECT TO: and mark an X in the top or bottom pair of each of the seven issues

Step 3. Read the definitions of each future issue. Turn the page over and now fill in Part B with plan of action in mind and say, I KNOW YOU WILL: and mark an X in the top or bottom pair of each of the seven issues.

Step 4. Open the page and connect the X's across the page

If you have a parallel line in your most upsetting issue, you have resolved your upset. Congratulations! You have changed the way you look at situations and upsetting events using communication tools to empower you.

If you still have a diagonal line in your most upsetting issue, you have not been able to resolve the upset. Your strategy and plan of action didn't work. You have some more work to do. Read Catch 22 and apply it to your upset. If you've changed your attitude as a result, redo the Supplier Future Upset Analyzer® choosing a strategy and a plan of action that will now work for you.

If you have diagonal lines in other issues, not your main issue, then perhaps you've uncovered the main issue of your upset, not the issue you thought it to be. Do another future analyzer.

4. EXPLANATION OF THE 7 ISSUES

4. EXPLANATION OF ISSUES - CONSUMER PAST

Part A (Your Expectation)

Issue I   If you expected an unusual response, i.e. the other person to do something you've never seen him or her do or say before, put an X in the top box. If you expected the same response you've gotten before, put an X in the bottom box.

Issue II   If you expected something different than arranged, or the other person to break a promise, put an X in the top box. If you expected the same arrangement as agreed or the other person to keep his or her promise, put an X in the bottom box.

Issue III   If you expected to negotiate or discuss new options; put an X in the top box. If you expected no choices, options, or discussions, put an X in the bottom box.

Issue IV   If you expected the other person to see your side and point of view, put an X in the top box. If you expected the other person to act in his or her own best interests, put an X in the bottom box.

Issue V   If you expected to be responsible for, or be the cause of, your own feelings, put an X in the top box. If you expected the other person to be the cause of your feelings, put an X in the bottom box.

Issue VI   If you expected to decide when the situation or event would happen, put an X in the top box. If you expected the other person to decide when, put an X in the bottom box.

Issue VII   If you expected to tell the other person how or what you felt, put an X in the top box. If you expected to not tell the other person how or what you felt, put an X in the bottom box.

Remember, this is <u>your own reconstruction</u> of what you expected <u>before</u> you got upset. If you feel an issue is not relevant to your upset, go to the next issue.

Part B (The Reality)

Issue I   If the other person surprised you or said or did something different, put an X in the top box. If the other person answered as he or she always does, put an X in the bottom box.

Issue II   If the other person made a different arrangement with you, or broke his or her promise, put an X in the top box. If the other person continued the same arrangement or kept the original promise, put an X in the bottom box.

Issue III   If the other person negotiated or discussed different options with you, put an X in the top box. If the other person offered you no choices, options or discussion, put an X in the bottom box.

Issue IV   If the other person saw your side and point of view, put an X in the top box. If the other person acted in his or her own best interests and didn't see your side, put an X in the bottom box.

Issue V If you were responsible, or caused your own feelings, put an X in the top box. If you blamed the other person for how you felt, put an X in the bottom box.

Issue VI   If the situation or event happened when you decided it would, put an X in the top box. If the other person decided when, put an X in the bottom box.

Issue VII   If you told the other person how or what you felt, put an X in the top box. If you didn't tell the other person how or what you felt, put an X in the bottom box.

Remember, this is your own reconstruction of what you expected before you got upset. If you feel an issue is not relevant to your upset, go to the next issue.

4. EXPLANATION OF ISSUES - CONSUMER FUTURE

Part A (Your Expectation)

Issue I   If you will want the other person to do or say something different or surprising, put an X in the top box. If you will want the other person to answer how he or she always does, put an X in the bottom box.

Issue II   If you will want a different arrangement, or a promise to be broken, put an X in the top box. If you will want the same arrangement or the other person to keep his or her promise, put an X in the bottom box.

Issue III   If you will want to negotiate or discuss different options put an X in the top box. If you will want no choices, options or discussion, put an X in the bottom box.

Issue IV   If you will want the other person to see your side and know what you need and want, put an X in the top box. If you will want the other person to act in his or her best interests not yours, put an X in the bottom box.

Issue V If you will want to be responsible for, or be the cause of your own feelings, put an X in the top box. If you will want the other person to be the cause of your feelings, put an X in the bottom box.

Issue VI   If you will want to decide when the situation or event will happen, put an X in the top box. If you will want the other person to decide when the situation or event will happen, put an X in the bottom box.

Issue VII   If you will want to tell the other person how you feel, put an X in the top box. If you will not want to tell the other person how you feel, put an X in the bottom box.

Remember: <u>this is what you think will really happen.</u> If you feel any issue is not relevant to your upset, go on to the next issue.

Part B (The Reality)

Issue I   If the other person will do or say something different or surprising, put an X in the top box. If the other person will answer how he or she always does, put an X in the bottom box.

Issue II   If the other person will make a different arrangement, or break a promise put an X in the top box. If the other person will continue the same arrangement or the other person to keep his or her promise, put an X in the bottom box.

Issue III   If the other person will negotiate or discuss different options, put an X in the top box. If the other person will offer you no choices, options or discussion, put an X in the bottom box.

Issue IV   If the other person will see your side, and know what you want and need, put an X in the top box. If the other person will act in his or her best interests, put an X in the bottom box.

Issue V If you will be responsible for or be the cause of your own feelings, put an X in the top box. If you will let the other person be the cause of your feelings, put an X in the bottom box.

Issue VI   If you will decide when the situation or event will happen, put an X in the top box. If you will let the other person decide when the situation or event will happen, put an X in the bottom box.

Issue VII   If you will not be able to tell the other person how you feel, put an X in the top box. If you will not want to tell the other person how you feel, put an X in the bottom box.

Remember: <u>this is what you think will really happen.</u> If you feel any issue is not relevant to your upset, go on to the next issue.

4. EXPLANATION OF ISSUES - SUPPLIER PAST

Part A (Your Expectation)

Issue I   If you expected to do or say something different or surprising, put an X in the top box. If you expected to answer how you always do, put an X in the bottom box.

Issue II   If you expected to make a different arrangement or break a promise, put an X in the top box. If you expected to maintain the same arrangement or keep your promise, put an X in the bottom box.

Issue III   If you expected to negotiate or discuss different options put an X in the top box. If you expected to offer no choices, options or discussion, put an X in the bottom box.

Issue IV   If you expected to see the other person's point of view, put an X in the top box. If you expected to not be sympathetic to the other person's point of view, put an X in the bottom box.

Issue V If you expected to not interfere with the outcome for the other person, put an X in the top box. If you expected to interfere with or determine the outcome, put an X in the bottom box.

Issue VI   If you expected to decide when the situation or event would happen, put an X in the top box. If you expected the other person to decide when, put an X in the bottom box.

Issue VII   If you expected the other person to tell you how or what he or she feels, put an X in the top box. If you expected the other person to not tell you how he or she feels, put an X in the bottom box.

Remember: this is <u>your own reconstruction</u> of what <u>actually happened</u> at the time of the incident. If you feel an issue is not relevant to your upset, go on to the next issue.

Part B (The Reality)

Issue I   If the other person wanted you to say or do something different, put an X in the top box. If the other person wanted you to answer as you always do, put an X in the bottom box.

Issue II   If the other person wanted you to make different arrangements or change the agreement, put an X in to the top box. If the other person wanted you to continue the same arrangement or keep an original promise, put an X in the bottom box.

Issue III   If the other person wanted you to negotiate or discuss different options, put an X in the top box. If the other person didn't want to negotiate or discuss different options, put an X in the bottom box.

Issue IV   If the other person wanted you to see his or her side, put an X in the top box. If the other person did not want you to see his or her side, put an X in the bottom box.

Issue V   If you did not interfere with the outcome for the other person, put an X in the top box. If you determined the outcome for the other person, put an X in the bottom box.

Issue VI   If the situation or event happened when you wanted it to, put an X in the top box. If the other person decided when, put an X in the bottom box.

Issue VII   If the other person told you how or what he or she felt, put an X in the top box. If the other person did not tell you how he or she felt, put an X in the bottom box.

Remember: this is <u>your own reconstruction</u> of what <u>actually happened</u> at the time of the incident. If you feel an issue is not relevant to your upset, go on to the next issue.

4. EXPLANATION OF ISSUES - SUPPLIER FUTURE

Part B (The Reality)

Issue I   If the other person will want you to say something different or surprising, put an X in the top box. If the other person will want you to answer as you always do, put an X in the bottom box.

Issue II   If the other person will want you to make different arrangements or change the agreement, put an X in the top box. If the other person will want you to continue the same arrangement or keep the original agreement, put an X in the bottom box.

Issue III   If the other person will want you to negotiate or discuss different options, put an X in the top box. If the other person will not want you to negotiate or discuss different options, put an X in the bottom box.

Issue IV   If the other person will want you to see his or her side, put an X in the top box. If the other person will not want you to see his or her side, put an X in the bottom box.

Issue V   If the other person will let you determine the outcome, put an X in the top box. If the other person will not let you determine the outcome, put an X in the bottom box.

Issue VI   If the other person will not decide when the situation or event will happen, put an X in the top box. If the other person will decide when the situation or event will happen, put an X in the bottom box.

Issue VII   If the other person will tell you how or what he or she feels,, put an X in the top box. If the other person will not tell you how he or she feels, put an X in the bottom box.

Remember: this is what you think <u>will really happen</u>. If you feel any issue is not relevant to your upset, go on to the next issue.

Part B (The Reality)

Issue I   If the other person will want you to say something different or surprising, put an X in the top box. If the other person will want you to answer as you always do, put an X in the bottom box.

Issue II   If the other person will want you to make different arrangements, change the agreement, put an X in the top box. If the other person will want you to continue the same arrangement or keep the original agreement, put an X in the bottom box.

Issue III   If the other person will want you to negotiate or discuss different options put an X in the top box. If the other person will not want you to negotiate or discuss different options, put an X in the bottom box.

Issue IV   If the other person will want you to see his or her side, put an X in the top box. If the other person will not want you to see his or her side, put an X in the bottom box.

Issue V   If the other person will let you determine the outcome, put an X in the top box. If the other person will not let you determine the outcome, put an X in the bottom box.

Issue VI   If the other person will not decide when the situation or event will happen, put an X in the top box. If the other person will decide when the situation or event will happen, put an X in the bottom box.

Issue VII   If the other person will tell you how or what he or she feels,, put an X in the top box. If the other person will not tell you how he or she feels, put an X in the bottom box.

Remember: this is what you think <u>will really happen</u>. If you feel any issue is not relevant to your upset, go on to the next issue.

5. THE MEANING OF THE CONNECTIONS

The meaning of the connection patterns will give you some insight into why you got upset. When you understand why you got upset, you can choose a strategy to help you resolve your upset.

[X]--[X]   A parallel line across the top means you are not
[ ] [ ]   upset about this issue. You are open and sensitive
to what comes along and can respond in the moment, appropriate to the situation.

[ ] [ ]   A parallel line across the bottom indicates that
[X]--[X]   while your expectation is in line with the reality, there is minimum communication between you and the other person. This pattern occurs frequently in business and family relationships. If you have three or more bottom to bottom connections on the Analyzer, you might want to re-examine what your relationship is about.

[X] [ ]   A diagonal line, upper left to lower right indicates
[ ]\ [X]   that you wanted some type of action or response from the other person and you didn't get it. You had an expectation that the other person would understand how you felt and what you wanted, and he or she would listen to you or give it to you. You didn't get what you wanted and you didn't like it!

[ ] [X]   This diagonal pattern indicates that you wanted things
[X]/ [ ]   to continue the way they have always been, the status-quo, and the other person surprised you and you didn't like it!

[ ] [ ]   Blank boxes on both sides usually imply that this
[ ] [ ]   issue was not relevant to your upset. It can also indicate that it is the most serious symptom of the entire set. If you continue to see the same issue as not meaningful or relevant to your upset, you may be blocking something that is getting in the way of your relationships.

It may help you to switch roles and play the part of the other person in your upsetting situation to give you a new perspective.

[X] [ ]   This incomplete connection indicates that you knew what
             you wanted but you didn't know what happened in the
[X] [ ]   situation.

[ ] [X]   This incomplete connection indicates that you knew
              what happened but you didn't know what you wanted.
[ ] [X]

The meaning of the connection patterns will give you some insight into why you got upset. When you see your expectations -- what you wanted to happen -- and see the reality -- what actually happened -- in each of the seven expectation areas, you can then plan a strategy to resolve your upset based upon your most upsetting issue.

Plans of actions for both the Consumer and the Supplier role for each of the seven issues follow on the next page.

6. Plans of Action

6a. Plans of Action - Consumer Past & Future

I EXPECTED: **IN REALITY I GOT:**

Part A   **Part B**

                                           I

An unusual response   [X] [ ]   [ ] [X]   **An unusual response**

                                    \\   /

A usual response   [ ] [X]   [X] [ ]   **A usual response**

         Things should change!   **Things shouldn't change**

RESPONSE: As the upset Consumer, change roles and be the Supplier. What can you supply, or not supply, to the other person to resolve your upset? Suggestions:

1. Tell the other person very clearly how you feel about the situation in a way that won't further create an upset for you.
2. Satisfy the other person's needs, so you in turn will get the response you really want. Sometimes it's the way that you say it, not what you say.
3. Give yourself permission to stop being upset and realize that the other person has already made a choice in how he or she wishes to deal with and respond to you.
4. Don't give the other person what is asked for simply because it is requested or demanded. Did you have an agreement to do or give it?
5. Don't counterattack and make the other person wrong when you are responded to with unacceptable behavior.

What are you going to do now? This may not be the first time that you wanted something from the other person and you didn't get it. Can you think of other cases where you didn't get what you wanted?

How many times have you been able to change the other person? Think about the fact that you may never get what you want from the other person! Knowing that you may never get what you want, how will you treat the other person in the future? You are upset about a situation that happened in the past. That cannot change. You can only change how you will handle this or a similar upsetting situation in the future.

What will you do differently?

The left box above is your expectation and the right box is the reality. You need to either change your expectation in each box to match the reality, or change the reality to match your expectation. If you choose to leave the relationship, there is nothing to change and you do not need a plan of action.

When your expectation is parallel with the reality, you will no longer be upset

Choose a strategy:

1. Change your expectation
2. Change the reality
3. Leave the relationship

If you do nothing, you will continue to be upset.

Based upon your choice of changing your expectation or changing the reality, think of what you are going to do so that you don't get upset the next time this or a similar situation happens again.

By seeing which upset issues trigger your present concern, you can choose a strategy and a plan of action to help you get what you want --without the emotional baggage attached to the anticipation of something that may or may not happen.

Fill out a Consumer Future Analyzer® to test the plan of action and strategy that you came up with. You will see if you have really changed the way you will react to the same or a similar upsetting situation if it happens again

If you still have diagonal lines, read Catch 22. If one of the suggestions hits a nerve, choose a different option and again fill out another future analyzer.

6a. PLANS OF ACTION-CONSUMER PAST & FUTURE

I EXPECTED: **IN REALITY I GOT:**

Part A   **Part B**

II

A changed agreement   [X]   [ ]   [ ]   [X]   A changed agreement

\   /

The old agreement   [ ]   [X]   [X]   [ ]   The old agreement

Things should change!   **Things shouldn't change**

CHANGES TO AGREEMENTS: As the upset Consumer, change roles and be the Supplier. What can you supply, or not supply, to the other person to resolve your upset? Suggestions:

1. Supply forgiveness when the other person breaks an agreement. As long as you remain in the Consumer role – wanting the other person to 'repent' -- you will remain upset. The other person can do nothing to get rid of your upset. It has already happened. It is in the past. The other person cannot repair the break.

2. Take responsibility and repair the relationship – if you want to. It always rests with the person who is upset, not the person who broke the agreement! It is your upset; you created it so you have to let go of it. The other person can't do it for you. You have to forgive the other person. To forgive is to give yourself permission to stop being upset with the other person. You can say it face-to-face, write a letter, or say it to yourself.

3. Consider changing or getting out of a relationship with someone who consistently breaks agreements. Be wary of another promise to atone for a broken promise – "I'll never do it again." You can bet that the other person will do it again!

4. If you are asked or pressured to give something – your time, money, or your support – that you did not agree to, supply the other person with the facts of the situation and the terms of the arrangement. State exactly what you are going to supply, or not supply. No is a wonderful response to agreeing to anything.

5. Express your feelings, do not vent them. It will only antagonize the other person and make it more difficult to focus on the facts and the issues if you attack.

What are you going to do now? This may not be the first time that you wanted something from the other person and you didn't get it. Can you think of other cases where you didn't get what you wanted?

How many times have you been able to change the other person? Think about the fact that you may never get what you want from the other person! Knowing that you may never get what you want, how will you treat the other person in the future? You are upset about a situation that happened in the past. That cannot change. You can only change how you will handle this or a similar upsetting situation in the future.
What will you do differently?

The left box above is your expectation and the right box is the reality. You need to either change your expectation in each box to match the reality, or change the reality in each box to match your expectation. If you choose to leave the relationship, there is nothing to change and you do not need a plan of action.

When your expectation is parallel with the reality, you will no longer be upset

Choose a strategy:

1. Change your expectation
2. Change the reality
3. Leave the relationship

If you do nothing, you will continue to be upset.

Based upon your choice of changing your expectation or changing the reality, think of what you are going to do so that you don't get upset the next time this or a similar situation happens again.

By seeing which upset issues trigger your present concern, you can choose a strategy and a plan of action to help you get what you want -- without the emotional baggage attached to the anticipation of something that may or may not happen.

Fill out a Consumer Future Analyzer® to test the plan of action and strategy that you came up with. You will see if you have really changed the way you will react to the same or a similar upsetting situation if it happens again

If you still have diagonal lines, read Catch 22. If one of the suggestions hits a nerve, choose a different option and again fill out another future analyzer.

6a. PLANS OF ACTION-CONSUMER PAST & FUTURE

I WANT: **IN REALITY I GOT:**

Part A   **Part B**

                                           III

Alternatives   [X]   [ ]   [ ]   [X]   **Alternatives**
                            \   /
No alternatives   [ ]   [X]   [X]   [ ]   **No alternatives**

      Things should change!   **Things shouldn't change!**

EXPLORING ALTERNATIVES: As the upset Consumer, change roles and be the Supplier. What can you supply, or not supply, to the other person to resolve your upset? Suggestions:

1. You make the suggestions and offer alternatives that will work for you. Look for ways that will satisfy both you and the other person. Supply what is needed to make it work!
2. If the other person doesn't come forward with a willingness to help solve the problem, forget it; it isn't important enough to the other person. If it is to you – express it.
3. If you don't get satisfaction, forget it, you're wasting your time. Find someone willing to work with you, not against you.
4. Providing alternatives is a way to negotiate – anything! It is also the way to reduce the heat of a confrontation. Emotions often get in the way of solving the problem. Establish your limits – the point beyond which you will not negotiate.
5. If you are emotionally attached to your point of view, you will take an uncompromising position, even if you think you are being objective and rational.
6. Don't accept or reject whatever is offered to you unless you really want to. If you are unable to decide among a set of alternatives that are presented to you, you are showing an unwillingness to live with the consequences of your choice. Get in touch with your feelings. Flip a coin! Choose. When it lands, are you happy with the result? If so, go with it. Wish it had flipped differently? If so, go with the other choice!
7. Present alternatives of your own. Take another look at what the real issue is in this situation.

What are you going to do now?

The left box above is your expectation and the right box is the reality. You need to either change your expectation in each box to match the reality, or change the reality in each box to match your expectation. If you choose to leave the relationship, there is nothing to change and you do not need a plan of action.

When your expectation is parallel with the reality, you will no longer be upset

Choose a strategy:
1. Change your expectation
2. Change the reality
3. Leave the relationship

If you do nothing, you will continue to be upset.

Based upon your choice of changing your expectation or changing the reality, think of what you are going to do so that you don't get upset the next time this or a similar situation happens again.

By seeing which upset issues trigger your present concern, you can choose a strategy and a plan of action to help you get what you want -- without the emotional baggage attached to the anticipation of something that may or may not happen.

Fill out a Consumer Future Analyzer® to test the plan of action and strategy that you came up with. You will see if you have really changed the way you will react to the same or a similar upsetting situation if it happens again

If you still have diagonal lines, read Catch 22. If one of the suggestions hits a nerve, choose a different option and again fill out another future analyzer.

6a. Plans of Action-Consumer Past & Future

I EXPECTED: **IN REALITY I GOT:**

Part A   **Part B**

              IV

Your understanding   [X] [ ]   [ ] [X]   **Your understanding**

                    \\   /

No understanding   [ ] [X]   [X] [ ]   **No understanding**

        Things should change!   **Things shouldn't change!**

BEING UNDERSTOOD/ACCEPTED: As the upset Consumer, change roles and be the Supplier. What can you supply, or not supply, to the other person to resolve your upset? Suggestions:

1. Tell the other person how you wish to be treated if you are being treated in a way you don't like. If the other person doesn't respond to your wishes, recognize that he or she has a problem – not you!

2. When you are confronted with unacceptable treatment or behavior, respond with how you feel about it. If you attack, the other person will get upset and counter-attack. This only aggravates and perpetuates the upset.

3. Recognize that the other person will treat you as he or she wants to, unless you express yourself. Listen very carefully to what the other person is saying. If you are satisfied, let the other person know how much you appreciate his or her understanding. If you're not satisfied, you need to make changes in the relationship.

What are you going to do now?

The left box above is your expectation and the right box is the reality. You need to either change your expectation in each box to match the reality, or change the reality in each box to match your expectation. If you choose to leave the relationship, there is nothing to change and you do not need a plan of action.

When your expectation is parallel with the reality, you will no longer be upset

Choose a strategy:

1. Change your expectation
2. Change the reality
3. Leave the relationship

If you do nothing, you will continue to be upset.

Based upon your choice of changing your expectation or changing the reality, think of what you are going to do so that you don't get upset the next time this or a similar situation happens again.

By seeing which upset issues trigger your present concern, you can choose a strategy and a plan of action to help you get what you want -- without the emotional baggage attached to the anticipation of something that may or may not happen.

Fill out a Consumer Future Analyzer® to test the plan of action and strategy that you came up with. You will see if you have really changed the way you will react to the same or a similar upsetting situation if it happens again

If you still have diagonal lines, read Catch 22. If one of the suggestions hits a nerve, choose a different option and again fill out another future analyzer.

6a. Plans of Action-Consumer Past & Future

I EXPECTED: **IN REALITY I GOT:**

Part A   **Part B**

                                        V
To not blame you   [X] [ ]   [ ] [X]   To not blame you
                                       \   /
To blame you   [ ] [X]   [X] [ ]   To blame you

Things should change!   Things shouldn't change!

OWNERSHIP OF FEELINGS: As the upset Consumer, change roles and be the Supplier. What can you supply, or not supply, to the other person to resolve your upset? Suggestions:

1. Tell the other person how you feel in a very clear and strong voice.
2. Do not allow the other person to manipulate, dictate, provoke, or pressure you into anything you don't want to do!
3. Supply yourself with the knowledge that you can take control and regain the power over your own actions and response – anytime you want to!
4. Depending upon the circumstances, you can give what is needed to yourself, to the other person, or to both. You already have the resources within yourself. You just need a reminder once in a while.
5. Don't blame the other person for how you feel, and expect him or her to make amends. You will be powerless and remain upset.
6. Take responsibility for your feelings, then you won't blame the other person. In other words, "own" your feelings and deal with them – a process that does not have to involve the other person. Although it seemed that someone else made you upset, the truth is you chose to respond the way you did. What you wanted to do or say, you did!
7. Don't fool yourself when you say, "You made me do or say it." Recognize that you will always be upset if you let yourself believe that others control your feelings. That's giving your power away! It's the consequences that you don't like. Don't now blame it on the other person.

What are you going to do now?

The left box above is your expectation and the right box is the reality. You need to either change your expectation in each box to match with the reality, or change the reality in each box to match with your expectation. If you choose to leave the relationship, there is nothing to change and you do not need a plan of action.

When your expectation is parallel with the reality, you will no longer be upset

Choose a strategy:

1. Change your expectation
2. Change the reality
3. Leave the relationship

If you do nothing, you will continue to be upset.

Based upon your choice of changing your expectation or changing the reality, think of what you are going to do so that you don't get upset the next time this or a similar situation happens again.

By seeing which upset issues trigger your present concern, you can choose a strategy and a plan of action to help you get what you want -- without the emotional baggage attached to the anticipation of something that may or may not happen.

Fill out a Consumer Future Analyzer® to test the plan of action and strategy that you came up with. You will see if you have really changed the way you will react to the same or a similar upsetting situation if it happens again

If you still have diagonal lines, read Catch 22. If one of the suggestions hits a nerve, choose a different option and again fill out another future analyzer.

6a. PLANS OF ACTION-CONSUMER PAST & FUTURE

I EXPECTED: **IN REALITY I GOT:**

Part A   **Part B**

                         VI

To initiate   [X] [ ]   [ ] [X]   **To initiate**

                        \\   /

To not initiate   [ ] [X]   [X] [ ]   **To not initiate**

       Things should change!   **Things shouldn't change!**

SETTING OF PRIORITIES: As the upset Consumer, change roles and be the Supplier. What can you supply, or not supply, to the other person to resolve your upset? Suggestions:

1. Operate on your own schedule and set the priorities. Don't let the other person disrupt your timetable.
2. Realize that you may have given up control of some portion of your life and the other person may get upset when you try to take it back. Ultimately you may find it healthier to end the relationship.
3. If the other person wants something at an inconvenient time for you, say so! Express it as, "The timing won't work for me." Pick a time that works for both of you.

What are you going to do now?

The left box above is your expectation and the right box is the reality. You need to either change your expectation in each box to match the reality, or change the reality in each box to match your expectation. If you choose to leave the relationship, there is nothing to change and you do not need a plan of action.

When your expectation is parallel with the reality, you will no longer be upset

Choose a strategy:

1. Change your expectation
2. Change the reality
3. Leave the relationship

If you do nothing, you will continue to be upset.

Based upon your choice of changing your expectation or changing the reality, think of what you are going to do so that you don't get upset the next time this or a similar situation happens again.

By seeing which upset issues(s) trigger your present concern, you can choose a strategy and a plan of action to help you get what you want -- without the emotional baggage attached to the anticipation of something that may or may not happen.

Fill out a Consumer Future Analyzer® to test the plan of action and strategy that you came up with. You will see if you have really changed the way you will react to the same or a similar upsetting situation if it happens again. If you still have diagonal lines, read Catch 22. If one of the suggestions hits a nerve, choose a different option and again fill out another future analyzer.

6a. Plans of Action-Consumer Past & Future

I EXPECTED:						IN REALITY I GOT:
Part A						**Part B**
		VII				
To give feedback	[X]	[ ]		[ ]	[X]	To give feedback
		\		/		
Not to give feedback	[ ]	[X]		[X]	[ ]	Not to give feedback

Things should change!   **Things shouldn't change!**

FEEDBACK: As the upset Consumer, change roles and be the Supplier. What can you supply, or not supply, to the other person to resolve your upset? Suggestions:

1. Tell the other person how the incident affected you and what action you will or will not take.
2. Let the other person know how you wish to be treated, either specifically or in general.
3. Just listen and hear the other person out. If the other person attacks you, defends himself or herself, or gives you a deaf ear, perhaps you need to reassess your relationship.
4. If you know that the other person will not like what you have to say, don't say it. You can't put water into a filled glass! What are you going to do now?

The left box above is your expectation and the right box is the reality. You need to either change your expectation in each box to match with the reality, or change the reality in each box to match your expectation. If you choose to leave the relationship, there is nothing to change and you do not need a plan of action.

When your expectation is parallel with the reality, you will no longer be upset

Choose a strategy:

1. Change your expectation
2. Change the reality
3. Leave the relationship

If you do nothing, you will continue to be upset.

Based upon your choice of changing your expectation or changing the reality, think of what you are going to do so that you don't get upset the next time this or a similar situation happens again.

By seeing which upset issues trigger your present concern, you can choose a strategy and a plan of action to help you get what you want -- without the emotional baggage attached to the anticipation of something that may or may not happen.

Fill out a Consumer Future Analyzer® to test the plan of action and strategy that you came up with. You will see if you have really changed the way you will react to the same or a similar upsetting situation if it happens again

If you still have diagonal lines, read Catch 22. If one of the suggestions hits a nerve, choose a different option and again fill out another future analyzer.

6b. SUPPLIER PAST & FUTURE PLANS OF ACTION

I WANT TO: **I KNOW YOU WILL:**

Part A   **Part B**

                                       I

Give an unusual response   [X]   [ ]   [ ]   [X]   Want an unusual response

                                   \   /

The old agreement   [ ]   [X]   [X]   [ ]   The old agreement

      Things should change!   **Things shouldn't change**

RESPONSE: As the upset Supplier, change roles and be the Consumer. What can you ask or not ask, from the other person to resolve your upset? Suggestions:

1. Stop supplying the other person with advice or input and another opportunity to reject what you have to offer. If the other person isn't asking, why do you think it's necessary to respond?
2. Give the other person the opportunity to be responsible for him or herself. Start asking instead of telling. You'll be surprised at the response you'll receive and how fast your relationship will improve.
3. If you must play the role of Supplier, find someone who will accept what you have to offer.

So what are you going to do?

The left box above is your expectation and the right box is the reality. You need to either change your expectation, that is, choose the right upper box, to match with the expectation, or change the reality and choose the left lower box to match. If you choose to leave the relationship, there is nothing to change and you do not need a plan of action.

When your expectation is parallel with the reality, you will no longer be upset

Choose a strategy

1. Change your expectation
2. Change the reality
3. Leave the relationship

Based upon your choice of either changing your expectation or changing the reality, think of what you are going to do so that you don't get upset the next time this or a similar situation happens again.

By seeing which upset issue(s) trigger your present concern, you can choose a strategy and a plan of action to help you get what you want without the emotional baggage attached to the anticipation of something that may or may not happen

Fill out a Supplier Future Analyzer® to test the plan of action that you came up with. You will see if you have really changed the way you will react to the same or a similar upsetting situation if it happens again. If you still have diagonal lines, read Catch 22. If one of the suggestions hits a nerve, choose a different option and again fill out another future analyzer.

6b. SUPPLIER PAST & FUTURE PLANS OF ACTION

I WANT TO: **I KNOW YOU WILL:**

Part A   **Part B**

II

Change our agreement	[X] [ ]	[ ] [X]	Want changes
Not change our agreement	[ ] [X]	[X] [ ]	Not want changes

Things should change!   **Things shouldn't change**

CHANGES TO AGREEMENTS: As the upset Supplier, change roles and be the Consumer. What can you ask or not ask, from the other person to resolve your upset? Suggestions:

4. If the other person won't accept changes to agreements, make as few as possible -- and only those you know you can keep. All interactions and relationships are controlled by some type of agreement. Recognize that all agreements can change. Don't take every request for a change as a command.
5. Don't let the other person make changes without getting something in return, and ask by when.
6. If you have to make changes, do let the other person know about it and offer options to avoid an upset or a break in the relationship.

So what are you going to do? This may not be the first time that you want to offer something to the other person and he or she won't accept it. Can you think of other cases where you weren't able to give what you want?

How often are you able to change the other person? Think about the fact that you may never be able to give what you want to the other person. Knowing that you may never be able to give what you want, how will you treat the other person in the upcoming situation?

The left box above is your expectation and the right box is the reality. You need to either change your expectation, that is choose the right upper box to match with the expectation, or change the reality and choose the left lower box to match. If you choose to leave the relationship, there is nothing to change and you do not need a plan of action.

When your expectation is parallel with the reality, you will no longer be upset

Choose a strategy

1. Change your expectation
2. Change the reality
3. Leave the relationship

Based upon your choice of either changing your expectation or changing the reality, think of what you are going to do so that you don't get upset the next time this or a similar situation happens again.

By seeing which upset issue(s) trigger your present concern, you can choose a strategy and a plan of action to help you get what you want without the emotional baggage attached to the anticipation of something that may or may not happen

Fill out a Supplier Future Analyzer® to test the plan of action that you came up with. You will see if you have really changed the way you will react to the same or a similar upsetting situation if it happens again.

If you still have diagonal lines, read Catch 22. If one of the suggestions hits a nerve, choose a different option and again fill out another future analyzer.

6b. Supplier Past & Future Plans of Action

I WANT TO: **I KNOW YOU WILL:**

Part A   **Part B**

                                    III
Explore alternatives   [X]   [ ]   [ ]   [X]   **Want alternatives**
                                 \   /
Not explore alternatives   [ ]   [X]   [X]   [ ]   **Not want alternatives**

     Things should change!   **Things shouldn't change!**

EXPLORING ALTERNATIVES: As the upset Supplier, changes roles and be the consumer. What can you ask, or not ask, from the other person to resolve your upset? Suggestions:

1. Stop supplying alternatives. Let the other person come up with suggestions.
2. Find out what the other person wants and will be satisfied with. Offer to supply only what you're able to deliver. Stick to your guns!

So what are you going to do? This may not be the first time that you want to offer something to the other person and he or she won't accept it. Can you think of other cases where you weren't able to give what you want?

How often are you able to change the other person? Think about the fact that you may never be able to give what you want to the other person. Knowing that you may never be able to give what you want, how will you treat the other person in the upcoming situation?

The left box above is your expectation and the right box is the reality. You need to either change your expectation, that is, choose the right upper box, to match with the expectation, or change the reality and choose the left lower box to match. If you choose to leave the relationship, there is nothing to change and you do not need a plan of action.

When your expectation is parallel with the reality, you will no longer be upset

Choose a strategy

1. Change your expectation
2. Change the reality
3. Leave the relationship

Based upon your choice of either changing your expectation or changing the reality, think of what you are going to do so that you don't get upset the next time this or a similar situation happens again.

By seeing which upset issue(s) trigger your present concern, you can choose a strategy and a plan of action to help you get what you want without the emotional baggage attached to the anticipation of something that may or may not happen

Fill out a Supplier Future Analyzer® to test the plan of action that you came up with. You will see if you have really changed the way you will react to the same or a similar upsetting situation if it happens again.

If you still have diagonal lines, read Catch 22. If one of the suggestions hits a nerve, choose a different option and again fill out another future analyzer.

6b. SUPPLIER PAST & FUTURE PLANS OF ACTION

I WANT TO: **I KNOW YOU WILL:**

Part A   **Part B**

                                          IV

Understand your side   [X]   [ ]   [ ]   [X]   Want understanding
                                      \   /
Not understand your side   [ ]   [X]   [X]   [ ]   Not want understanding

   Things should change!   **Things shouldn't change!**

BEING UNDERSTOOD/ACCEPTED: As the upset Supplier, changes roles and be the Consumer. What can you ask, or not ask, from the other person to resolve your upset? Suggestions:

1. Stop trying so hard to understand the other person's point of view and consider your own.
2. Ask the other person if he or she understands what it is that you want. Is it so important for the other person to accept or understand you? If he or she doesn't want to, you might want to reassess your relationship.
3. Recognize that you may never get what you want from the other person!

So what are you going to do? This may not be the first time that you want to offer something to the other person and he or she won't accept it. Can you think of other cases where you weren't able to give what you want?

How often are you able to change the other person? Think about the fact that you may never be able to give what you want to the other person. Knowing that you may never be able to give what you want, how will you treat the other person in the upcoming situation?

The left box above is your expectation and the right box is the reality. You need to either change your expectation, that is choose the right upper box to match with the expectation, or change the reality and choose the left lower box to match. If you choose to leave the relationship, there is nothing to change and you do not need a plan of action.

When your expectation is parallel with the reality, you will no longer be upset

Choose a strategy

   1. Change your expectation
   2. Change the reality
   3. Leave the relationship

Based upon your choice of either changing your expectation or changing the reality, think of what you are going to do so that you don't get upset the next time this or a similar situation happens again.

By seeing which upset issue(s) trigger your present concern, you can choose a strategy and a plan of action to help you get what you want without the emotional baggage attached to the anticipation of something that may or may not happen

Fill out a Supplier Future Analyzer® to test the plan of action that you came up with. You will see if you have really changed the way you will react to the same or a similar upsetting situation if it happens again.
.
If you still have diagonal lines, read Catch 22. If one of the suggestions hits a nerve, choose a different option and again fill out another future analyzer.

6b. SUPPLIER PAST & FUTURE PLANS OF ACTION

I WANT TO:					IN REALITY:
Part A					**Part B**
		V			
Not Control	[X] [ ]		[ ] [X]		I didn't control
	\		/		
Control	[ ] [X]		[X] [ ]		I did control

Things should change!   **Things shouldn't change**

OWNERSHIP OF FEELINGS: As the upset Supplier, changes roles and be the Consumer. What can you ask, or not ask, from the other person to resolve your upset? Suggestions:

1. Don't try to control the other person's feelings. The issue is one of power. If your intentions are to control the outcome of the situation, you are mistaking the use of force for power. Your real power lies in allowing the other person to appreciate and benefit from what you have to offer and to accept what he or she has to offer you.
2. Don't let the other person push your "hot buttons." Respond to the issue, not your own emotional habit. Make your behavior an action that comes from within you, not a reaction to an outside force or stimulus.

So what are you going to do? This may not be the first time that you want to offer something to the other person and he or she won't accept it. Can you think of other cases where you weren't able to give what you want?

How often are you able to change the other person? Think about the fact that you may never be able to give what you want to the other person. Knowing that you may never be able to give what you want, how will you treat the other person in the upcoming situation?

The left box above is your expectation and the right box is the reality. You need to either change your expectation, that is choose the right upper box to match with the expectation, or change the reality and choose the left lower box to match. If you choose to leave the relationship, there is nothing to change and you do not need a plan of action.

When your expectation is parallel with the reality, you will no longer be upset

Choose a strategy

1. Change your expectation
2. Change the reality
3. Leave the relationship

Based upon your choice of either changing your expectation or changing the reality, think of what you are going to do so that you don't get upset the next time this or a similar situation happens again.

By seeing which upset issue(s) trigger your present concern, you can choose a strategy and a plan of action to help you get what you want without the emotional baggage attached to the anticipation of something that may or may not happen

Fill out a Supplier Future Analyzer® to test the plan of action that you came up with. You will see if you have really changed the way you will react to the same or a similar upsetting situation if it happens again.

If you still have diagonal lines, read Catch 22. If one of the suggestions hits a nerve, choose a different option and again fill out another future analyzer.

6b. SUPPLIER PAST & FUTURE PLANS OF ACTION

I WANT TO:						IN REALITY:
Part A						**Part B**
			VI			
Be the initiator	[X]	[ ]		[ ]	[X]	**I was the initiator**
		\		/		
Not be the initiator	[ ]	[X]		[X]	[ ]	**You were the initiator**

Things should change!   **Things shouldn't change**

SETTING OF PRIORITIES: As the upset Supplier, changes roles and be the Consumer. What can you ask, or not ask, from the other person to resolve your upset? Suggestions:

1. Let the other person make the first move or take the first step.
2. Communicate your timetable. Offer the other person alternatives if you can. Learn to say "no", with kindness and firmness.
3. If the other person repeatedly rebuffs your suggestions, or changes the timetable, stop initiating and evaluate what your relationship with this person is all about.

So what are you going to do? This may not be the first time that you want to offer something to the other person and he or she won't accept it. Can you think of other cases where you weren't able to give what you want?

How often are you able to change the other person? Think about the fact that you may never be able to give what you want to the other person. Knowing that you may never be able to give what you want, how will you treat the other person in the upcoming situation?

The left box above is your expectation and the right box is the reality. You need to either change your expectation, that is, choose the right upper box, to match with the expectation, or change the reality and choose the left lower box to match. If you choose to leave the relationship, there is nothing to change and you do not need a plan of action.

When your expectation is parallel with the reality, you will no longer be upset

Choose a strategy

1. Change your expectation
2. Change the reality
3. Leave the relationship

Based upon your choice of either changing your expectation or changing the reality, think of what you are going to do so that you don't get upset the next time this or a similar situation happens again.

By seeing which upset issue(s) trigger your present concern, you can choose a strategy and a plan of action to help you get what you want without the emotional baggage attached to the anticipation of something that may or may not happen

Fill out a Supplier Future Analyzer® to test the plan of action that you came up with. You will see if you have really changed the way you will react to the same or a similar upsetting situation if it happens again.

If you still have diagonal lines, read Catch 22. If one of the suggestions hits a nerve, choose a different option and again fill out another future analyzer.

6b. SUPPLIER PAST & FUTURE PLANS OF ACTION

I WANT TO: **IN REALITY:**

Part A   **Part B**

                                        VII

Get feedback   [X]   [ ]   [ ] [X]   **You gave feedback**
                                  \   /
The old agreement   [ ]   [X]   [X] [ ]   **You didn't give feedback**
Not get feedback

Things should change!   Things shouldn't change

FEEDBACK: As the upset Supplier, changes roles and be the Consumer. What can you ask, or not ask, from the other person to resolve your upset? Suggestions:

1. Find out how you're doing by asking the other person. If you can't get the kind of feedback you need, you might want to re-examine your motives, your expectations, and the kind of relationship you have with the other person.
2. Don't give answers when you are asked for agreement or reasons for your actions. Silence is a wonderful answer. You may also want to ask why he or she needs to know the answer.

So what are you going to do? This may not be the first time that you want to offer something to the other person and he or she won't accept it. Can you think of other cases where you weren't able to give what you want?

How often are you able to change the other person? Think about the fact that you may never be able to give what you want to the other person. Knowing that you may never be able to give what you want, how will you treat the other person in the upcoming situation?

The left box above is your expectation and the right box is the reality. You need to either change your expectation, that is, choose the right upper box, to match with the expectation, or change the reality and choose the left lower box to match. If you choose to leave the relationship, there is nothing to change and you do not need a plan of action.

When your expectation is parallel with the reality, you will no longer be upset

Choose a strategy

1. Change your expectation
2. Change the reality
3. Leave the relationship

Based upon your choice of either changing your expectation or changing the reality, think of what you are going to do so that you don't get upset the next time this or a similar situation happens again.

By seeing which upset issue(s) trigger your present concern, you can choose a strategy and a plan of action to help you get what you want without the emotional baggage attached to the anticipation of something that may or may not happen

Fill out a Supplier Future Analyzer® to test the plan of action that you came up with. You will see if you have really changed the way you will react to the same or a similar upsetting situation if it happens again.
.

If you still have diagonal lines, read Catch 22. If one of the suggestions hits a nerve, choose a different option and again fill out another future analyzer.

7. CATCH 22

You're still upset. To help you clear up some of the issues surrounding your upset and allow you to look at the situation in a different way, 22 suggestions are given to help you get off your position and resolve your upset.

As you read each suggestion, listen to the feeling that you get in your body. It may tell you when a suggestion has touched a tender nerve. Re-examine your strategy based on that suggestion and fill out another Future Upset Analyzer®. You may need to change your main upsetting issue or your strategy.

1. Change your role from being a Consumer to being a Supplier or vice-versa.
2. Role play the upset with a friend and listen to yourself.
3. Are you really upset?
4. Are you being honest with yourself about what really happened?
5. Ask someone else to talk to the other person.
6. Is this the situation that is really upsetting you?
7. Write down what the other person "should" do to resolve the upset. Now change the "should" to, "they chose not to", or "they chose to." Now what are you going to do?
8. Write it in a letter, saying it all. Tear it up or burn it, or put it in a shredder. The problem gets reduced to confetti.
9. Can you check your assumptions with the other person about his or her actions or statements? Do you want to? Are you afraid of what you might hear? What does that say about your relationship?
10. What are you trying to accomplish? Do you have to be right? If so, is there a way to be right and still get what you want?
11. Put yourself in the other person's shoes and listen to his or her side of the story.
12. Are you afraid of the consequences of what solving the problem means?
13. Take the same upset and apply it to someone you only slightly know. Do you have the same upset? If not, you might be upset with the person and not the situation.
14. Imagine yourself with only one week to live. Would you still hold the upset the same way?
15. If you could have anything in the world that you wanted, what would help you resolve this upset? What is preventing you from getting it?
16. Perhaps you are upset with a third party for doing something to someone you care about? Are you really upset with that person? Could it be your friend who didn't do or say what

you thought he or she should, or didn't handle the situation as you expected him or her to?

17. Are you holding onto a belief based on the way the other person "should" behave rather than the way that person did behave? Can you remember who taught you that belief? Tell that person it isn't working! Now what are you going to do?

18. Congratulations, you wanted to be upset, and you are. How long do you want to be upset to satisfy your sense of righteousness? A week, a month, a year, the rest of your life? What is it costing you?

19. Do you complain about your health because of stress? Isn't it worth giving up your anger and resentment to regain your health?

20. If you can't resolve your upset at this point, it's because you don't want to. How many other upsets like this one are you holding onto? This program can help you, only if you are willing to be open and honest about your relationships. Do you really enjoy being upset?

21. Re-read the chapter on the seven expectation issues.

22. Re-read the chapter on beliefs and don't 'should on yourself.'

SECTION III

PART II. THROUGH SUPPLIER EYES

This subject deals with concept tools. Without these tools we wouldn't know if we are the hammer or the nail!

Consumer and Supplier are roles we use every day when we give and take in relationships and interactions with others. We'll now focus specifically on the Supplier role, using this headset, and see the world through Supplier eyes.

Suppliers think differently than Consumers

Each headline and its accompanying theory offer you the opportunity to see 'possibilities' for change in your life. This can only be done through Supplier eyes. To be the Consumer means to be on the receiving end and we want to be the builder!

The choices in life are based upon whether you choose to think like a Consumer or a Supplier. As a Supplier, you create. As a Consumer, you initiate!

See if the concepts I'll expound upon agree or disagree with your own belief system. How will you reconcile or refute them based upon what works or doesn't work for you? Will you continue with what doesn't work for you, the status quo, or will you pick up new tools and make them work for you? You'll have to determine what to build.

If you are in conflict, fill out the Emotional Toolbox™ Analyzer choosing a Supplier or a Consumer Past Analyzer. To determine which one to fill out, read, "Which Analyzer to Fill Out", and follow the directions.

You would enter the following statement, "I am upset because you," and then fill in what you're upset about using me, Zalman, as the other person, being as specific as possible about what I wrote that upset you.

Eagles and Turkeys
I classify people for the purpose of identifying their basic nature: eagles or turkeys. Eagles live and fly in a rarified atmosphere. They need plenty of space in which to fly. They can see other eagles flying and all the turkeys below them. Turkeys can only see other turkeys. It's lonely being an eagle, but the benefits far out way the disadvantages.

When you meet a turkey, silently, under your breath say, 'gobble-gobble.' Chat awhile then fly back up to where you belong.

Creating and Cleaning

You are either creating something or you are cleaning something at any given moment. If you are not doing either, then where are you? We can't create and clean up at the same time. When we create something, build something, anything, we leave something to clean up after ourselves, the residue. Many people are just too lazy to clean up after themselves and then the problems mount up… to the point where it can become too overwhelming to even begin. Let's take a simple example of what I mean.

A Clean Sink

Consider this term a mantra[1], just like 'gobble-gobble.' You have a clean sink. You have a cup of coffee and put the cup and the spoon into the clean sink. What do you see?

A clean sink with a cup and a spoon in it.

You cut a piece of pie and eat it and put the plate and the fork in the sink. What do you see?

A clean sink with a cup and a spoon and a plate and a fork in it.

You open up a can of soup and put the soup bowl and the tablespoon in the sink. What do you see?

A dirty sink!

When the sink is dirty, you lose the ability to differentiate between a clean sink and what's in it -- plus you don't know what's been added into it!

Now translate this into your own life. You must always be cleaning out the garbage in your life to know when another piece of garbage is entering it. Yes, it takes time and effort to do this, but you have no other choice if you want to have your life exactly the way you want it to be.

If your head is swimming with all things that need cleaning up, both physically and in your relationships with others, you have some work to do. It's not that you don't have the tools to do it; it's just that you've been too busy with too much minutiae, the little stuff in your life, to pay attention to what's important.

Let's create the Empowerment party that I mentioned before. Its purpose is to empower the American people. Our platform will be:

We will give Americans what they want and not give them what they don't want.

We'll create campaign chapters in every state. It will be a grass roots ad hoc party that will rise above the political parties we have now, until we form a critical mass, and then we'll run for office in state and national elections.

Don't you think it's possible? If Rosa Parks could challenge and transform the racial fiber of our country by refusing to stand up and give her seat to a white person, then you and I can do it. The moral majority that runs our country isn't moral and they are not in the majority. Individually and collectively we can have it the way we want it to be.

[1]In Hinduism, a mantra is a sacred verbal formula repeated in prayer, meditation, or incantation, such as an invocation of a god, a magic spell, or a syllable or portion of scripture containing mystical potentialities and a commonly repeated word or phrase

First we need a plan. With a plan, we can choose the tools to build our party. In the process we need to get rid of all the self-serving politicians we voted in on every level of government. Let's get the campaign going and raise funds, bang the drums, blow the horns, get bumper stickers.

I checked, and the website www.empowermentparty.org was available so I went ahead and registered it for one year in my name. It's the first step in making it real!

If you want to join the party, send me your name and email address. Nobody else will see it. I'll have my web designer put password protection into getting into the website using your email address. We'll include a state blog, so we can communicate on things we need to share with party members like who to throw out of office, who to support, which issues to support, companies we're going to boycott and support …things like that.

The dues will be $5/year. This will support the websites and the paid members to run each chapter in each area in each state. Of course we'll have volunteers too, just as we had with the Obama campaign. Here's a few of the floorboards in our platform:

- No candidate can spend more than $25,000 per person in campaign financing and it cannot come from corporations.
- State level offices cannot be held for more than 4 years. If you can't get the job done by then, you don't deserve to be in office longer
- Only the president and his cabinet members, and senators and governors positions are full time. All other positions must be part-time, spending only one week a month on government business. They can work full time in other jobs.
- Anyone found associating with or holding clandestine meetings with lobbyists will be fined $1,000 for the first offense, and $5,000 for each subsequent offense – plus these offenses will be well publicized on our website.

This is just a start! Who's going to start the first chapter in their state by getting 10 members to join @ $5 each? The money as I said will be used to develop chapter websites in each state. Get constituents to buy my book and become empowered members. My email is zpuchkoff@carolina.rr.com to get in touch with me for where to send your membership fee.

Here is how I envision getting the grass roots issues and concerns up to the top echelon on a 24/7 basis:

1. Create a website for every chapter in each city and state, for example: www.empowermentparty.com/southcharlotte/nc/php and www.empowermentparty.com/university/nc/php and so forth,

Do this throughout the U.S. We can have over 1,000 different websites! We can solicit the emails of every person who wants to join our party.

2. Show the photos and email addresses of the top 9 cabinet officials and under each, show the issues the American people want changed and which cabinet member is responsible for it. Make it a vote for or against, so we can tally the votes up under each issue. You would vote for each issue but only one vote per issue.

3. Every time somebody registered their email and paid the $5 annual fee, the number of members in the party for that chapter would be shown in a separate field. We would now know how many voted for or against a particular issue. The specific issues would be decided upon by our top officials, filtered down to state chapter captains, down to city chapter captains to post on each website.

4. Here's the best part. Our president would have his pulse on the American people 24/7 on each issue! All he has to do is plug into his own website and get the tally of the total number of votes, yes or no, on each issue, and convey that to each of his cabinet members, who would also get the tally of what the American people want, not what they want to do but what the American people want them to do. Cross us and we'll vote you out of office! We will not be the Consumers of what we don't want to get or not want to receive. We will tell our elected officials as Consumers what we want them to do and not want to do for us!

5. Of course we'll have a blog on each issue to exchange views and share opinions.

If you can dream it, you can make it happen

Impedimentia

The Greek word for baggage or luggage is 'impedimentia'. The baggage could be physical or emotional. Get rid of your baggage and see how well you'll feel. If you're overweight, consider that weight is a 'withhold.' Get rid of the emotional baggage and see if the weight doesn't drop. The Emotional Toolbox™ is also a good tool to use to help resolve upsets that trigger the need to eat.

When we buy things, we really don't own them. We rent them for as long as they're useful to us, and then we pass them on when we pass away. Shrouds don't have pockets, so don't become attached to objects. I'll discuss more about this subject, collecting things, later on.

Abcd-efg-hijk-lmnop

Children from kindergarten on are taught various subjects so that when they graduate from high school or college, they can go out in the world and apply what they learned.

WRONG!

They are not taught how to build anything. They are taught how to use tools so that when they go out in the world, their employers will tell them what the company is building and expect them to have the proper tools to build it. That's the reality.

1. What to build
2. Which tools to choose
3. How to use them

How do children know what tools to learn in school if they don't know what they are going to build 10 or so years in the future? They need to be given things to build now and taught how to use the tools to build them so that when they get out into the world they can continue to build what they learned.

This approach to teaching can be a starting point for school administrative officials to design curriculums that compare academia's expectations for teaching students how to use tools with the reality of what they need to build in the real world. Consider a curriculum that included the time value of money, how to maintain and balance a checkbook, how to find out anything on the internet, how to start a business.

From your experiences, what would you have liked to be taught when you were in school? What are you going to empower your children to build, starting right now?

A few years ago I signed up as an after-school tutor in New York City. The program was sponsored by a not-for-profit organization to help public school students who needed remedial tutoring in math, reading, English, and writing.

I was assigned to help a 9-year old girl, Nancy, who had trouble in just about every subject. We met in a teaching classroom in a Catholic school on the upper west side of Manhattan every Tuesday and Friday at 4pm for an hour.

I was given a report of Nancy's progress the previous year with another tutor, and what progress she was making, as well as a form to fill out at the end of every session, including what I taught her, and her progress each session.

I could use whatever tools I wanted in any subject I wanted to teach. I had free reign. Not being a certified teacher with a degree, I 'Googled' everything that I needed to teach her. I worded it, "How do you…" and filled in the subject and printed it out, and 3-hole punched the topic and put it in a binder.

My intention was to build up Nancy's confidence in her ability so she would feel that she was able to learn, and to enjoy learning at the same time! I first started off by showing her some magic tricks, and she loved it! I asked her if she would like to learn one, and when she said yes, I knew I had a student!

Within one-half an hour, I taught her a simple trick and told her that she had to practice at home and do it for me the next time we met. This was the beginning of creating a structured routine of practicing – anything. Learning can be made fun!

I bought a soft-covered book of short stories and asked her to pick one out to read out loud to me. We stopped at every unfamiliar word so she could get the dictionary out and look up the word. At the end of every page, I asked her to give me a short summary of what was happening in the story.

Her reading was staccato; she pronounced each word independently. That was because she was looking at only one word at a time. I showed her how to look at 3 words at a time and to speak them one after the other, as in a conversation -- without having to first say them in her mind, which slows down the story telling enormously. Speed readers take in paragraphs at a time, and some people can take in whole pages at a time!

We recognize objects and words not by their attributes or their named identification but by our immediate cognizance of what they are. That is to say, we do not have to look at a telephone and say the word telephone in our mind first to be able to recognize that we are looking at a telephone.

And so it is with reading. We see the words and instantly know what it is that's being said. This takes some time, just as it takes time to learn how to walk. We do not deliberately put one foot in front of the other. Our footsteps flow one after the other. I demonstrated this for Nancy and seeing how I walked stilted style, she could associate it with how she had been reading.

To further help in developing a cadence, or a rhythmic pattern in reading out loud, I downloaded the most lyrical poem that I could find, "The Owl and the Pussycat" by Edward Lear. We went over the poem every time we met. In time, she learned the poem by heart and I told her that when she grows up and has children of her own, she could teach it to them. I believe she will.

I reproduced the poem so that you can teach it to your children or grandchildren. I had to look up the word 'runcible' and I now know what a runcible spoon is. Actually my mother used it when we ate grapefruit but I didn't then know its name. It's a combination spoon and knife, with ridges at one end of the spoon to cut the flesh out from the pulp.

The Owl and the Pussycat
By Edward Lear
I

The Owl and the Pussy-cat went to sea
In a beautiful pea green boat,
They took some honey, and plenty of money,
Wrapped up in a five pound note.
The Owl looked up to the stars above,
And sang to a small guitar,

'O lovely Pussy! O Pussy my love,
What a beautiful Pussy you are,
You are,
You are!
What a beautiful Pussy you are!'

II

Pussy said to the Owl, 'You elegant fowl!
How charmingly sweet you sing!
O let us be married! too long we have tarried:
But what shall we do for a ring?'
They sailed away, for a year and a day,
To the land where the Bong-tree grows
And there in a wood a Piggy-wig stood
With a ring at the end of his nose,
His nose,
His nose,
With a ring at the end of his nose.

'Dear pig, are you willing to sell for one shilling
Your ring?' Said the Piggy, 'I will.'
So they took it away, and were married next day
By the Turkey who lives on the hill.
They dined on mince, and slices of quince,
Which they ate with a runcible spoon;
And hand in hand, on the edge of the sand,
They danced by the light of the moon,
The moon,
The moon,
They danced by the light of the moon.

In furthering Nancy's education, I taught her how to differentiate between coins …from one cent to fifty cents without having to look at them, simply by feel. All coins have different sizes;

1¢, 5¢, 10¢, 25¢, 50¢, even the $1 coin. In addition, some coins have smooth edges, and other coins have ridged edges. Coins also have different thicknesses.

Within a week, she was able to put the coins in her pocket, and pull them out one-by-one when I asked her to give me the coin I wanted. What was I building?

I think you can answer that one.

Whenever Nancy wrote anything, she printed the words. I asked why she didn't write cursive, or in script. To my amazement, she told me that the public schools in the state of New York no longer taught cursive writing, as everybody has a computer with Word® and spell checker.

We'll see about that, I said!

I Googled, www.handwritingforkids.com and printed out practice sheets on basic handwriting. It's © 2000-2008 by Linda C. Readman, and contributions to her are appreciated. If you print out the sheets, her address is on it.

I also downloaded, www.howtotutor.com/cursive.htm, "How Should We Teach Our Children to Write? Cursive First, Print Later?" by Samuel L. Blumenfeld. In 3 days I was ready to teach Nancy how to write cursive.

Devoting three hourly sessions to just practicing, "The little brown fox jumped over the lazy dog", which contained the 26 letters of the alphabet, and practicing 26 lower and upper case letters, Nancy was ready to test her new-found writing tools.

She came in the next session with a big smile on her face and proudly told me, "My teacher said that I'm the only one in the class who can write cursive!" My intention showed up, as yours can anytime you want it to.

At the end of the spring term Nancy had read all of the short stories, had caught up on everything so I gave her the book to keep and said my goodby. I moved that May to Charlotte, NC.

The Eyes Have It
Watch people's eyes when they speak to you. You'll know when they've finished speaking because their eyes will drop. That's the sign that they have finished communicating what they have to say to you. Now it's your turn to speak. Test it out the next time you speak to someone.

Still watching while someone is speaking, you can see when they're telling the truth or not. I didn't make it up. If they are telling the truth, their eyes will move up to their right. If they are lying, their eyes will move up to their left. Don't you see my eyes are up to the right?

Do-be-do-be-do-be-do
It's not Frank Sinatra singing. It's the two different modes of being that we engage in at any given time. We either 'do', that is take action of one kind or another, or we 'be', that is we don't 'do'

anything, and allow ourselves to take in emotionally and spiritually what the world has to offer us. We are in effect replenishing our inner being, our well-spring.

We don't have to be doing something all the time. We don't have to look busy or 'make work' to make ourselves feel worthwhile. And that includes staying late at the office every night being a workaholic.

Nobody ever said on their deathbed, "I wish I spent more time in the office."

Simply put, when we are Suppliers we do, when we are Consumers we 'be.'

For many of us, it's very difficult to 'be.' It makes us feel that we're not accomplishing anything. But we are! We're replenishing our inner feelings as we need to be doing.

Nobody can give happiness to you and nobody can take it away unless you let them, and in so doing you give up control. You will never find happiness! I personally guarantee it. You have my word on it. I'm telling you the truth. Don't you see my eyes are turned up to the right?

Happiness is not found outside of yourself. It's not found in a new house, car, wife, job, in anything. Happiness comes from within, only you lost sight of this when the world caved in on you and you had to go out and fight the battles. A new car feeling lasts 2 weeks. A new office feeling lasts 2 weeks. A pay raise feeling lasts 2 weeks.

All you have to do is to get rid of the emotional baggage you've been carrying around for years to let the happiness that's been dormant inside you reappear.

Don't you remember how happy you were just to skip a stone across a pond? How about standing with a fishing rod in your hand when you were a little boy or girl? Can you remember how it felt? What's holding you back? What are you holding on to that you're afraid to let go of?

Nobody ever said on their deathbed, "I regretted many of the things I did in my life."

They didn't regret them. They did them because they wanted to. They only regretted the consequences or results of what they did!

What they aren't saying is that they regretted the things they didn't do! You don't want to wait until you're on your deathbed, so why not starting right now, do-be-do, and do the things you've always wanted and not do the things you don't want to be doing.

In 1997 I woke up one morning and I said to Janet, we're going to Australia. Call the travel agency and pack your bags. I've never been there and I want to go there. And we went, spending 2 weeks there and one week in New Zealand. And we went back to New Zealand in 2000 to see the millennium come in. I did it!

Karma

Dictionary definitions are wonderful to look up. I've heard people say, "That's my karma", as if it was predestined to happen regardless of the actions or deeds by that person.

1. *Hinduism & Buddhism* The total effect of a person's actions and conduct during the successive phases of the person's existence, regarded as determining the person's destiny.
2. Fate; destiny.
3. *Informal* A distinctive aura, atmosphere, or feeling: There's bad karma around the house today.

That doesn't sound like the same thing! One definition says that's cause and effect. What an individual does will determine where he will wind up. So if I do good things, then I'm going to wind up in a good place? Wrong!

It's a total package theory. You have to be of one mind in thought and action on a continuous basis in your existence to arrive at the effect of what you created. You can't go to church or Synagogue on Saturday and Sunday and pray for forgiveness or repent for sins, and then go back on Monday to a dog-eat-dog world existence.

I am reminded of a book that I read many years ago by Somerset Maugham, The Razor's Edge, which was turned into a movie, starring Tyrone Power. It's the story of a playboy who went to Tibet in search of the truth (that's my recollection) and came back enlightened and a new man. He had discovered that he had to tell the truth at all cost, and to do it required him to walk through life metaphorically as if he was on a razor's edge. If he was not true to himself, he would trip and in so doing he would fall off the razor's edge and cut himself.

Each of us needs to be on a razor's edge if we are to commit ourselves to having our intentions show up in life.

Let's take this one step further in examining the true nature of karma, and that is cause and effect. I will use examples taken from business terms, as that's what I'm familiar with.

If a customer asks you for something, that something could be a product, a service, or space. Those are the only three things or 'deliverables' that you are going to supply to that request. The term is arbitrary, perhaps because you deliver it to the customer, even though it may be picked up.

The customer is the Consumer, the requester of the deliverable, and you are the Supplier, the giver of the deliverable. Now that we have that in place, let's use actual situations, questions and answers to ponder using the headsets of Consumers and Suppliers.

When you're traveling 45 miles an hour down Main Street in a 25 mile per hour zone, what are you requesting as a Consumer?

Answer: **A ticket from a policeman who is the Supplier.**

That's karma!

When you put on a U.S. military uniform, what is the deliverable that you are asking for?
Answer: **A bullet from the enemy**.

That's karma!

If you flunk the mid-term and the final exam in a subject, what is the deliverable that you're requesting?

Answer: **You know the answer!**

Cause and effect might not be readily apparent in a short time range, but ultimately cause and effect connect. That is why we cannot judge reasons why things happen because, first of all, we cannot see the whole picture at any one time, and secondly, our memory cannot hold all the cause and effect connections over a long period of time.

> Joe was a kind, good man who was faithful to his family and honest to his friends, and gave to charity; and he never made it big.
> He would pray to God every day to win the lottery -- every day, every day.
> One day a booming voice came out of the void saying, "Joe, give me a break and buy a ticket!"

Guess why cause and effect didn't happen this time?

Listen Up!
People can only tell you who they <u>are</u>, not who they <u>are not</u>. That is to say, if we use our eyes and our ears and listen very carefully, in the first few sentences, we will get a clear picture of the person we're talking with when we first meet. We won't if we're interested in impressing him or her or we're not paying attention to what is being said.

Our instinct is to size people up when we first meet them. We do this because we want to feel comfortable. Pre-judging takes the work out of finding out who they really are. The trick is to trust your inner feeling, because it's the best tool you'll ever have for judging people.

When I couldn't tell who someone was when I first met them, I would ask if they would like to see a magic trick. If they said 'No', I had my answer. If they said 'yes' I would do a trick and by their reaction, I would know who they are. Here are the tools that I used in sizing them up, but first you need to know that the purpose of doing magic is to entertain your audience, not to fool them.

If that person was more interested in finding out how I did the trick or tried to make me look foolish, I knew I had a control freak on my hands. Here's a person to stay away from. They'll shut you down at every opportunity. If that person appreciated what I did and went along with my presentation, I knew that person was open and accepting to what comes along.

What tools are you using to judge people?

Inventory Control

If you care about something, you'll keep an inventory of it. You can keep it on a computer, a piece of paper, in your head, anywhere, but you will know how much of it you have, perhaps not exactly but you'll be pretty damn close. Why?

If you run out, there will be consequences that you won't like. A businessman knows that certain numbers are vital to his business, such as sales, inventory, accounts receivables, and he keeps track of these vital numbers. A chef must know his stock of food on any given day, to order what he needs filled in. My wife Janet keeps track of how many rolls of toilet paper we have in the bathroom, and how many bars of soap and toothpaste are in the bottom cabinet. Why? She doesn't want to run out of any of these items. It's important to her to know when we're running low.

It's not important to me. As a joke teller, it's very important that I remember and categorize a joke that I like and put it into my inventory of jokes when someone tells one to me so I can repeat it.

'I can never remember a joke.' 'I can never remember a name.' Does this apply to you? If so, the reason is because you're a Consumer, and you don't have any intention of remembering jokes or names. You don't put them into your inventory of jokes and names of people. They go in one ear and out the other. It's just that simple!

If you want to remember anything, change roles and be the Supplier (to yourself) and create the inventory of names and jokes or anything else that's important to you. So when a joke is told, associate it with something familiar, especially the punch line, and remember where you filed it away. Associate a persons name with a feature about them, either a physical attribute or an attitude they have, and then repeat it as a mantra. Otherwise, don't keep on saying, I can never remember…

Meditation

I've often heard this word, and I'm perplexed as to what to do. Do I sit with my hands folded, my feet crossed? Is this important to do? Am I supposed to think about a particular subject or do I allow anything to cross my mind?

I think I'm sounding like Andy Rooney on 60 minutes. I don't like using the 'meditation' word as it conjures up religious trappings and I'm against all religious trappings, because they're 'traps' to me. I prefer empowerment thinking. That is, making up my own mind as to my own moral codes of conduct.

If you agree with me act now, and you can receive a 10% discount if you join the empowerment party. It's only $5 but you need to join today and become a member for only $4.50 a year. We'll let you meditate as long as you need to. My email address again is zpuchkoff@carolina.rr.com and I'll add your name to our membership list.

Remember I just discussed keeping an inventory of things you care about and things to do. Here's another way. Sit in a comfortable chair with the door closed and no distractions --g no TV, radio, or pets and you're all alone. Now just relax, and think of nothing....and don't try to! Close your eyes or keep them open, whatever is comfortable for you. And don't have anything in your hands.

Whatever is in your space will show up in your mind. It will appear as a 'to do' list, those things that need your attention. Don't do anything about them. Allow all those thoughts to enter your mind, and simply note them. Do this for 2 minutes.

I'm being kind because I don't think you can stand doing and thinking of nothing for 5 minutes. Try 15 minutes and you'll go crazy! After 2 minutes get up and go and write them down. These are things that you need to clean up and do ASAP. Duh! This is not rocket science. It's just the way your brain works, and it's a blessing to find out how to use it to clean out the impedimentia that's in the way of you realizing the happiness that you can have, if only you are willing to clean out your own sink.

Do this 3 times a week, every week for the rest of your life. Six minutes a week is not a lot unless you fight it, like doing 20 minutes of exercise 3 times a week. You're getting off too easily if you expect to make positive changes that you don't have to work at. If you don't want to, put the book down and continue to complain as you've always done.

Hey! Who said life was fair? Life is what you make it! Are you a Supplier to yourself or a Consumer of what you don't have? Remember the ruthless rules of reality, dear reader.

Judgment Day
This is not about after you die. It's about who does the judging in any situation where you play the role of the Supplier: as an actor, an artist, or an entertainer.

The moment you stop being the Supplier to your audience and start judging yourself -- if your work or performance is good enough -- you become a Consumer and at that point you've lost touch with your audience.

Do you get the jitters when you have to get up and give a speech or act? People who were queried answered that doing just that was the most frightening thing they could think of. Richard Burton was said to have drunk a bottle of liquor before he ever would go onstage. Helen Hayes would get the shakes before she went on stage before every performance.

Janet is a cabaret performer, and before working her act one night in New York City, she called me at home and said she had the jitters, even though she had performed this same act before.

I told her, don't be a Consumer and judge yourself during the act. Be the Supplier right to the end. Let the audience judge you and they'll do that by the applause you'll get at the end of your performance. She did it, and they gave her a standing ovation – no more jitters.

Once you judge yourself, you lose confidence and it's very difficult to change roles, that is go from being a Supplier to a Consumer, and then recover to become a Supplier again.

Stay in the same role in which you started.

Athletes have this same problem. Books have been written about the inner game of tennis or golf or any other sport. They're playing great, they're winning and all of a sudden they take a bad shot, and it's all downhill from there. You've seen it happen. What caused it?

They went from being a Supplier (of good performance) to being a Consumer (judging themselves for bad performance). They have no tools or time to recover, unless they are seasoned pros. They have lost self-confidence. From then on, it's a downward spiral to defeat. We've seen this many times at tennis games or golf matches.

You cannot be in both roles at the same time

You are in one role or another at any given time. The winner is the person who can switch roles instantly, recover and remain in the Supplier's role and never ever think as a Consumer until the event is over.

Chain Saw

The language that we use has power. When we speak harshly to someone, those words can never be taken back; the damage has been done. As an allegory, imagine yourself in a forest with a chainsaw. Whatever the chainsaw comes in contact with is cut off, never to grow again. So you have to be very careful how you use it. Now imagine all your words to be chain saws and the people you communicate with are trees. So whenever you feel the urge to say something you'll regret, say 'chain saw', as a mantra.

You can always stop yourself from getting upset with someone by repeating to yourself, over and over: wigwam, tepee, wigwam, tepee, wigwam, tepee.

It shows that you're too tense (2 tents)

Time out - Substitution

If you never heard the word 'bad,' what other word would you have never heard? 'Good', that's right. Just imagine how many words we bring into being just by uttering their counterpart. How about the word wrong? Then 'right' wouldn't exist. These are judgment words which are subjective in nature and are liable to cause conflict and retaliation.

How about substituting words that improve the situation not hurt it, and are objective in nature and can move a conversation forward, even though different opinions are expressed?

Suppose we substituted win or lose with 'effective' and 'ineffective.' Gives a more objective tone to the situation and it still gets the point across. You have an opportunity to redesign your vocabulary so that the words you use express exactly what you want to say without instilling fear, hostility, or anger in someone else. The dictionary is your best friend.

If you use positive words, you will get back positive feedback; if you use negative words, you'll get negative feedback. The world is a mirror, and you cannot see a reflection different than what you created. Here's a puzzle: why is the reflection in a mirror left to right, opposite than what is real, yet top to bottom it's exactly the same?

In our universe, there is a left and right, so it's recreated in a mirror, but there is no up and down, so it remains the same view. Hmmm…so why is heaven depicted as being up and hell being below if they are the same?

The Dating Game

Many years ago, I went to a reunion of EST graduates who were volunteers during the year. EST was the 'training' created by Werner Erhard in the mid 70's. I talked with a woman in her early 30's who was a sex surrogate and she did this for a living. She would help men overcome their fears in having sex by having sex with them.

She told me that she was very successful in what she did but she was having trouble getting a man for herself. What! I said. I asked her what she did to advertise, and she said she put many ads in the personal columns of magazines but none of the men who replied appealed to her.

Delving further, I asked 'how did you word the ad'? Now all you single guys and gals listen up!

She said she described herself and what she was looking for in a man.

She was playing the part of a Consumer, asking for what she wanted. And all the men who answered were playing the part of Consumers, asking what they wanted. In order to have a relationship one party needs to be the Consumer, the other needs to be the Supplier.

I told her that she needed to promote what she could give or offer a man and be a Supplier, not a Consumer of what she wanted from him. If she did this, she would have them knocking down her door to get to her. She did it and sure enough, that's what happened and I didn't hear from her again.

Along the same lines, Janet is a guru when it comes to direct mail. She created sweepstakes for magazines across the country. A client told her that she was advertising to adopt a baby but so far, nobody answered her ads. Janet offered to reword the ad and here's what happened:

The woman had featured who she and her husband were as Consumers. Janet changed it around and promoted what the woman and her husband could give the baby and the pregnant mother as Suppliers, stating the benefits the baby would have in her care.

Two weeks later the phone rang, and the baby was adopted! Are you getting the picture?

Get off it!
This old expression means literally, to get off your position. That is, change the way you are looking at something right now, as you can only see a very small part of the picture through your eyes from where you are standing.

So literally, with both feet together, move one or the other about two feet apart and then put them both back together in your new position. You will now see something differently from that position.

When we say this, we are asking someone to emotionally to get off the position they are holding onto and let go of it so that they can listen to and take in another person's viewpoint.

How many times have you made a decision and you judged it immediately as good or bad, only to find out weeks, months, years later that it didn't turn out the way you expected it to go?

I was reading a book, The Illustrated Religion's of the World, by Huston Smith, © 1958, and in it was a story that I want to relate to you about Confucius because it had such an impact on me:

> A Chinese farmer had a small house with a little corral in back with a stallion in it. One day the stallion jumped over the fence and ran away.
> > His neighbor said, *that's a terrible thing that happened to your horse!*
> > He said, *I don't know if it's such a terrible thing.*
> The next day the stallion came back leading a whole herd of wild mares into the corral.
> > His neighbor said, *that's a wonderful thing that happened.*
> > He said, *we'll I don't know if it's such a wonderful thing.*
> The next day the farmer's son broke his leg when he fell off one of the mares.
> > His neighbor said, *that's a terrible thing that happened.*
> > He said, *well I don't know if it's such a terrible thing.*
> The next day the Chinese army rode through looking for teenagers to recruit into the army and couldn't take the lad with a broken leg.

Good thing, bad thing; we are always making immediate judgments when we don't have a big enough picture or don't have all the information at hand.

More than Time on Your Hands
The Upset Analyzer™ in the Emotional Toolbox™ will help you resolve upsets. It's not that you won't get upset, but that it teaches you not to hold onto an upset because if it is not attended to, it may cause dis-ease in your body. A case in point:

If I held up a glass of water in my outstretched hand and asked how much the water weighed, you would give me some answer. It's not how much it weighed that would cause a problem with my arm. It would be how long I kept my arm stretched out.

If I held the glass up for a minute, my arm would ache. If I held it up for an hour I would have severe pains, and if I held it up for 3 hours, I would have to be taken to the hospital.

And so it is with an upset that is held over time. The longer you hold onto it, the worse it will get.

Peeling an Onion

As human beings we want to protect our image of who we think we are, and what we've become. Ask someone who they are and they'll give you different answers. One person will extend a business card. 'Oh, you're a business card?' Another will say their name. Another may say, I'm the president or CEO, or whatever his title that may include a high ranking position in the military, religious order, institution, government, etc.

Is that who the person is, or is there more? Stripped of name, title, and job, how would you answer someone if they asked you? You could say that you were kind, considerate, charitable, loving, perhaps adding many more desirable attributes. But that wouldn't tell them who you really are. So what's the answer?

We are in effect, like onions. When you strip an onion of its layers right down to the core, what do you have left? NOTHING! That's right, nothing. It sounds a lot scarier than what it really is. We all have layers and we work very hard to protect them, so as not to have others peel them away to expose our vulnerabilities and inadequacies. It's very painful to have them revealed.

Each layer revealed takes away what we have always believed is a part of us, because we have lived with it all our lives. "How dare you try to take away a part of who I am?"
The truth is, it's not a part of you and never was. It's impedimentia, the baggage that you've been carrying around all these years.

If you allow someone to help you strip it all away or do it by yourself, you will find that you are still you -- without the baggage -- free to be anything you want to be, at any time, in any place! Can you envision that? Can you feel it?

If you can, then your transformation is complete, and you've allowed yourself to accept new ideas and a philosophy that feels right to you.

You can now become a charter member of the Empowerment party!

If you can't strip it all away, the world will settle for what you can strip away, and thank you for your willingness and ability to do something to bring you closer to yourself. You too can join our movement. Now go out and start a chapter in your state!

In every Reality Analysis™ analyzer there are seven issues which originate from a single source; the Chakras. These are discussed in detail in The Emotional Toolbox™ program, which is the core technology as to why people get upset. The words in each issue are different, but they have a connecting thread. The Reality Analysis Systems® methodology and the 7 factor comparisons in other areas are shown in the Reality Analysis Systems® chapter.

To give you a specific example, in the business comparison, one of the questions asked is: do you rent or sell your product? Applied to a relationship, the inherent issue is: do you rent yourself or sell yourself to your partner? Important implications, because a man may feel that once he gets married, he owns his wife or vice versa.

When you sell something, the buyer can do whatever he or she wants with the product. But if rented, it must be returned in the same condition, less wear and tear. A person cannot own another person in a relationship or in a marriage. You can only rent yourself to the other person and you can always leave if the other person does not take good care of you.

Institutions
According to the dictionary, the definition of an institution is ...

> ...an established entity or activity in society comprising rule-bound and standard behavior patterns. It includes any enduring activity by groups or organizations (e.g. the family, education system, law, polity, economy, or religion), which address important and persistent societal problems.

My theory on institutions, marriage, and religion through Supplier eyes: I'm for all religions and certainly for marriage; they're great, if they help you. Otherwise, why would you want to be a part of one?

Every institution I can think of is a Supplier; they give the Consumer something, whether tangible or intangible and provide a deliverable: a product, a service, or space. The only two institutions I can think of that are in business to perpetuate themselves are government and religion.

Think about it. They appear to be Suppliers but in fact they are closet Consumers. They really want to take from you, usually money to keep themselves going. Would you voluntarily give them money if you didn't have to?

The institution of marriage provides a product. That product is a document – a marriage license provided by the state in which you get married, usually officiated over by a member of the clergy in your faith.

The question I put to you is: when is a marriage successful? If you answered yes to the question, "...till death do you part" at the ceremony, the answer would be until one partner dies.

I'll back up. You had to sign a contract, and you promised that you would stay with your partner until one of you died. At that point the contract is over, and you've fulfilled your obligation under the contract. That's the context of the relationship.

But what if they weren't happy?

That's the content of the marriage, whether it was good, or bad. In my generation, we stayed married, 'no matter what!' It's not that way today, and it doesn't have to be the way it was. And, you have to work at keeping a marriage alive and well.

I was married for 25 years when I left my first wife – and not for another woman. I was too much of a Supplier for my wife who was too much of an emotional Consumer. I could not give her what she needed in the amount she needed. In the four years that I was on my own I learned more about myself than I ever did living with her.

I had two relationships after leaving my wife and I asked each woman to marry me. They both declined. In retrospect, if I had married either one of them, I would have left them or they would have left me. What I did not know then was how to find the right woman. Here's what I needed to do, as some of you may need to do:

Use the tools in this book and find out what your intended partner needs and let that person know what you need!

Sit with pen and paper in hand and ask each other the following questions:

What do you need materially and how much?
What do you need emotionally and how much?
What do you need sexually and how much?
What do you need spiritually and how much?
What do you need …(fill in anything you need)

Write it all down and see how much you can supply to each other. Perhaps you can give 80% in one area, 90% in another area, or 40% in another area. Balance it out and the question to ask yourself, can you LIVE with it? You are in effect, playing Supplier/Consumer to each other.

If you can't supply enough to each other's needs, then take another piece of paper and go find someone else to interview.

I found out that I could live with any woman on earth!

All I had to do was to find out what needs the woman required and supply them to her!

Isn't it simple when you put it down on paper?

Religion

I mentioned that there were only three deliverables: products, services, or space. What does a religious organization supply to its members? My answer will be looking through Supplier eyes, so I invite you to put on my glasses to see what I see.

1.   A seat in the congregation – space
2.   A place for social interaction -- a service

3.   Religious instruction for children – a service

These are deliverables that are independent of the value or benefit that the organization may or may not give to its members. The quality of the deliverable must be judged by the Consumer, not by the Supplier organization. Unfortunately, too many religions dictate to the Consumer what must be accepted as value or benefit or the Supplier will stop supplying.

This is fear-driven, based upon belief systems that are taught to children and perpetuated by parents to the next generation.

If God wants you to have the good life why be afraid to express it when you have it?

Do you believe in Santa Claus? You did as a child, so why don't you still believe in him? That's because someone told you at one point in the growing up stage that he wasn't real. How did that make you feel?

If nobody told you that he wasn't real, would you still believe in Santa Claus? If you said no, I don't believe in Santa Claus, your belief systems are showing, not your rational thinking.

To proselytize a religion is to ask me to take off my glasses and put on your glasses so I can see what you're seeing and to then say to me, don't you see much better now?

> *When I express my abundance*
> *I'm afraid God will change my luck*
> *When I express my misfortune*
> *I never expect God to change my luck*
> *Who set this up, me or God?*

- There are thousands of religions espoused by many spokespeople. If the messages are different, where are they all getting it from?

- If my religion says I was born in sin, if I leave will you come with me?

- If I knew then what I now know, I wouldn't have learned it!

Colleges and Universities
These are also considered institutions. What is the deliverable that each of them offers its students?

Is it an education, a degree, a place of learning, a scholarship, an opportunity to learn?

Space -- a seat in a classroom

I'll back up. You don't have to get an education; you can flunk out of school. You don't have to attend classes, and you don't have to receive a diploma. When you pay your tuition, the only thing that you are guaranteed is a seat in the class. When the enrollment equals the number of seats available in the classrooms, the enrollment is closed. Case closed.

The college would have to add to its infrastructure to support additional students -- housing, cafeterias, instructors and teachers, social and athletic facilities, more classrooms probably and at considerably more cost than the increased tuition gained. What can be done so that more students at every level of education, from elementary/grade school up can get a better education? Provide virtual classrooms!

Many colleges are doing just that, providing classroom teaching with at-home computers, but they need funding from endowments, municipalities, state agencies, increased school taxes, to create a real 'no child left behind' program that is substantial in reality, instead of in expectation.

To shell out $20-$40 thousand dollars a year to send a child through college is a bit much to ask a parent. If we could provide virtual classrooms throughout the country starting at state colleges, we could provide every student who wanted one, with a college education that would cost no more than $5,000 a year. Where did I get that price? I made it up. And we could pay professors and teachers the kind of salary that top execs get.

What do you think would happen to enrollment in Ivy League colleges? And what effect would that have on tuition costs? Can I enlist a Supplier out there who is a state university official to create a pilot program in his state?

If you find it uncomfortable with my glasses on, and you know you need to change the prescription in the glasses that you're wearing, what are you going to do? You'll have to decide that for yourself as it's your life and only you know where you want to be going.

The roadmap of your life is not where you are really going

Unfortunately, as I said before … too many people are driving through life looking through their rear-view mirror.

Don't you trust me?
This is one of those expressions that supposedly put you on the spot to answer the other person, "Of course I do!" when in reality you don't. Let's take this scenario apart to see exactly what's happening and why. Putting on your Supplier/Consumer earphones, you will be able to hear what's going on in each person's mind, which is in italics.

The Supplier says, "I promise I'm going to be at the meeting." *I don't think I can make it.*

The Consumer replies, "It's urgent that you be there, because your vote counts a lot." *I don't trust him because he's missed meetings before.* "Promise me that you're going to be there." *I hope I can get him to keep his word this time.*
The Supplier responds; "I told you I'm going to be there. *He's thinking I'm not going to be there.* Don't you trust me? *That will get me off the hook.*

If you give positive feedback, "Of course I trust you!" that gives the other person the opportunity to not have you continue the subject. You have let him off the hook.

If you give negative feedback, "I don't trust you!" you will antagonize the other person and give him good reason to use it as an excuse to say, "In that case, if you don't trust me, you're not my friend and I'm not going!"

You're being put on the spot as a Consumer of a question that you don't want to hear. You are proverbially on the horns of dilemma. Neither answer will suffice. What do you do?

Change roles and be the Supplier of information that you know about the other person; it needs to be objective not subjective. The reply, " I trust you to do what you usually do, and that is to not show up at meetings, and I'm asking you if I can trust you to show up to this one."

The answer to a 'trust me?' question must always come from knowing that the other person will always do what is best for him or herself and not for you. If the other person does show up, you can be surprised, and, tell the other person, "I knew I could count on you!"

Let's use another scenario. You've answered the question as the Supplier. How about changing roles and be the Consumer and say, "Why do you ask?" Now the other person is on the spot to answer you. He has to defend himself with a reason that you question, that may force the other person to prove that he can be trusted. His response of, "Because I don't think you trust me", is the opportunity to say that he has missed many meetings and you want to be sure that he shows up.

The Consumer inherently trusts the Supplier right up to the time when he can't be trusted and that's when a promise is broken. The decision is yours as to which role you are more comfortable in, and the circumstances surrounding the interaction as to whether to be the Supplier or the Consumer.

So many seemingly entangled emotional issues can be dealt with in an unemotional and rational manner using Consumer and Supplier roles to play out the scene.

Let's use the same scenario in business.

You have a long standing customer who has open account terms and always pays on time. The last 2 invoices were paid 15-20 days past due. He's placed another order and you send him an acknowledgment with 'prepayment required.'

He calls you and says, "I've always had open account with you, don't you trust me?" If you get hooked into answering this question, you're going to lose one way or the other.

1. If you say, "sure I trust you", you'll have to give him open account terms and chances are you won't get paid at all, or have to wait a long time for your money again.

2. If you say, "I don't trust you", you've made it subjective and personal.

It's not a matter of whether you trust him or not. Past transactions show that he's late in paying invoices, and that extending credit to him is based upon current performance. You can ask him for full prepayment or negotiate and offer an option. Ask for half, the balance on open account and if he pays on time, then extend full credit.

If he doesn't agree to your terms, you're being conned!

Breakfast Anyone?
As a businessman, I've hired many people to fill customer service positions. The duties include taking orders over the phone, entering them into the computer, following up orders, sending purchase orders to vendors. It's a very detail oriented position.

I've used my Interview Analyzer™ to show me if my expectations for the job match the reality of the person I'm interviewing. It does not help me determine if the person can follow a very structured, detailed, and methodical routine the job requires. Resumes can't tell me that either.

What I do is tell the person that I've never cooked anything before and I want to cook breakfast consisting of scrambled eggs, bacon, whole wheat toast with butter, and coffee with half & half. I ask that person to describe in detail how to do it and have it on the table all at the same time.

I listen very carefully, and at the end of the story, I say either you're hired or thank you, we'll be in touch, which I never will. I don't need to give that person a long explanation as to why he or she is not qualified.

I'll put the question to you. What am I looking for in this person?

While you're thinking, what are the two things that you can't eat for breakfast?

Lunch and dinner!

Breakfast is the hardest meal to make. That's because each ingredient takes a different length of time to prepare and cook. There's a lot about detail, when and how each is prepared, and the length of time each step takes. It requires someone who is methodical, structured, and can clearly explain each step in sequence.

Isn't it simple when you put it down on paper?

For or About
Here's another distinction that I categorize people. Are you a 'for' or 'about' person?

'It's going to rain today.' 'Did you catch the game on TV last night?' 'Who's your favorite singer?' These are subjects that are <u>about</u> things. They deal with reporting information about the past.

There's no action in the present or possibilities for creating something in the future. They don't build or advance things. This is the role of a Consumer.

When you talk <u>for</u> something, there is the opportunity to create things, build for the future. This is the role of a Supplier. Think in terms of possibilities. Remember when you used to daydream? I still do, and when I let my mind go where it wants to, I envision what I want to build. Using that as a starting point, I then say, what are the tools that I need to use and do I have the resources to build it. If not, I look to where I can get them.

All the World's a Stage
That's according to William Shakespeare. If we are the actors in it, we certainly should have the ability to determine what roles we want to play and be the producer and the director and star in our own play, which is our life.

We can do this is if we decide what kind of a play we want to produce, that is, an opera, a tragedy, a farce, a drama, a comedy, or a musical. Next we need to choose the cast of characters we want in our play taken from a pool of actors which includes our family, friends, and business associates. Let's not forget cameo roles, extras and walk-ons. Who is suited to play each part that we've written into our play?

We wrote the script but no matter how often we do a re-write, the actors keep on messing up their lines, missing cues, and not following what we want them to do or say. At this rate, no one will want to come see our play!

Wait, it's our life so who cares who comes to see the play! The problem is, we are so concerned how our life looks to other people that we are afraid to be the star and not care what others think of our play.

We have become spear carriers in our own opera.

Throw down your spear and get back to what you're supposed to be doing in your own play: directing, producing, orchestrating. Be the Supplier to yourself, and not the Consumer of whatever part is given to you by others.

So whenever you feel that your life isn't going the way you want, and you're in a scene that is not to your liking or you're not acting in your best interests, say the mantra word, 'Spear' and you'll know what you need to be doing.

There! It took me all these words to get to the punch line.

A Successful Failure
So many of us feel inadequate that we just can't imagine or feel that we are able and capable of being a success at anything, and I mean anything. It doesn't make a difference what it is:
Cooking – Oh, I can't cook. Can you read? If so, you can cook
Sewing – Oh, I can't sew. Can you read? You can sew.

The list goes on and on. Well, what have you tried doing? What have you stayed with doing so that you can become successful at it? If nothing, I don't see your intention showing. We all know what failure is and we're comfortable with where we're at even though we don't like it, and we can only dream of being successful.

I know a few people who are absolutely successful - at being a failure in their lives. No kidding, whatever they do it always fails. That is because of wrong thinking. Their premise is wrong to begin with.

I'll back up. Your expectation for success will not lead to the reality you envision. You have to work it the other way! If your expectations are not grounded, you have to jump start and deal with your reality first and allow your expectations and emotions to catch up with you, even though you're not comfortable in so doing. Let's take a closer look at the three relationships between expectation and reality in diagram form.

People have different views of their expectations and their reality, and no pair of eyes are the same. Imagine the top box to represent the expectation side, the left eye, and the bottom box to represent the reality side, the right eye.

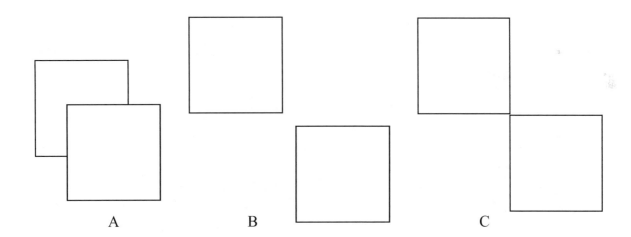

In diagram form, it's easy to see the three types of connections that exist between an individual's expectation and the reality of a situation.

   A. Expectation and Reality overlap; no distinction is made between the two
   B. Expectation and Reality disjoined; can't connect cause with effect
   C. Expectation and Reality connected; cause and effect are in direct sequence

Isn't it easy when you put it down on paper?

If you only did something when you were comfortable about it, how many things would you get done? You had to go into unchartered areas, and make your way through, with the uneasy feeling that it would not work – and it did! How did you then feel?

Apply the same tactics. Imagine yourself being successful at what you do best. Apply the principles and use the tools that create the reality, independently and without regard to your expectations, which seem to lead down the path to failure. Your expectations are only what you think, and it's what you do that makes the difference in your life. If your result is a failure, you planned it that way!

As an example: I have no regard to whether I can build a new political party or not. I do not have an expectation that it will take off. I'm creating it just the same, and I will enlist the people who do know how to run campaigns, and get the resources and tools to help it grow.

I don't care what you think! I don't even care what I think! What's important is what I do. And the same applies to you!

If you regard yourself as a failure, liken it to a person who has always been fat who finally loses the weight and looks in the mirror and sees a fat person. You will always see yourself as a failure even when you achieve success at something – unless you change roles. Stop being the Consumer of failure and start being the Supplier of success.

I'll back up. To consider whether you are successful or not successful, there are three questions that must be answered first:

1.   How do you measure success?
2.   What areas of your life are you focusing on?
3.   Are you thinking as a Consumer or a Supplier

The book cover shows a tape measure (of success) whereby we can measure quantitatively how much success we have achieved in terms of money, friends, our family, and personal accomplishments. This is subjective as we all have our own ideas of what success looks like.

Some of us are happy to use a 25' tape measure as a criterion, whereas others aren't happy unless they're carrying around a 100' tape measure. How much is enough can never be answered as an absolute value. Many of us are using yardsticks as substitutions for fulfillment, or what we don't have in our lives.

*The need for fulfillment can never be satisfied by someone
getting too much of what he or she really doesn't want.*

The answer to #1 rests with you, dear reader.

Just as there are areas of 'smartness', there are judgment areas of success that bear focusing upon because they are important to us. The areas can be easily identified because we keep an inventory of them. If it's not important to us, we don't concern ourselves if we're successful in that area or not.

Here are the judgment areas of success that I focus upon in answer to question #2:

1. My marriage, the quality of my relationship with my wife
2. My relationship with my children
3. My business, the ability to pay my bills, make a profit, and provide a comfortable lifestyle
4. My relationship with my friends, how many I have and for how long
5. My ability to take care of my health and my peace of mind

My judgment of being successful or not is predicated upon whether I'm thinking as a Consumer or as a Supplier. When it comes to doing magic, I don't need to concern myself with whether I'm successful or not. I let my audience do the judging, and by their response, I'm a success!

If I judge my success against another magician who is in the limelight, I'm going to have a problem, because I'm not measuring my success in terms of my accomplishments, but with my abilities compared to someone else; and that's a different measurement.

My answer to #3 is I do my best to think like a Supplier to my audience.

> *Are you thinking like a Consumer or a Supplier when*
> *you measure your successes in each of your areas?*

Create a market

Near the outskirts of a small city in a rural area, a gas station stood at one of the corners of an intersection. The other three corners were vacant lots. Business was not good even though there was traffic going by.

An enterprising man happened to be driving by the gas station one day and saw both a possibility and an opportunity.

A possibility is something that can be achieved or has potential in the future. It usually requires a series of steps. It may or may not be an opportunity to take advantage of, as the timing or the circumstances may not be favorable. These two viewpoints are entirely different.

One person may see a possibility but may not know how to take advantage of an opportunity. This is the Consumer role. Another person may see a situation as an opportunity, and may or may not be concerned with its possibility at the moment and create it as he builds. This is the Supplier role. Now that you have the distinction, let's see what the man did.

He approached the gas station owner and asked if he would be interested in selling the gas station. Sure, said the owner.

So the man went to the city hall of records and found out who owned the other 3 lots and contacted them. Each of them were more than happy to sell him their lot, which he bought with little down and monthly payments spread over a long period of time.

Then he went back to the gas station owner and bought his station. What did he do next?

He contacted a competing gasoline company and bought a franchise and erected another gas station on one of the corners and started a price war with big signs up and down the intersection. Every car that passed stopped to fill up at the cheapest station.

With a little more money in his pocket he again contacted another competing gas company and did the same thing. So now he had three gas stations on three corners, all competing with one another.

I think you get the picture. In time he had four gas stations going, each promoting a different brand, each advertising different prices for gas in a continuing gas war. Word got out in the city and cars would line up to get his gas. From high prices to low prices, he still made money no matter which station a car stopped at.

When you're holding both ends of the stick, there is no stick!

Did you ever take notice that certain intersections now have four different gas stations? What makes you think they are not all owned by the same person?

How can you create a market with a business or service that you are in or want to go into? Does the possibility exist, and can you see an opportunity to do it?

To achieve the results, you need resources. See The Competitive Advantage™ program in this book for help with developing your plan.

A beginning, a middle and an end
When you build something, that's the beginning; while you're building, that's the middle, and when you finish building that's the end of being the Supplier.

You can enjoy it, admire it, and even show it off; after a while you tire of it as the Consumer -- and that's the time to move on. Unfortunately, too many of us don't know where we are in our own life cycle. We've stayed too long at the fair. It's time to move on, and we don't want to!

We've become too complacent, too comfortable in a dead-end job or situation. We're galvanized to the point where we can't even think of moving on – to what? we say. We're afraid of giving up our comfortable position unless the benefits of moving on exceed the benefits of staying where we are.

Janet and I moved into a contemporary house in Connecticut, in Litchfield County, fifty feet from the Housatonic River, right on Route 7. It had 5 acres with a wrap-around deck and a hot tub in it, all-glass windows, 2 fireplaces – everything we always wanted.

I did the mowing, the gardening, and everything else to make the place a showcase. After a while I hired a landscaper to add trees and shrubbery. And then more shrubbery was added. Then I added a gazebo right off the water. Railroad tie steps were added to walk down to the river. I got tired of watering so I added automatic underground sprinklers.

After 12 years my dream house became a nightmare to maintain and all I could see was work and a sieve for money to go down the drain! I had stayed too long at the fair. Everyone who saw the for sale sign asked me why I would want to leave such an idyllic setting, a haven.

They couldn't understand because they were not in my life cycle, and explaining didn't help. The expression "everyone dances to a different drummer" means the same thing.

I'm going through a similar situation right now.

I'm 3rd generation in a family business, started by my grandfather and following in my father's footsteps. I'm an only child and my two sons are established in what they are doing: I have no one to leave the business to. It is not feasible to sell because it requires years of experience to understand how to market the products we offer. In 2010 the business will be 100 years old.

Janet keeps on telling me that if I close the business our financial life style wouldn't change. It's not a matter of money, and we would have more time to travel and enjoy our life. So what's holding me back?

The same fears that we all have either real or imaginary. I have to use the same tools that I have been teaching you to use to solve a problem, so allow me to use you as a sounding board for where this scenario will take me.

Parenthetically, if you have a similar problem, use a friend to talk it out with. You'd be amazed at the outcome just by airing it.

I cannot change my expectation that I can spend less time in the office because I moved my business down to Charlotte NC recently and the customer service person I hired will not ever be able to run the business without my constant presence.

Because after 50 years in it I no longer have the enthusiasm nor the drive or ambition to build, I cannot turn it into a cash cow or self-generating business.

Right now I'm upset and I do not want to continue to be upset. I have to leave the relationship!

That's what I'm going to do. My plan is to close the business by the end of 2009, sell off the inventory, pay off the creditors, close the office, shut down the website, and take a nice long holiday with Janet.

I know I'm not going to sit in the park and feed pigeons!

So much for Supplier Eyes!

Part III. Through Consumer Eyes

We need to switch roles and become Consumers if we are to understand the thinking process that goes on and the actions that Consumers take.

Consumers think differently than Suppliers

We know that a Consumer initiates all requests and that nothing takes place or manifests itself unless a request is made by the Consumer to the Supplier. If a Supplier initiates a request it is an unsolicited request the Consumer does not have to respond or reply ... more about this subject later on.

The Consumer's power comes from two sources:

    1. As the initiator of all requests
    2. As the non-Consumer of what is offered

The first ability is manifested when the Consumer says to the Supplier, "Do you have...?" or, "I want...." This role is explained in The Emotional Toolbox™ program under the 'Consumers and Suppliers' chapter.

The clerk in a retail store or a waitress in a restaurant may precede the Consumer's request for something with, "May I help you?" simply because the Consumer has not made up his or her mind as to what to order. The interchange between Consumer and Supplier is still the same.

To tell or not to tell
The second ability is to be a non-Consumer, and this has much greater power. As long as the Supplier fulfills the request of the Consumer matching the expectation of the Consumer, we have a happy and satisfied Consumer. When the expectation of the Consumer is not fulfilled by the Supplier and the Consumer gets something that he doesn't want or doesn't get something that he wanted, another question arises:

Does the Consumer tell or not tell the Supplier of the problem?

If the Consumer does not tell the Supplier of the problem, and accepts what is given out of embarrassment or fear that the Supplier will not listen or make restitution, guess what? We will have an upset Consumer.

If the Consumer tells the Supplier of the problem, the Supplier may still not listen or make restitution, in which case we will still have an upset Consumer. In either case:

It is incumbent upon the Consumer to tell the Supplier of the problem.

Here's an example.

Janet and I had lunch in a delicatessen that had recently changed hands. We usually ordered a corned-beef sandwich which we always liked. This time we ordered a brisket sandwich which we split. It was terribly dry. We asked the waitress to please bring us some hot gravy for the sandwich. She brought over a thick brown sauce that we put on the sandwich which made it worse!

We ate the sandwich, paid for it and left the restaurant saying to each other that we were never going back there again!

I'll back up. The scenario that took place was that we went into the deli as satisfied Consumers as we had eaten there before and we expected to walk out as satisfied Consumers. Our expectations were not fulfilled when we tasted the sandwich. We did not solve our problem in the Consumer role! By asking for gravy, we wanted to solve our own problem, so we became Suppliers to ourselves.

But we did not become non-consumers (of the sandwich), change roles and become the Supplier (to the waitress) of our discontent (of the sandwich), we allowed ourselves to get upset and remain upset when we walked out of the restaurant.

The universe will supply

The inherent question here is, do you believe it or do you know it? To believe it is to take someone else's word for it based upon their experiences. To know it is to experience it yourself as the Consumer.

As a Consumer, if you don't put what you want out in the world, nobody is going to hear it and supply it to you. I know it to be true because I've experienced it many times. A few years ago when we lived in Sharon, CT, Janet wanted to make a turkey and realized she didn't have a turkey pan. I said, don't worry, we'll find one at a tag sale, and that Saturday we actually did.

It makes no difference what you want. It could be a hot water bottle or a used car. Believing or not believing that it works is not the issue. "I'll never find the right man." "I'll never find the right woman." These are self-defeating prophecies. Know that the right person will come into your life and your intention will show up.

Intention is doing what you need to do to make something happen

It may not happen immediately, but if you put it out in the universe, sooner or later, it will appear. I promise you. Can't you see that my eyes are turned up to the right?

Put up and shut up

Do you put up with waiting; in line to be seated in a crowded restaurant? How about waiting before someone comes over to your table to take your drink order? If you say 'yes' then I ask you, why put up with it?

If you say 'No', then you are a non-Consumer, unwilling to accept whatever is given to you. As the Consumer, you pay good money to get what you want, and not get what you don't want.

If not you, who? And if not now, when?

When was the last time you walked out of a restaurant without leaving a tip because the service was terrible? Be honest! If you ever did it, I'll bet you did it only once, and you probably felt guilty for doing it.

I'm going to tell you the secret of how to never ever feel guilty again in your whole life. But you may be afraid to hear it. It may upset your whole belief system and religious training.

Always take responsibility for your words and actions.

That's it! Sound too simple? Understand its meaning. Every single thing you do and say, you will own up to and take responsibility for. No sneaking around, no lying, no spin, no fudging, no shifting the blame, no asking for forgiveness, no defense, no excuses - ever. If you can do that, stand up in any situation, emotionally naked, and say, 'yes it was me,' then you're a free person. You now have the tool to never feel guilty again. Are you willing to get up to bat and take responsibility?

A tip is not a given; it's a reward for good service. And if you think that TIP is an acronym for 'To insure promptness', you're mistaken. Besides, you would give it at the beginning of the meal not at the end of the meal.

Here's a test. The next time you have a meal out, walk out without leaving a tip. Do it for no reason whatsoever other than to feel the experience and to know that you are in control of your own feelings as a Consumer. You don't have to make excuses to anyone!

I can't do that, you'll say. Guess what? Your belief system is showing! OK, wait until the service is terrible. The waiter doesn't bring bread to the table, takes a long time in getting to you, doesn't bring you exactly what you ordered, doesn't stop by to ask if everything is OK with the meal, and do you need anything, and worse, has someone else bring your meal, and only stops by to leave the check on the table. Will that make you feel justified in not leaving a tip?

What is the job of the waiter who takes your order in a restaurant? If you say, to take your order and bring you the food, that's the wrong answer. Nowadays, at many restaurants, other wait-staff bring the food.

The answer is, to make sure the food you ordered is exactly the same food brought to your table, checked by the waiter before it's served to you. And if it is not exactly what you ordered, then to tell the chef it's not as ordered, and not bring it to you.

How many times have you received food that was not prepared as you ordered it? How many times has the waiter told you that your food order had to be returned to the kitchen to be redone because it was not prepared as you ordered it?

This micro study in food service illustrates the need to separate the Consumer role from the Supplier role.

Managing vs Doing

The two modes of expression, 'managing' and 'doing', are entirely different jobs. To 'do' is to perform specific tasks like bringing food from the kitchen to your table. That's doing something. To manage is to be responsible for the entire range of activities from beginning to end, the whole nine yards. (The expression is attributable, among others, to making a suit which takes nine yards of material.)

You cannot manage and do at the same time.

When you are doing something, you are the Supplier. You are supplying something to yourself or to your boss or superior. When you are managing you are the Consumer. You are responsible for all the individual tasks from beginning to end in a series of activities that encompass a job. These are called life-cycle steps and they can be found in the 'Competitive Edge Analyzer™' program.

I'll back up. When you are a manager, you must be responsible for what is being done or is not being done by everyone under your supervision or control. In the case where you only are involved, then it is your sole responsibility to manage the entire process.

In the case of being a manager in a restaurant, it would include as part of the process to make sure that all the waiters and waitresses were doing their jobs taking orders promptly at tables, making sure the customers received their food within a reasonable length of time, they were satisfied with the service, and the busboys or wait-staff cleaned the tables off and reset them quickly. A manager must take in what is going on around him or her, and that's the definition of a Consumer.

So if we equate Supplying with doing and Consuming with managing, we can easily see that we cannot do and manage at the same time.

We cannot be in both roles at the same time!

I think the reason there are so many small business failures is that one person takes on both jobs, ignoring the fact that doing and managing cannot be combined.

Anytime you feel you have to do something, your belief system is showing. You don't have to do anything you don't want to do. The solution is, change roles and be the non-Consumer – of inferior and bad service. Then you don't have to supply – anything.

What or who is preventing you from exercising your power as a non-Consumer? Who do you think is judging you -- society, your friends, a spouse?

A little secret …

No matter what you do or don't do, you're going to be judged anyway, so why pay attention to what people think? If it upsets you being in one role, switch roles! These decisions are not hard to make, which reminds me…

If you take responsibility for your actions as a non-Consumer of bad or inferior behavior or service and not reward it, you're a free person. You too are qualified to join the Empowerment Party. We allow both upset Suppliers and Consumers to join us, to oust the government officials who are draining our treasury by bailing out conglomerates who ought to be left to go into bankruptcy!

You're selfish!
These are words we've heard before, and they were probably thrown at us by people who thought that we were doing what was in our own best interest, not theirs.

Guess what?

They were absolutely right! The definition of selfish is: not doing what someone else wants you to do. You're doing and acting in your own best interest and that's what you must always do – be the Supplier to yourself first.

Shakespeare said it, "To thine own self be true." That's you and me, and I come first, and you come second in my world. If you're not numero uno in your own world, then you can't take care of anyone else. If you don't agree with me, fill out a Consumer past Upset Analyzer™.

Civil Servant
This label to me sounds like an oxymoron. It's an expression that contains exact opposites, such as "giant shrimp", or a "little lot." Public and government officials are called civil servants, and by far, most of them do not seem to me to be civil, nor do they serve.

Have you ever called a public utility company, like the phone company, electric company, the gas company, or any other monopoly? Did you call them to thank them for the wonderful service they give you, sending the correct bill that you can easily read, on time all the time?

Stop laughing!

Every time you call, it's because there's a problem, a situation, and you're primed to expect feedback that you're not going to like. Worse, you're going to be connected to someone who seems not to care because that person knows that when that phone rings, he or she is going to hear from an irate Consumer demanding retribution or a pound of flesh!

How do you handle situations like this?

Change roles from being an upset Consumer of getting something you didn't want to get, such as a large bill from the company, to being a Supplier. Your job as the Supplier will be to supply the customer service person with the facts of the situation as you know them to be.

And you need to be patient while the person looks up your records, asking you for every type of personal identity so that they are not infringing on any local or state or federal law. At the end, I ask if they need to know my jockey shorts size to keep the conversation humorous.

As long as you maintain your composure, thanking that person for their help in clearing up a problem or a misunderstanding, the longer that person will stay with you to help you. You are the breath of fresh air in an otherwise unhealthy arena. You are the Consumer of the information given to you over the phone and the Supplier of the facts as you know them; you're also the creator of a positive relationship with the person at the other end of the phone. In effect, you set the stage and the tone of the conversation.

Outsourcing
"Thank you for calling, may I call you by your first name?" It's got to be someone from Bangladore, India, Malasya, Indonesia, or some other foreign country asking!

Hate it, hate it, hate it! But it's a reality and we need to approach the problem much as we do with civil servants, only we have a language problem here. We tell them our problem and they read from a prepared script.

What is the solution?

As the Consumer, always ask to speak to a supervisor … in a very firm voice, maybe ask more than once. You may not get anywhere with the supervisor, but you'll know that you've spoken to a top echelon at that location. If you can't get resolution, see if the company has a U.S. contact on their website.

As the Consumer, you can send an email saying you can't understand what the customer service person is saying and that you are switching over to a company that has U.S. customer service people. If enough people do it, guess what will happen?

Pay your bills offline
The worst hype ever goes to companies that want you to sign up online to pay your monthly bills. They say you will save postage, etc. etc. It's pure garbage. And if you believe it's to your benefit as a Consumer, then you're being conned.

You lose the control of tracking when your money goes out of your account unless it's on the same date every month and you can't do anything to stop it, except go through a lot of red tape. It's hard to dispute the bill because it's always automatically paid!

The company saves postage, mailing costs, envelope and forms expenses, etc. and they get to keep your money sooner -- on the day it's pulled from your account.

Do they tell you they're lowering their cost when you do this – and give you a discount? Of course not! Take back control of your finances and send a letter to every company that you signed up for this disservice, cancelling it.

Let me see your license!
I drive fast. I drive at least 10 miles above the posted speed limit. I'm a NY driver and a defensive one. But living in NC has changed my attitude about drivers down here. This is NASCAR country and I think every driver sees himself or herself around the oval on the track. They tailgate at 65 mph on interstate 485!

I figure that if I'm pulled over for a speeding ticket every 3-4 years, I'm still ahead and I've traveled a lot further in less time than I would have at normal speed limits. As a Consumer who has been pulled over a few times, and was asked for license and registration, I ask the policeman, "how fast was I going?" Whatever speed the officer says, I respond with, "I thought I was doing 80!"

I'll back up. No matter what I say, the officer has radar to tell him exactly how fast I was going, so no matter what I say, he has the exact speed. By making a joke of it, it takes the emotion out of the situation because the policeman always expects some type of confrontation with the driver; this is an upset in the making.

I take the heat off the situation with humor. He doesn't expect this. I switch roles from being an upset Consumer of getting a ticket, to being a Supplier of unexpected information. Guess what?

It usually works! I get an official warning to drive slower. Try it. What do you have to lose?

What's your job?
Years ago, Janet was afraid of flying. She would sit in the seat with white knuckles showing as she grasped the armrests. Every little up and down bump in the aircraft caused her to turn white. "What if this happens, what if that happens" jwas her concern. She was a very upset Consumer, getting something she didn't want to get and that was, motion in the aircraft.

I told her that her job as a passenger, a Consumer, is to make sure that her behind remains in the seat at all times. That is to say, she needed to feel that she was physically attached to the seat cushion under her. And especially when the aircraft bounced up and down due to air turbulence.

She needed to concentrate on that one activity, with her seat belt firmly fastened around her, all focus on being in her seat, and that's all she was to be responsible for.

It worked! She went from being an upset Consumer who was getting something she didn't want to get, insecurity as a passenger, to being a Supplier of safety to herself. By putting herself in this role, her fear and the white knuckles disappeared very quickly.

Role playing

Many an upsetting situation can be resolved amicably when two people role play it out and recreate the incident together. This time they reverse the roles that they had during the interaction. Each party acts out how they think the other person acted and what was said. It usually devolves into, 'what was this all about?' This has a way of diffusing explosive situations.

As an example, if you and the other person are upset over the same issue, agree to switch roles and have each of you act out the other person's role – become the other person – and behave as the other person; say what the other person said to you and vice versa.

Remember the saying:

> *Never judge an Indian unless you walk a mile in his moccasins.*
> *Then you'll be a mile away from him and you'll have his moccasins!*

Better yet, before an argument escalates into throwing things, both parties must agree to take off their clothes and hold both hands high over their heads. Then they can holler all they want. Humor has a way of diffusing explosive situations.

Consumerism

Getting back to Janet's fear of flying, she would often say while we were in the air, "I could never be a pilot." I said, "You're right, and you don't have to worry about that, because you're not a pilot." I added, "And the pilot could never write award winning direct mail pieces like you did."

If you ever compare yourself to someone else, seeing an ability which you do not have, you will always lose. Trust me; can't you see my eyes are turned up to the right?

"I wish I could do that." "I wish I could be like him or her." "I could never do that." Guess what? You are not that person. You are YOU and to make any comparison on any level, will only demean you and your own abilities.

> *Balls said the Queen, if I had them I'd be King.*
> *The King laughed, not because he wanted to*
> *but because he had two!*

Janet is a very good cook. She even took lessons at a famous French cooking school in Hillsdale, NY. That was the week that I had to do my own cooking at home alone! The next time we went out to dinner I asked the owner's wife if she needed any help in the kitchen. Maybe this was a way to learn what it takes to run a restaurant which Janet had thought about. Sure, she said. We need a busboy. Janet said, OK, when do I start?

A day later she started and the day after that the owner's wife said, "I'm sorry, but you won't make it to waitress." She was fired. In retrospect, she wasn't trained to be a busboy as she had no experience.

Two days later Janet received a contract for $26,000 to write a direct-mail package for a national magazine. I hope you're getting the message. Sometimes all that's needed is a little push, a reminder, of what you already know that makes you stand out in the crowd that makes you different from other people with your own special talents. Somehow the message got lost in the shuffle somewhere.

We all do magic

Whenever I perform in public, doing magic for the checkout personnel at supermarkets, for tellers at the bank, wherever and whenever, at the end I always tell them that they are magicians too, doing what they know best, only they don't look at it that way.

I say that I can teach them how to do magic but they would have teach me to do what they do and it would take them a lot of time too to teach me. You are a magician in what you do, only you don't look at it that way because you are so used to doing what you've been doing all these years, that it's become second-nature to you.

Realize that if you don't get out of bed in the morning and go to your job and help other people, you will be missed! Trust me my eyes are turned up to the right.

> "Marvin, get up, it's time to go to school."
> "I don't want to!"
> "Why not, Marvin?"
> "Because I don't like the kids and they don't like me!"
> "Be sensible, Marvin, you're 54 years old and you're the principal!"

Protection

Sorry, this is not about sex. It's about life insurance, and the many ways life insurance companies want to take your money and make you feel that you can't do without life insurance.

When I was 21 my father told me that he had bought me the 1st annual premium of a 30-year whole-life insurance policy. At the end of the year I cancelled it.

Since then I've never bought a life insurance policy. Consider the money I've saved over 54 years! Let's look a little closer at what really needs to be called 'death insurance.' The insurance companies dreamed up this palliative expression so as to not get you upset. You only collect; excuse me, your heirs collect the money when you die.

Nobody passes away. You can pass gas, you can pass go and collect $200 but you can't pass away. So why do people say he or she passed away? Does it lessen the feeling that it's not real and it didn't happen? People are born and people die.

The insurance companies want you to not only insure your life but to also use the payments to create a savings account within the plan. They want to use your money to make more money for them, and in return pay you less interest than you can earn if you were to buy term life insurance only.

Take the savings portion of the payments and put it into a savings account

In effect, they want you to be an uneducated Consumer. Change roles and be the Supplier of information to yourself to help you make decisions that help you, not them.

Worse, they advertise to parents and grandparents to take out life insurance policies on their children and grandchildren. The real question is: what is the purpose of life insurance?

It is to provide a lump sum payment or an annuity to a family that no longer has a living breadwinner to provide for the family's income. If a child dies, does the income of the family suffer? You decide.

Social Security
I hate this term too. There's nothing social about it and I don't feel secure about how much money I'm going to get each month as Congress is playing around with privatizing it and you know what happens next. Costs go up, benefits go down.

I heard an 'expert' on a radio show say that it was better to wait until you were 65 to collect social security than it was to collect it at 62, because you would collect more money in the long run.

So as a consummate Consumer, I took a closer look at this statement and here's what I came up with.

Use $1,000 a month at age 62 as an example. That's $36,000 in 3 years that you'll collect when you turn 65. You put the money in the bank each month and collect 4% interest. I have my trusty HP12C calculator at hand and it tells me that at age 65 you will have $38,308.83 including interest.

If you wait the 3 years, keep on working, and have withholding and social security and Medicare payments taken out of your salary, you'll start to collect about $300 more each month. That's $100 a year more for the 3 years that you didn't collect.

OK, you now collect $1,300 a month, $15,600 a year starting at age 65. You blew $38,308.83 that you didn't collect over the past 3 years! Guess how many years you have to wait before you make up that money that you lost because you didn't apply at age 62?

Do you want to be a Consumer of bad information or the Supplier of good information to yourself?

On the Horns of Dilemma

This is a situation that requires a choice between options that are or seem equally unfavorable or mutually exclusive.

I went through a situation when my mother was in a nursing home, dying of cancer. Wanting to be a Supplier to my mother, there was nothing that I could supply except to be there at her side, when I could be. In effect, I was an upset Supplier.

On the other hand I was also an upset Consumer, because I didn't like getting what I didn't want to get, and that was the knowledge that my mother was dying. I felt helpless. I could not leave the relationship and so I remained upset until my mother died.

A pebble thrown into a calm lake makes a concentric circle of waves, moving outward, ever decreasing in energy, until there's nothing moving. Only the memory of the incident lingers on.

Then I took the time to heal and forgive myself.

I recalled this incident because my accountant called me the other night and told me that her father had 3 heart attacks and he was not likely to survive. She felt guilty because she couldn't do anything to help her father and she anguished over the situation. She was taking it out on herself, remaining constantly upset.

We've all done it when it comes to seeing a loved one suffer.

No matter what we feel or what we do, whether the decision we make to prolong or terminate a loved one's life, it still puts us on the horns of dilemma.

There is no answer, but there is a question that we need to ask ourselves. If death is a part of life, why not accept what it is and celebrate someone's life all the time? And the time to do it is when they are alive so that we have no regrets, and not say, "I should have…"

Be the consummate Supplier!

I'm late because…

No one has ever been late in his or her life. They are late because…

Does it really make a difference why they are late and that their excuse excuses them from being responsible for their actions?

As an example, your friend is always at least 15-20 minute late for an appointment with you. You always come on time because you're always punctual and expect others to be on time too. Whether you say nothing when that person comes late or you ask them to please come on time, he or she is always late and it bothers you.

If you show up 15-20 minutes late it will still bother you that the other person is late too. It goes against your belief system as you don't want to be late to accommodate your friend.

You have to change the reality and that means telling your friend to show up on time and that you will give him or her 5 minutes leeway, otherwise you are going to leave. So you do leave the next time. That's changing the reality.

But wait! You can't do that. It's not your nature to do that and it would cause friction with your friend and you don't want to create a situation that may cause you to lose a friend or make you look like you're not a nice person. Sound familiar? So what's the solution?

You can leave the relationship; that is, put off making an appointment with the other person. How does that sound? If you don't like it and you don't want to lose your friendship, continue to make appointments, show up on time and wait for your friend to be late, and continue to get upset. This scenario goes on in everyone's mind at one time or another, except the situation changes with different people.

If you have been playing the role of the consumer in this scenario you are concerned with what you are getting or not getting out of the relationship with the other person.

It's time to switch roles and play the part of the supplier and consider what you want to give or not give to your friend. The reality is that this person is not your friend! The other person does not care about your feelings and is concerned only with his or her feelings and will not accommodate you. So as the non-supplier to your friend, you are going to leave the relationship and not call your friend. If your friend calls to make an appointment, you will say that you will not make appointments because he or she is always late and inconsiderate of your feelings. This is what it means to leave the relationship, and then you don't need to change your expectation or the reality.

The Emotional Toolbox™ explains in detail the core technology of why people get upset and what they can do to resolve their upsets. You can fill out an analyzer using this same upset if it applies to you. You will then see what choice you are going to make.

Just say NO

The word NO is a wonderful tool. You don't need to give a reason for saying it. It's also a full sentence. If this is too blunt, how about, 'I decline'. Is that softer? As a Consumer, you have a right to say NO, to anything. An unsolicited request for something, from anybody, deserves a NO answer. If you find it difficult to say NO, you are giving up your power to another person. How does that make you feel? How do you handle phone calls for donations, or solicitations from strangers? Does it upset you? Think about the control that you're giving away.

I sometimes get phone calls from companies doing surveys asking for my opinion. I ask the person if they get paid to give the survey. The answer is always yes. I tell them that I never answer a survey unless I get paid too. End of discussion. How about using silence? It's a wonderful tool. Better yet, if you have caller ID, don't pick up the phone if you don't know who is calling.

Nothing happens when you say NO, but a YES puts action into being, and that's probably why YES may be a problem too. That means you have to do something, commit to something, and that's scary at times. We all ask others to help us and we hear answers like, 'I'll think about it.' or 'Maybe later.' 'I don't know.' 'I'll see.' 'Speak to me later.'

Anything other than a YES is a NO!

Money talks

If you don't think money talks, you're deaf! It's saying; don't spend me, save me! And if you know the rule of 72 you would be saving it. This is not rocket science.

1. If you get 4% interest a year, it will double in 18 years
   72 divided by 4 = 18
2. If you get 6% interest a year, it will double in 12 years, saving 6 years!
   72 divided by 6 = 12; that's how important every single percentage point is, so if you know the % of interest you're getting, you'll know how long it will take to double your money by dividing it into 72.
3. Conversely, if you want your money to double in 10 years, divide it into 72 and you'll know that you need to get 7.2% interest a year; 10 into 72 = 7.2%. If you want it to double in 8 years, divide it into 72 and you'll need to get 9% a year interest.

So what can you do with this tool? BUILD! And that is, create a retirement plan for yourself. How? Take whatever money you can put away each month, that is, not spend on junk, trinkets, expensive toys, Christmas presents (that's right, Christmas presents), and put it in the bank that will give you the highest interest rate you can find. Retailers won't like you during the holiday season, but your friends and relatives will still love you when you send things you made yourself, like poems, a precious book, or a personal item of yours that you want them to have. Wasn't it supposed to be the 'spirit' of Christmas, not the 'gifts' of Christmas? Why go into hock for a year?

You can now do some figuring. Whatever your age, you can tell exactly how much money you will have saved in the future using an example of 4% interest a year, doubling in 10 years.

Hmmm…I'm figuring that you can save $100/month. Cut the total saved in half if you have to. Add more if you can.

That's $1,200 a year saved, and it will double to $2,400 in 18 years. Get the math?

$2,400 will double to $4,800 in 36 years. That's a multiple of 2 in 18 years and a multiple of 4 in 36 years. If you can save $500/month your savings will be $24,000!

So what's stopping you from sitting down and going over the things that you can do without so you can build a nest egg? If you don't pay your financial dues now, you'll pay dearly for it later.

So if you're in your 20's, every dollar that you spend today is really worth $4 in the future. And if you can save $500/month, every dollar that you spend today is really worth $20 in future dollars.

The American Nightmare
You're told by everyone, and especially real estate people: BUY A HOUSE! It's the American dream. Get married, don't get married, but buy a house.

I think it's the American nightmare. The worst thing you can do is buy a house unless it's for cash and I don't care if it's a new or an old house.

Never buy anything that you can't afford to pay with cash

You'll tell me that you will never be able to buy a big ticket item and I say, not so! What will drive you into bankruptcy are the interest payments. Look at the debt load that the American economy is carrying right now. Just look at the number of bank foreclosures taking place and the domino effect it has on jobs, the real estate market and the auto industry.

Before credit cards, everybody paid cash or knew what they could afford to buy. I say, tear up your credit cards right now if you can't afford to pay off the amount owed every single month. TV commercials abound with paid actors proclaiming, "I don't know how I built up such large credit card debts, but I got help from…." This is a lot of garbage!

The tool to use in learning how to use money is, 'cash is king.' Here's how you use it to build.

- Find a nice house to buy that you can afford with a minimum of 10% down payment. The House Buyer's Analyzer™ (HBA) will tell you exactly how much house you can afford. Figure a 6% mortgage for 30-years fixed, and what the mortgage payment is each month. Add insurance, taxes, maintenance every month, and repairs. Don't forget to add all the outside gardening stuff, and don't be stingy about it. Get an accurate monthly figure you'll have to shell out.

- Now go and find a nice apartment or house to rent that you'll be comfortable in and allow for family expansion. Pay your financial dues now and wait while building up your cash.

- Take the difference between what your rent cost and what you would have to pay monthly if you bought the house and put it in the bank every month and figure how much money you will have in 10 years including the interest earned.

Go out and buy an HP32C financial calculator and you'll know exactly how much money you'll have in future dollars for any period of time at any interest rate. Here are some figures that I plugged into it based on how much you put away each month at 4% for 10 years for you to ponder: N=number of months (120) I=monthly interest payment; PMT=amount you put away each month; PV=initial sum you put away (zero) FV=future value of your savings.

N	I	PMT	PV	FV
120	4	500	0	73,870
120	4	750	0	110,805
120	4	1,000	0	147,740
120	4	1,250	0	184,675
120	4	1,500	0	221,611

If it's not enough to buy a starter house and you still can't wait to buy one, make it your down payment keeping 10% of it for reserves. So when anyone tells you that paying rent is like throwing money down the toilet or burning it, smile and say gobble, gobble.

- Once a year, make an additional monthly payment to the bank. This will reduce the mortgage time in half! If you don't believe me, ask your mortgage company. Can't you see that my eyes are turned up to the right?

- When your mortgage is paid off, continue to make the same monthly mortgage payment into your bank account. Don't spend it otherwise you'll be at the mercy of the government when all you'll have is your social security check to count on. That's planning for retirement. If your mortgage is paid off, and you're retired, all your money is in the house.

- But before it's paid off, refinance it and put the money in the bank. You don't have to pay taxes on refinancing it! Then you can move into a nice condo, rent the house out to pay the mortgage, or sell the house. You have a high mortgage; chances are you won't have to pay a lot of taxes on the sale. Discuss this with your accountant.

Here's a plan that can help everyone stay out of debt and keep the housing industry and the U.S. auto industry afloat. In the 30's and 40's, there were lay-away plans. You put a down payment on something, and you made a payment every week towards the purchase price, and at the end you owned it free and clear. What's the matter with that?

If you think like a Consumer, you want it now!
If you think like a Supplier, you'll create for the future!

Buy My Problem
Every time you see a 'For Sale' sign, it's really saying, 'Buy My Problem.' The person who's selling something wants to get rid of it. You may not know the reason or ever will, but that person has to get rid of it one way or the other. No matter what story the person makes up, he has to get rid

of it and wants you to buy his problem. His role is that of a Supplier and he wants you to be the Consumer – of his problem, to take it off his hands.

When you know what role you are in, you know which tools to use to decide if you want to take his problem off his hands and at what price. Nobody sells anything that is a benefit to them. Only when it becomes a liability is a 'for sale' sign put out. So 'buy my problem' is the mantra to use when negotiating, and always be prepared to walk away from a deal that is not to your satisfaction. The definition of negotiating is not to always get the best price. It's the ability to get what you want, regardless of what it is; so remember, it's not only the price.

The House Buyer's Analyzer™ is a good tool to use when you're in the market to buy a house because it addresses the emotional needs of a buyer first, which are important considerations. If you're in the market to buy a house, make sure you read the instructions and fill out the analyzer.

Selling is a different matter, because now you become the Supplier, and you have to be prepared to accept a price lower than what you want to get. This is especially important when a house is involved. Most people have an expectation of what their house is worth, far beyond the reality of what comparable houses have sold for in the neighborhood. Get a real estate broker to give you 'comps' of houses sold in the last year in your area.

The best time to sell a house is when you have a buyer.

No matter what price you ask for, you can't sell a house if you don't have a buyer. Work with the buyer -- if you have one. You wouldn't sell it unless you had to, so make the deal! I've been through this scenario a few times and no matter what I felt about what the price 'should be', the market and the buyer dictate it Let me spell it out for you so you will clearly understand the selling process and what you have done when you refuse an offer or fail to renegotiate the price.

You want to sell your house for $229,000 because that's your expectation of the value of the house. A buyer comes along and makes an offer of $209,000. You refuse it. What have you in effect done?

You bought back your house for $209,000!

OK, I'll back up. If you sold the house for $209,000 you would have the $209,000 in the bank, right? You refused the offer so the value of the house that was established by the buyer at $209,000 is in the house, even though you refused it, still thinking it is worth $229,000. So the value of the house becomes $209,000 – you bought back your house for $209,000.

Another buyer comes along and offers you $215,000. You refuse it also. You bought back your house for $215,000 and made $6,000 on paper, the difference between $209,000 and $215,000.

Another buyer comes along and offers you $210,000 and you accept it. How did you really make out on the deal? Don't tell me you lost $19,000 because you expected to get $229,000! That figure was only in your head. You lost $5,000 because you bought back the house for $215,000 when you could have sold it and you sold the house for $210,000. The math is there for you to see.

Supply and Demand

Consumers are on the Demand side. So what would happen if they stopped demanding, that is, became non-Consumers? There would be an overabundance of supply, and that would cause prices to drop because the Suppliers need to get rid of their over supply and recoup their money.

It's not rocket science, but it's the tool to use when you want something to happen, to change. You need to be a non-Consumer to the Supplier – stop demanding!

Let's use a specific example. Skyrocketing oil prices are controlled by a handful of oil companies and all the other oil companies follow suit in raising prices. Stop buying Citgo® gas and Texaco® gas which comes from Venezuela. Buy gas from any other oil company, but not from these two companies.

'You', are not alone; you are every single person who drives an automobile in the United States. The price of gas would drop to under $1 over time. But how do you get the word out to all Americans?

Advertise!

Take out full-page ads in newspapers across the country; spread the word on TV and radio. That's how!

Where do you get the money?

Hmmm…if gas could cost $1 instead of $4 at its high, that's $3/gallon savings and if the average mpg is 20 miles and the average mileage driven in a year is 12,000 miles, then 600 gallons used in a year would save you $1,800 each year.

Would you kick in $100 to save this amount each and every year?

The same principle can be used to get whatever you want. Remember, your job is to get what you want to get and not get what you don't want to get as the Consumer.

As of this writing, Ford is in trouble, General Motors is in trouble, the American car industry is in trouble. The big three execs went to Washington with their hands out to be bailed out. Why? Because they were too stupid and greedy to pay attention to what Consumers wanted.

They decided what they wanted to build, not what the American people wanted to buy! And so the American people bought foreign cars. We could use some of the gas money and make up T-shirts with:

> **I'm a non-Consumer** written across the front
> **I'm a non-Supplier** written across the back.

You would be effective in both of these roles, switching anytime you want and get the same results!

> 1. What do you want to build?
> 2. Which tools are you going to use?
> 3. Do you know how to use them?

I know!

This expression is probably the most difficult to suppress the urge to say to someone. Broken down to its intimated meaning when you say this to someone, you are in effect conveying that you don't need his or her input, interference or commentary.

And it makes no difference if you do or don't know. The damage has been done. As the Consumer you are saying to the Supplier, 'don't supply to me!'

The underlying communication is that person wants to help by giving information that he or she feels the other person doesn't have or know at the moment.

When you reject the other person's contribution to the interaction, you are negating the other person. Guess what you're NOT going to get the next time? Any input from the other person, and that may get you into trouble if you do need input.

You must change roles from being the Consumer of information (that you know or don't know) and be the Supplier. What do you need to supply to the other person?

A thank you!

No matter what the other person tells you, say, thank you! You are saying to the other person that you appreciate the contribution. It does not diminish your knowledge of the subject or your abilities.

Case in point: You're driving with your wife next to you and you're coming home from shopping at the supermarket. You're two blocks from home and your wife says, "stay to the right, we're almost home."

You say, "I know." WRONG! You say, thank you! Why?

Your wife is making a contribution to you when she supplies you with information. Say I know, and guess what you're going to get from your wife? Less input. It doesn't make a difference what anybody says to you, regardless if their input is the truth or not. Input from any source is the signal for you to say 'thank you. It doesn't mean that you have to take that input as a command.

The words that you may remember hearing your parents say when you were a child were, 'say please and thank you.' They still hold today as door openers. You'll be amazed at the way people will respond to you when you say these two words that acknowledge them.

Take up a collection
The following questions may help you ask yourself why you need to collect things.

1. Does it have sentimental value, like every family picture framed?
2. Does it have utilitarian value, like every Craftsman tool ever made?
3. Does it have esthetic value, like 75 Norman Rockwell plates on the walls?
4. Does it add to your collection, like 2,000 beer cans from every country?
5. Does it have informational value, like 3 rooms of books and magazines?
6. Does it give you a feeling of status, like 15 vintage autos in the rented garage?
7. Does it have investment value, like the whole series of Franklin Mint coins?

Is it an addiction? Do you feel the need to consume to fill an emotional hole somewhere … are you really looking for something more substantial? Suppose you switched roles and became the Supplier; what would you give to yourself that would replace your need to collect things?

Remember that Suppliers think differently than Consumers, so you have the opportunity to test it out and take on a project that is fulfilling to yourself. You probably spend a lot of time with your collection. Maybe you can spend more time with friends, relatives, and forge new relationships instead of time with your collection? I'll bet you'll spend less time with your collection, or better still, put it away or sell it.

In which role do you feel you have power? Can you emotionally afford to give up your collection? Can you stop using your collection as a crutch and open your space to create relationships in your life?

I've always wondered why some people have so many pictures of their family, children, grandchildren, wedding pictures, pets -- you name it -- on their furniture, including the grand piano. If this is you, what is it that you're saying? Can it be that you love your family so much that you need to be reminded of what they look like?

If you're holding on to memories for dear life through pictures, perhaps it's time to get a life. Put most of the pictures away. You'll always have the memories in your mind and in your heart. You'll also have less dusting to do!

"I want to live closer to my children or my grandchildren." That's what I hear retired couples say. Is it because they want to be Suppliers to them, because they think their children can't live without them around, or is it because they are Consumers and they believe they can't live without being near their children?

In 23 years of marriage, Janet and I moved 11 times but it didn't help. The children still found out where we lived!

Raising Children for Fun & Profit

I've never seen a book with this title in a bookstore. I wonder why some couples have so many children except to emotionally profit by them, and it certainly isn't fun raising them. Perhaps it's because they need children to take care of them in their old age or having children keeps the couple busy raising them and further space between them.

I'll put the question to you: what is your job as a parent? A wise woman who brought up 4 daughters gave me the best answer I've ever heard.

You give them roots and you give them wings

The roots are the education they need, the tools to help them build things, the love and compassion you instilled in them, and the emotional and spiritual foundation of the family. The wings are the willingness to let go and allow them to grow and learn and be individuals in the world, confident in their own abilities.

"You did your job." That's the phrase every parent wants to hear. You can then put your tools down and know that after you're gone, you won't hear, "You left me, and I don't know how to fend for myself or take care of myself. I hate you!"

"Tough love" is not an idle statement. It's born out of doing the job that has to be done regardless of what a child says to you or feels about you. The job is not to have a child like you or love you. Your children are not your friends. These are another two of the ruthless rules of reality. Break them and you're in deep do-do. Nobody said it was easy raising children and there's no book that will tell you how to raise your own. Dr. Spock is long dead, and his methods are not used anymore.

"I'm scared of my child." That's a familiar statement today. What really is the problem? That the child will run away? Whatever it is, fill out an analyzer in The Emotional Toolbox™. In the space that says, I am upset because you…enter what you're upset about, and be very clear about what you're upset about.

Do a past Consumer upset if you're not getting something you want (from your child), or you're getting something you don't want (from your child). Fill out a past Supplier upset if you can't give your child something you want to give (a lecture or a scolding, or perhaps a smack in the ass.)

Find out exactly what the issues are and then create a plan of action of what you will do the next time a similar confronting situation arises. The cognitive word is DO, and you do need to do something. Are you really afraid of your child or are you afraid of what others will say about what you want to do, including your spouse?

After the plan of action is made, fill out a Future Consumer or Supplier analyzer to see if your plan of action will work. If it will work and you have all parallel lines across the page, congratulations. If it won't work, you have some work to do and rethink your strategy.

A child can never be older than his or her parents

If you remember this statement, you'll know that you must always be in control of the situation and that you are the parent, your child is not.

Uh-Huh!

When my two sons were in their teens, they would tell me things that would make me upset, and I told them so. I would admonish them. What that did was to have them not tell me things and they clammed up.

I was a Consumer of things I didn't want to hear and I was a Supplier to them of things they didn't want to hear. That makes for a great relationship!

What I needed to do was to change roles and be a non-Supplier to them of my feelings and be a non-Consumer, and that is, not be at the effect of their input to me. Here's the scenario I followed whenever they decided to tell me anything. The italics are my unspoken internal conversations to have them move their story forward. Perhaps this communication tool can help you too.

Son's comment; "I got into an accident"
My comment; **Uh-Hu!** *Continue, I'm listening*
Son's continued comment; "The car is totaled."
My comment; **so then what?** *You still have my attention*
Son's comment; "Nobody got hurt and I had it towed to the service station."
My comment; **so what are you going to do about it?** *It's your life so you make the decision of what to do.*
Son's comment; (Any option he came up with was negotiated)

It worked!

I didn't scold them. I didn't tell them what to do. I just listened. I was not their friend, I was their parent, and I empowered them to make their own decisions. And that's when our relationship changed for the better.

That was over 30 years ago. I live in Charlotte, NC now. One son lives in Staten Island, NY and the other lives in Wayne, NJ. They call me when they need to connect with their father. They speak, I listen. I've done my job.

You're Stupid!

This is a generalization that we sometimes throw out at people when we're upset or angry. And it's often thrown out at us. If we look a little deeper we will find that people are intelligent and have 'smarts' in specific areas:

1. Street smarts
2. Book smarts
3. Sexual smarts
4. Mechanical smarts
5. Mathematical smarts
6. Intuitive smarts
7. Psychological smarts

Can you identify with one or more of these attributes? Have I left any out? What tool are you going to use to handle the situation? Humor!

Now the next time someone says to you, "you're stupid", you can answer them, "yes, but in what area?" And if they can't tell you that, then they're stupid too!

What did I do in this scenario? I turned a potentially upsetting situation into a farce, a joke that only I understand, not the other person. As the receiver, the Consumer of something I got that I didn't want to hear, I changed roles and became the Supplier of an answer that satisfied me that didn't have anything to do with the other person.

Sidestep a potentially upsetting situation
by taking the heat off -- use humor!

You got the finger!

Similarly as in the scenario above, someone gives you the finger while you're driving. Do you give him the finger back? If so, you've allowed someone to control your emotions with a gesture and you've responded in kind. You're now an upset Consumer because you got something you didn't want to get and you've changed roles to become a Supplier and give the other driver something that he doesn't want to get.

In certain instances, depending upon the emotional tolerance of each driver, this could escalate into road rage. How do you create a plan of action to handle the situation? What tool are you going to use to dissipate a potential upset? Humor!

What is the difference between an asshole and a hemorrhoid?

An asshole has a use!

So the next time someone gives you the finger, holler back, "Oh, you know me?"

156

What did I do in this scenario? I again turned a potentially upsetting situation into a farce, a joke that only I understand, not the other person. As the receiver, the Consumer of something I got that I didn't want to hear, I changed roles and became the Supplier of an answer that satisfied me, that didn't have anything to do with the other person.

You are now empowered to control your emotions, your actions and reactions because you are using communication tools that you didn't have before. And what are you building?

You are building confidence in your own ability to control your life

Do the best job that isn't!

Does the quarterback throw the football to where the running back IS or to where he ISN'T? I'll back up. Does he throw it to where he is at that moment, or to where he will be in a few seconds?

He throws it to where he isn't, to where he will be.

This sets the scenario for why CEO's of major companies are paid such staggering salaries, with stock options, perks, and benefits. They are paid for work that isn't.

I'll back up again. When something isn't working properly in a company, a specialist is called in to fix the problem. He does something as a Supplier, and he's paid accordingly. An advertising agency is replaced with another agency to produce better ads. The software company is replaced with another software company that provides better security, better customer relations management, CRM for short.

When there's a major problem that has no simple answer, no fast fix or cure, somebody has to be brought in to do something that isn't; that is, create something that isn't a resource at hand to turn the company around. He isn't paid the big bucks to fix something that's broken. He is paid to be creative, to bring into being something that isn't there.

There are also critical positions staffed with people who are paid to fix what isn't broken – yet! You might call them future Suppliers. They are on-staff – electricians, computer technicians; -- to be on call just waiting for something to break down. They manage the process of what is working now, so you might call them present Suppliers.

Isn't it easy when you think in terms of Consumers and Suppliers and put it down on paper? Makes hiring the right people a lot easier.

If you're not satisfied where you are, you can't move on.
If you think you can, you'll still be where you are.
Be satisfied so you can move on.

So much for Consumer eyes!

SECTION IV

PART IV. PERSONAL AND BUSINESS ANALYZERS

The analyzer forms for each of the six programs and the mini Upset Analyzer™ forms are reproduced in triplicate at the back of the book to cut out where shown and fill out. You may also make copies of the forms.

1. Using The Relationship Analyzer™ you will build:

A better relationship with the person you're dating
A better relationship with your children
A better relationship with your spouse
A better relationship with your boss, co-workers
A better relationship with someone new
…and more

2. Using The Interview Analyzer™ you will:

Find out when you're hiring the wrong person for the job
Save the company time and money
Build a better a job for yourself
Make more money
Help your company grow faster
…and more

3. Using The Career Analyzer™ you will:

Find out what you're good at doing
Find out what you're not good at doing
Find a better career
Learn to use the skills you have
… and more

4. Using The House Buyer's Analyzer™ you'll find out:

What you don't like in a house
What you do like in a house
How to go about buying a house

When to buy a house
How much you can afford for a house
How to work with a Realtor®
How to keep track of houses you've seen
…and more

5. Using the Competitive Edge Analyzer™, you will:

Build a more profitable company
Build a bigger company
Find out what's not working in the company
Find out what resources you need to achieve a competitive edge
Find out why your competition is beating you
…and more

1. THE RELATIONSHIP ANALYZER™

We all want a relationship with someone who matches our expectations of our ideal mate. Some of these qualities might be; handsome, pretty, tall, muscular, buxom, sexy, sensual, rich, have a sense of humor, caring and considerate, playful, earthy, intelligent, be understanding, sensitive, or be a good listener.

We all have our list which we've been carrying around for so long we know it by heart. You know the words, "I'm looking for someone who…", or, I need somebody who…" You fill in the blanks.

In matching our needs with the qualities we see in another person, we identify traits based upon our expectations for a successful relationship, which may be unrealistic, self-indulgent, or well-founded.

Many of us don't know or can't express what we really need in order to have a successful relationship. We certainly know when we're not getting what we need when a relationship doesn't seem to get off the ground or when once started, begins to fall apart.

The Relationship Analyzer™ lets you see at a glance when your expectations are mismatched with the personality attributes you see in another person. If the expected qualities that you're looking for can be closely matched with the qualities in another person, there is a greater chance to have a successful relationship with that person.

Focus will be on defined qualities as they relate to ones needs, as opposed to one's wants, with the purpose of creating this distinction for you to use as a guide in determining if a particular relationship issue is indeed considered a need, as sustenance, or a want – as a wish fulfillment.

1. *THE RELATIONSHIP ANALYZER*™
A guide to improving your relationships

Part A			**Part B**
I need someone who:			**This person:**

1. Wisdom

Is spontaneous	[ ]	[ ]	Is spontaneous
Is predictable	[ ]	[ ]	Is predictable

2. Perception

Always keeps agreements	[ ]	[ ]	Always keeps agreements
Allows agreements to change	[ ]	[ ]	Allows agreements to change

3. Communication

Offers alternatives	[ ]	[ ]	Offers alternatives
Does not offer alternatives	[ ]	[ ]	Does not offer alternatives

4. Heart

Is understanding	[ ]	[ ]	Is understanding
Is objective	[ ]	[ ]	Is objective

5. Power

Does not control	[ ]	[ ]	Does not control
Controls	[ ]	[ ]	Controls

6. Pleasure

Initiates	[ ]	[ ]	Initiates
Does not initiate	[ ]	[ ]	Does not initiate

7. Security

Gives feedback	[ ]	[ ]	Gives feedback
Does not give feedback	[ ]	[ ]	Does not give feedback

FILLING OUT THE RELATIONSHIP ANALYZER™

Copy the Relationship Analyzer™ form or cut out the form at the back of the book with the meaning of the issues at hand. Fold the analyzer form lengthwise exposing only Part A.

Read the meaning of the first issue then mark an 'X' in the most appropriate box in the first pair of statements on the Analyzer, based upon what you need from the other person. Do this with each of the other six issues.

Then turn the form over to hide Part A and mark an 'X' in the most appropriate box in each statement pair in Part B, based upon your perception of what you are getting or not getting from the other person.

When you have filled in all seven issues, open the form and connect the 'X' marks from Part A to Part B in each statement pair. The pattern of connections, parallel lines or diagonal lines, will reveal a diagram or X-ray of your relationship. There are seven different connection patterns that are possible in each of the seven sets of statements.

1. Upper left to upper right
2. Upper left to lower right
3. Lower left to upper right
4. Lower left to lower right
5. Left side only blank
6. Right side only blank
7. Both sides blank

Read the meaning of the connections and the meaning of the issues as they relate to each one of the connections you have made on the form. Next, read the choices that you have in any relationship to help you choose a plan of action to help you get what you need:

THE MEANING OF THE ISSUES

1. Wisdom

The key issue here is getting an unusual response or a usual response from the other person. Do you like surprises or habitual behavior? If you show a diagonal line in either direction indicating a mismatch, your role in the relationship will be revealed in statements like these:

As the Consumer: Why don't you do it the way I want it done? I know exactly what you will do.
As the Supplier: Why aren't you ever satisfied with what I do or say?

2. Perception

The key issue here is keeping agreements or breaking promises. Does the other person keep his or her agreements and discuss changes when necessary, or break promises without discussing them with you? Do you expect the other person to always keep his or her agreements? Can you live with a person who is fallible and changes agreements? If you show a diagonal line in either direction indicating a mismatch, your role in the relationship will be revealed in statements like these:

As the Consumer: What do you mean you changed your mind? Now you tell me?
As the Supplier: I told you things might change. Why don't you ever listen to me? What's the big deal?

Consumers keep track of changed agreements. Suppliers keep track of lies. Can you accept the other person's behavior? Can the other person accept your behavior?

Which can you change; what you need or the reality of what you are getting?

3. Communication

The key issue here is one of negotiation versus stipulation. If you communicate your wishes and the other person doesn't want to listen to what you have to offer, where does that put you? Do you feel that you'll always have to agree or submit to the other person's wishes? If you show a diagonal line in either direction indicating a mismatch, your role in the relationship will be revealed in statements like these:

As the Consumer: Why do you always have it your way? Why can't we do it my way too?
As the Supplier: Why can't you make up your mind? Why can't I win too?

4. Heart

The key issue here is one of understanding, and the role each partner plays. Do you want the other person to see you as an individual and treat you as such? Or do you wish the other person to treat you in a stereotype role? If you don't communicate how you wish to be treated, the other person will treat you as they wish. What do you think your chances are of getting the other person to understand you?

A woman marries a man with the expectation of changing him. A man marries a woman with the expectation that she will never change. Guess what? She changes and he won't! If you show a diagonal line in either direction indicating a mismatch, your role in the relationship will be revealed in statements like these:

As the Consumer: Why don't you want to understand me? You're not listening to me!
As the Supplier: I don't understand where you're coming from! Why aren't you like everyone else?

166

5. Power

The issues here are of control and blame in the relationship. Does the other person want to have control? If you both want to control and be Suppliers, you'll always be fighting. If neither one of you controls, you'll have a better chance of allocating responsibility based upon your individual strengths and weaknesses. When you blame the other person, you're giving up your power and not taking responsibility for your own actions and words. Issues can always be discussed and resolved if neither party pulls a power play or blames the other person. Does the other person take responsibility for his or her actions and words or try to put blame on you?

If you show a diagonal line in either direction indicating a mismatch, your role in the relationship will be revealed in statements like these:

As the Consumer: Why do you always want to control everything? Why are you so argumentative all the time?
As the Supplier: Why are you always blaming me?

6. Pleasure

The key issues here are priorities, timing, and responsiveness: when to give or get. Are you willing to wait or do you want immediate gratification? Is the other person on the same wavelength? Does the other person make suggestions as to what to do and when, all or most of the time? Do you? When you clash, what do you do? This issue includes sexual fulfillment. Initiating is being the Supplier. Not initiating is being the Consumer. If you are not getting your needs fulfilled, have you conveyed exactly what you need, what you like and what you don't like, to your partner? Has your partner told you? Being explicit may sometimes feel awkward and embarrassing. If either one of you always plays the same role, switch roles. It may allow each of you to get to know each other more intimately.

If you show a diagonal line in either direction indicating a mismatch, your role in the relationship will be revealed in statements like these:

As the Consumer: Why aren't you doing it when I want it done?
As the Supplier: Why won't you let me do it when I want to?

7. Security

The issues here are of approval, disapproval, and acknowledgement of what is said and done. The first issue, response, deals with an answer to what is said or done. The response may come from you or the other person. Feedback is what you or the other person answers in return to the response. Are you secure in listening to what the other person has to say? Do you take feedback as negative criticism or positive support?

Anything that can't be discussed creates a void in the relationship. Are you willing to live with this? How secure are you in being able to discuss any issue with the other person? The other person must be your best friend.

If you show a diagonal line in either direction indicating a mismatch, your role in the relationship will be revealed in statements like these:

As the Consumer: Why are you criticizing me all the time?
As the Supplier: What did I say or do that was so bad?

THE MEANING OF THE CONNECTIONS

No. 1
[X] -- [X]
[ ]   [ ]

A parallel line across the top shows that your need in this area matches the quality that you see in the other person. What you need is what you are getting. The more parallel lines you have across the top, the closer the other person comes to filling your needs.

Now that you know what the optimum connection is, don't try to force the connection. Don't look at what you have marked on what you need to make it align with what you're getting from the other person.

If the form shows seven matches across the top, and you still feel unfulfilled in your relationship, you're not telling the truth about what your needs are. You need to look a little deeper to find out what it is you're holding on to that you don't want to give up.

No. 2
[X] [ ]
      \
[ ] [X]

This diagonal line, upper left to lower right, indicates a mismatch. The other person, as you see him or her, is not filling your needs in this area. Are you so sure? Have you communicated to the other person what you need? Do so if you have not. Nobody is a mind reader! If you know you will not get what you need, how important is it? Only you can decide. Consider this; how often have you been able to change the other person? Can you change your expectation of what the other person can give to you? What are you going to do?

No. 3
[ ] [X]
    /
[X] [ ]

This diagonal line, upper right to lower left, indicates a mismatch; you are having problems in this area. You want the status quo. You're sure of what you're getting and you don't want to make changes, and the other person wants to both give you what you don't want – and perhaps keeps on telling you that you 'should' accept what he or she wants to give you – for your own good! Do you want to continue getting what you don't need? What are you going to do?

No. 4
[ ]   [ ]
[X] -- [X]

This bottom-to-bottom parallel line indicates that while your expectation is in alignment with what you are getting, there is minimum communication between the two of you. Perhaps you're suppressing discussing issues that have been dormant for quite a while. Or that have been discussed before and bringing them up now will only cause resentment and upset.

If so, what are you really afraid of? Not wanting to hear the other person's response and not wanting to give feedback? Would that open up a hornet's nest that you're not prepared right now to deal with? In how many other areas do you have a bottom-to-bottom connection? Perhaps you need to re-evaluate your relationship with the other person. Consider discussing a changed agreement to the one you have now. Trust your feelings as you listen to the other person. Bottom-to-bottom connections usually occur in business and in family affairs where no one wants to rock the boat.

No. 5
[ ] [ ]
[X] [ ]

This incomplete connection is considered a diagonal line. You know exactly what you need and you don't know if you're getting it from the other person. Are you sure you know the other person? If not, perhaps you need to get to know him or her better. Is it that you don't really care about the relationship that much and you would rather recreate and just have fun together? Or is it that you're afraid of finding out that the other person is not capable of giving you what you need in this area? Why don't you take the time to find out? You may surprise yourself.

No. 6
[ ] [ ]
[ ] [X]

This incomplete connection is considered a diagonal line. You don't know what you need, and yet you know what the other person is giving you. Is there some reason why you don't want to consider what you need because you don't think the other person can give it to you? Perhaps you're trying too hard to hold the relationship together out of your desire to please the other person. What are you holding on to that you don't want to express? Which will upset you more, not asking for what you need or not getting what you need? What are you going to do?

No. 7
[ ] [ ]
[ ] [ ]

Blanks on both sides indicate that this issue is not relevant to your relationship ... or it may also indicate that this issue is the most important one to address.

If you feel that your expectation may never be fulfilled, you may not want to have one. You may not want to look for what you think you will never get. This may be your way of avoiding getting upset.

You probably spend a lot of time arguing over issues that don't contribute to the relationship. Instead of a relationship, you have an entanglement! You and the other person are tied up in what the both of you are not getting you have lost sight of the name of the game. And that is, giving to each other what is needed and wanted. If the both of you are so needy that neither one of you can play Supplier to the other , you have two Consumers, no communication – and no relationship!

One of you must be the Supplier and the other must be the Consumer. It makes no difference which one of you goes first as the Supplier to the other. Flip a coin, arm wrestle, or base it upon which one has a bigger emotional hole in his or her stomach.

As long as one person is willing to play Supplier to the other and wait to get his or her needs filled in return, mutual trust and confidence will be maintained. If the satisfied Consumer does not switch roles and be the Supplier to the other person, there is not only an upset in the making, there is a break in the fiber of the relationship – causing emotional scar tissue!

WHAT CHOICES DO YOU HAVE?

In any relationship where you are upset and not getting what you need, you have three choices:

> **1. You can change your expectation**
> **2. You can change the reality of the situation**
> **3. You can leave the relationship**

If you do nothing, you will continue to remain upset. To change your expectation means that you recognize that you are not going to get what you need from the other person in a way that satisfies you and you will not expect the other person to give it to you. Can you do this with each issue where you have a diagonal line?

To change the reality of the situation is to change the attitude and behavior of the other person in what he or she does or says so that you get what you need. How often have you been able to change the other person? If you are able to do one or the other, you have an opportunity to continue in your relationship. How long do you think any change will last before it reverts to the old agreement?

If you cannot change your expectation and you cannot change the reality, and you do not want to remain upset in the relationship, then you have one other alternative. You have to leave the relationship!

If you found out what you already know about your relationship -- that it isn't working -- your choice to leave the relationship can be both a relief and also very frightening. It forces you to see that you have to do something about it. You need to be the Supplier to yourself, and that is to give yourself permission to leave the relationship.

Two objects cannot occupy the same space at the same time. The same can be said for relationships. Unless you provide the space for a new relationship, the old one will prevent you from forming a new one. Have you come to the decision that you are going to leave?

If you have three or more diagonal lines or incomplete connections that you cannot resolve and you are continually upset about these issues -- it's time to move on. You're getting about 60% of your needs fulfilled!

THE CONTENT ISSUES

We have addressed the context of the relationship; the satisfaction of needs. There are also content issues that are often overlooked. Here are a few examples of how to avoid potentially upsetting situations that can cause friction between partners.

1. Anytime there is confrontation or friction between the two of you, stop and ask yourself:

"Is my relationship with my partner more important than... " (fill in the issue).

If your answer is yes, then use the communication tools to discover what the problem is really about and what the both of you can do to resolve it.

If your answer is no, then instead of a <u>relationship</u>, you have an <u>entanglement</u> and it may be time to end it.

2. Never make your partner wrong. We cannot say that a person's teeth are wrong, a person's hair is wrong, anymore than we can say that a tree is wrong. Likewise, saying a person is wrong is to attack the other person personally and subjectively. To say that you disagree with what the other person did or said is to be objective and sensitive to the other person's feelings. Attacking someone with, 'you're wrong' only creates a defense mechanism leading to an escalation of hostility and charged emotions.

3. Avoid using the word 'but'. What it says is, "I negate what you have just said and I'm sticking to what I believe." In effect, you are erasing what the other person said. You've closed down the discussion. Using the word, 'and' is far more inclusive. It allows what was said to remain and it allows a contribution by each person. You have not broken the fibers of the communication. Further clarification on this subject is discussed in "Through Supplier Eyes."

4. Don't go to bed angry at each other. All too often, an upsetting situation will cause one or both partners to go to bed upset, angry, withdrawn, as upset Consumers. Time and a night's sleep may not help the parties to resolve the upset. It will be held until the appropriate time comes when it will be flung in the other person's face. We will keep score! We've all done it!

An agreement by both parties to never go to bed until an upsetting situation that occurred has been resolved will prevent the same argument from echoing in the future. Both parties must say it or lose the right to ever bring it up in the future: not tomorrow, next week, not ever! This agreement prevents both of you from becoming a closet Consumer or Supplier, just waiting for the right moment to drop a shoe on one another.

5. Marriage is NOT a "50/50" proposition. If it is, then each partner is only getting 50% of what he or she needs. Would you be satisfied in a relationship like that?

In a successful relationship, both parties get 100% of what each needs. Impossible you say? If you work at giving your partner whatever he or she needs and he or she does the same, then you're each getting 100% -- a partnership called WIN/WIN!

6. If you want to have a fantastic relationship, always support your partner in what he or she wants to do. Support can be emotional, physical, and financial -- anything that helps the other person to achieve his or her goal.

WHAT'S NEXT?

Let's play a game. At the top of piece of paper, write 'Supplier' on the left side and 'Consumer' on the right.

Then each day, list under Supplier something you did for or said to someone else -- or to yourself -- that you felt good about. And under Consumer list something you allowed someone else to contribute to you in word or deed that you really appreciated. It doesn't matter how small or how large, just that it's something you acknowledged someone else for giving to you. Do this for 30 days.

Then look at your list and see how you've learned to use the tools of relationship to help yourself and others. And go to the mirror and say, "Congratulations!"

2. THE INTERVIEW ANALYZER™

*How to tell when you're interviewing
the wrong person for the job*

I WANT SOMEONE WHO: **IN REALITY THIS PERSON:**

Part A   **Part B**

I

Responds in an unusual manner   [ ]   [ ]   Responds in an unusual manner
Responds in a usual manner   [ ]   [ ]   Responds in a usual manner

II

Adapts to changes   [ ]   [ ]   Adapts to changes
Sticks to the rules   [ ]   [ ]   Sticks to the rules

III

Looks for alternatives   [ ]   [ ]   Looks for alternatives
Follows instructions   [ ]   [ ]   Follows instructions

IV

Is people oriented   [ ]   [ ]   Is people oriented
Is task oriented   [ ]   [ ]   Is task oriented

V

Lets the result speak for itself   [ ]   [ ]   Lets the result speak for itself
Proves each point   [ ]   [ ]   Proves each point

VI

Sets own priorities   [ ]   [ ]   Sets own priorities
Follows the schedules   [ ]   [ ]   Follows the schedules

VII

Discusses issues   [ ]   [ ]   Discusses issues
Accepts conditions   [ ]   [ ]   Accepts conditions

Applicant's Name _____ Date _____
Job description _____
Comments _____

© **Copyright 2009 Zalman Puchkoff**

174

THE INTERVIEW ANALYZER™

Directions:

Copy the analyzer or cut out the Interview Analyzer™ form at the back of the book with the meaning of the issues at hand. Fold the analyzer form lengthwise exposing only Part A.

Turn the form over and do the same with 'The Reality Is' side, then open the form and connect each pair of X's across the page. Open the form and connect a line to each 'X' in each pair of statements. The lines may be parallel across the top, parallel across the bottom, diagonal in each direction, or there may be blank boxes on either side of the form.

It's expensive to interview, hire, and train an employee. It's even more expensive to have to fire that person in a short term and re-train someone else. That expense can be eliminated with the help of proper tools. The Interview AnalyzerJ is one of those tools.

Interviewing is an art, not a science. It requires experience, good judgment, and the willingness to use the tools that are available to help match the person to the job.

As interviewers, we all have views about ourselves and other people. We look for people who have attributes that match our expectations about how a job should be done. Some of these qualities are: aggressive, assertive, dedicated, adaptable, patient, outspoken, shy, determined, or sympathetic.

Our expectations of the job requirements and the applicant's personality traits may be unrealistic, self-indulgent, or well founded. If we can quantify the qualities we're looking for, we have a better chance of getting what we <u>do want</u> and not getting what we <u>don't want</u>.

The Interview AnalyzerJ will let you see when you're interviewing the wrong person for the job. It lets you see what your relationship is with the applicant. It gives you an X-ray of what the problems are in your search for the right person for the job, and affords you the opportunity to correct them.

It allows you to be objective about your own feelings regarding the person you are interviewing. It gives you a way to determine, in a short time, which applicants most likely <u>will not</u> work out.

If you interview people who will be reporting directly to you, your requirements will be more or less set by your own experiences and standards. Use The Interview AnalyzerJ as a yardstick for evaluating your expectations against the applicant's qualities.

If you're a personnel manager, an executive recruiter, human resources manager, work for an employment agency, or do the hiring in your organization, the Interview AnalyzerJ can make your job much easier. While it cannot measure the technical and mechanical abilities of the applicant, -- so difficult to define -- it can, and does, quantify the communication skills you're asked to look for by your client or department manager, against those qualities you look to see in the applicant.

If you know what you want and what to look for, you'll have a better chance of finding what you want when you see it. If you have little or no experience in interviewing people and you don't know what to look for, you will have no way of knowing if and when you get what you're looking for.

The Interview AnalyzerJ helps you do just that -- get the kind of person you want and not get who you don't want. By matching up the traits required to the traits of the applicant, the seven expectation issues help you save time and money.

The Analyzer helps you weed out those candidates who can be seen to be definitely not eligible. You can concentrate on selecting the best applicant from a group of prospects you know are suited to the job.

How it works
The underlying structure of The Interview AnalyzerJ is based on seven interpersonal expectation issues that form the basis of our relationship and interaction with other people. In defining these seven expectation issues, you will have a clearer picture of what it is you are measuring in this case, the specific attributes required for the job against the applicant's qualifications.

When we identify each of the seven issues and relate them to each of the paired statements on the Interview AnalyzerJ, the purpose of this interview tool will become apparent to you -- to help you make the right decisions.

There are seven pairs of statements on each side of the form which correlate to the seven interpersonal issues. The left side, Part A, is the expectation side, the attributes you're looking for. The right side, Part B, is the reality side which represents the qualities you perceive in the applicant.

Consumers and Suppliers
The words consumer and supplier are terms that most people, especially those engaged in business, are familiar with.

Consumers are people who use, buy, consume, or accept things from suppliers. Suppliers are people who make, sell, supply, or give things to consumers. In business, employers are the Consumers. They are the receivers or recipients of the work. The employees are the Suppliers. They are the givers -- the doers of the work. This Consumer/Supplier relationship works on every level in a company.

To subordinates, you are the Consumer. They are the Suppliers. To superiors, you are the Supplier. They are the Consumers. To peers, you can be both the Supplier and the Consumer -- but not at the same time!

Unfortunately, many businesspeople tend to confuse their roles in their relationships with peers, subordinates, and superiors.

The Interview Analyzer™ identifies and clarifies the roles that are played when hiring people, to put Consumers together with Suppliers and vice-versa.

The top statement in each sentence pair represents the Supplier role -- the giver or doers of the work. The bottom statement represents the Consumer role -- the askers or acceptors of the work.

If you are a Consumer (employer) to your subordinates, your job is to get what you want from them and not get what you don't want. They are Suppliers to you and their job is to give you what you want. If you find yourself getting what you don't want or not getting what you do want, you may find yourself getting upset.

If you are a Supplier (employee) to your superiors, your job is to give them what they do want and not give them what they don't want. If you find yourself giving what you don't want, or unable to give what you do want, you may also get upset.

Relationships start to strain when people forget what role they are in and what their primary job function is. If not corrected, long term stress and upsets lead to dis-ease in the body.

In dealing with your peers, someone must be the Supplier and someone must be the Consumer. When two people talk to each other at the same time, they are both supplying. No communication takes place. When two people "hold it in" and don't talk to one another, no communication takes place. They are both consuming -- a cause for stress -- and an upsetting situation in the making.

Using the terms Consumer and Supplier to identify the roles of the players will allow you to establish realistic expectations for the job and let you focus on the qualities that you're looking for in an applicant.

As the interviewer, you are the Consumer. If you're looking for a Supplier type of person and you're interviewing a Consumer, you'll see diagonals on the Interview Analyzer] going from upper left to lower right. If you want a Consumer type of person, and you're interviewing a Supplier, you'll see diagonals on the form going from lower left to upper right. In determining the type of individual you want for the job, decide whether you need a Supplier or a Consumer type person. Also consider what type of relationships you have with the other people in your organization. It may give you further insight into the type of person you want to work with.

What to look for

The more diagonals you see, the more the applicant is not suited for this position. If you see three or more diagonals or incomplete connections at the end of the interview, this is a definite red flag. What you expect of someone in those areas is not what you are going to get.

The Interview Analyzer™ offers you two views:
1. It measures the personality traits you require for the job against those you see in the applicant.
2. It shows you the interpersonal (Supplier/Consumer) relationship that you're having with the applicant at the time of the interview.

How to use the form
Make a test case. Choose a position or job where you know the attributes required for a job. Make some copies of the Interview Analyzer™. Now fill in this side using the person who has that job as your model, placing an X in the most appropriate box in each pair of statements that you think apply. If you know a little about this person's personality, you'll know what boxes to mark.

When this is done, open the form and connect the X's across each pair of statements. What you will see is an X-Ray of parallel and/or diagonal lines across the page.

If the person is suited to the job, you'll see few or no diagonals. On the other hand, if you think that person is not suited to the job and is not doing it well, or doesn't get along well with other people, you'll see many diagonals.

The Interview
Before the actual interview, take another Analyzer and place an X in Part A in the most appropriate box in each pair of statements for the qualities you want for the job. Then fold the sheet in half lengthwise on the numbered issues and turn it over, with the reality side, Part B facing you.

During the interview ask the applicant the kinds of questions that provide you with the information you need to fill in the boxes on the reality side. You can mark the boxes either during or after the interview.

Again, the Interview AnalyzerJ will not tell you if the right person is being hired for the job. It is designed to let you see, graphically, the difference between your requirements (or expectations) for the job with the qualities you see in the applicant.

When they match (parallel lines from Part A to Part B) you get what you expected and when they don't match, (diagonal lines in either direction from Part A to Part B), you get what you don't want.

Most of us don't know what really works, but we certainly know when something doesn't work. The Interview AnalyzerJ lets you see very quickly when the wrong person is being interviewed for the job.

If you can match the expected qualities for a job with the actual qualities of an applicant, there is a better chance to hire someone who will succeed in the job.

Continual mistakes in choosing an employee might indicate that you need to change your requirements or expectations for the job, or you need to change the reality of the type of person you're interviewing; that is, look for different attributes in an applicant.

Put another way, you might want to re-examine the job description based upon different guidelines.

Understanding the issues

To understand what each statement pair means, we need to relate them to seven interpersonal issues. You will then be able to see the relationship of each communication issue to the statements on the form. They may give you insight into the requirements that you have for the job measured against the qualities of the person you're interviewing.

THE 7 EXPECTATION ISSUES

1. RESPONSE

The basic issue is, are you looking for an unusual response, or a predictable response? How do you want the person in this job to respond or reply? Are you looking for someone who can think independently, or a person who will respond in a manner that is expected for this position?

If you want someone to think independently, then you'll want to hear new and unusual responses during the interview. On the other hand, if you want to hear answers that are always appropriate to the occasion, what is expected, you'll look for predictability and no surprises in the applicant's replies.

What is important to you, new or unusual responses to the issues at hand or predictable responses? If you anticipate one type of response and you get another, will it upset you?

2. AGREEMENTS

The basic issue here is changes to agreements. Do you want someone who is able to adapt to and make changes to agreements with you, whatever they are, or hold rigid to the rules as laid down by you or the company?

It's your choice. What type of person do you want? If you recognize that all interactions and relationships are controlled by some type of agreement, and that all agreements change, you create an important shift in your outlook towards your expectations for the applicant you're interviewing.

3. ALTERNATIVES

The basic issue here is supplying options. Do you want someone who is able to offer and suggest alternatives to problems and suggest alternate ways to get the job done, or someone who follows instructions and assignments, and reports when a problem or difficulty is encountered or arises?

Is the applicant willing to negotiate and explore alternatives during the interview. If one of you wants to explore alternatives and the other does not, there's cause for an upset -- and possibly the end of the interview. Negotiation is the tool to reduce the heat of a confrontation. If the applicant negotiates with you, then be prepared to negotiate with this person if you hire him or her. If you want to stipulate and lay down the rules, and the applicant responds with an unusual answer and wants to negotiate and you don't like it, recognize that this type of relationship is what you're going to get if you hire this individual.

4. UNDERSTANDING

This issue deals with the qualities of acceptance and understanding. Successful communication at every level of relationship requires that these be present in every interaction, no matter how trivial or deeply important the subject matter.

We sometimes view the other person in a stereotype role rather than as an individual. If you expect the applicant to be like you (no one is) and to behave and act as you do, this is another form of stereotyping. When we meet someone new, as during an interview, we want to instantly size that person up and assign him or her a role. We feel more comfortable in knowing "who they are", according to our standards.

Be objective about who the applicant is, not what you want him or her to be. To deal effectively with people, you have to have an understanding of who they are. This is often expressed as, "I know where you're coming from", or simply, "I know what you mean."

When you're doing tasks, you have to have an understanding of the job to be done and how to do it. Interacting with the public or being in a sales position requires tact, diplomacy, and a willingness to understand the other person.

Will the applicant be working mostly with people, or things? A technician who has to explain and demonstrate the workings of a complicated piece of equipment, such as a computer or an industrial generator, may need qualities in both areas, but what is the predominant and most important quality needed?

As the Consumer in the interview, if you will not or cannot listen to the other person because you see him or her in a stereotype role, you may not understand what the other person wants to communicate to you. You may need to get your ego and emotional baggage out of the way and go into neutral and just listen without judging the other person. Feed back what the other person said to you to insure that you got the right message. Rephrase it with, "As I understand it, you are saying," or, "As I see it…"

What is your goal? Are you looking for a good will ambassador, a salesperson, or a technical wizard?

5. CONTROL

The issue here is one of power. As long as a person is in control, power is maintained. If that person loses it, he or she may blame another individual. When we blame someone else, we're giving that person our power, and letting that person control how we feel, either good or bad.

In the same way that a material possession can be owned, so can a feeling. Likewise, in the same way that you can deny that you own a material possession, you can deny owning a feeling. "That dog destroyed your flowerbed? "No, that's not my dog." "Hostility towards you?" "I'm not aware of any bad feelings between you and me."

A person who lets the result speak for itself doesn't have to be defensive and can take responsibility for his or her feelings and actions. On the other hand a person who proves each point is either a cautious individual, concerned about each decision and its consequences, or perhaps a person who is not generally sure of himself or herself and has to defend each action.

Are you going to be working with this person? Do you see a power struggle in the making or a tendency to avoid responsibility and blame others?

6. PRIORITIES

The issue here is who does what on whose priorities. If you want someone to be a self starter who doesn't need to be reminded when and what to do, you'll choose a Supplier type of person. On the other hand, if you want someone to follow whatever the schedules are, without an option for change in timing or sequence, you'll want a Consumer type of person.

7. FEEDBACK

The issue here is comeback or retort and is essential to good human relations, even in business. As the Consumer -- the employer -- you may get upset if the applicant says something you don't like or says it in a way you don't want to hear.

Are you looking for someone who can tell you how he or she you feels and discuss the issues with you, or not give you any feedback or commentary?

The difference between the first issue, response, and this issue is, response is defined as whether the other person gives you a usual or unusual comeback or retort. Feedback is defined as a commentary on the issue or subject under discussion. It may also be the response, and it can be positive or negative.

Basically are you looking for someone who speaks his or her mind or a 'Yes' person?

THE MEANING OF THE CONNECTIONS

There are eight different connection patterns that are possible in each of the 7 sets of statements.

- Upper left to upper right
- Upper left to lower right
- Lower left to upper right
- Lower left to lower right

- Left side only blank
- Right side only blank
- Both sides blank
- Two X's in one set

[X]--[X]
[ ] [ ]

A parallel line across the top in any issue shows that your expectation for the job matches the qualities that you see in the applicant. What you expect is what you will probably get. The more parallel lines across the top, the more this person matches your job requirements.

Now that you know what the optimum connection is, don't try to force this connection during the interview by looking to see what you marked on the expectation side, Part A, before the interview.

If the interview form shows 7 parallel lines across the top, you may have found yourself the perfect candidate or, you're pressing to find the right person and it's a wish fulfillment on your part that this is the right person for the job. Better to be on the cautious side; take some more time with this candidate.

[X] [ ]
    \
[ ] [X]

This diagonal line in any issue indicates that the applicant does not possess the "take charge" or entrepreneurial qualities you expect of someone you hire for this position. This person is not aggressive or forceful. This type of person usually fits well as a team player in large organizations.

Did the applicant know beforehand what the job entailed? This may not be the first time the applicant has applied for a position that requires abilities that are outside of his or her domain. Are you willing to gamble?

[ ] [X]
    /
[X] [ ]

This diagonal line in any issue indicates that you expect the applicant to be a team player and carry out all responsibilities as assigned and the applicant surprised you. Is this job in a large organization where you want a team player? If so, this individual may feel stifled because his or her creativity and self assertiveness needs to be fully expressed.

A small company might be a better place for this individual unless you can handle an assertive "take charge" person. Can you work with this person? Can everybody else work together harmoniously?

[ ] [ ]
[X]--[X]

This parallel line in any issue indicates that there is a match between your expectation and the applicant's traits. Recognize that the applicant is not generally expressive or communicative, and neither are you. Bottom to bottom connections indicate minimum communication, usually occurring in family or business relationships.

The applicant is better adapted to task oriented projects, rather than dealing with people in social environments. Do you expect to fill a sales or customer service position with this person? Think again!

[ ] [ ]
[X] [ ]

This incomplete pattern in any issue is regarded as a diagonal connection. You know what you want, what's required for the job, but you haven't discovered if the applicant has the qualities you want. You will have to ask more pointed questions, or listen more closely to what the applicant is or is not revealing.

[ ] [ ]
[ ] [X]

This incomplete pattern in any issue is also regarded as a diagonal connection. You have no expectations for the position. You don't know what attributes are required for the job, but you do know the characteristics the applicant possesses. How do you know if what you found is what you need if you have no measurement for the job? Do some more homework! Find out what qualifications are needed for the job.

Blanks on both sides in any issue indicate that this issue is not relevant to the job and you didn't look for this quality in the applicant. Are you sure? It may also indicate that this issue is the most important one to look at. If you feel that the qualifications for the job might never be fulfilled, you may not choose to have one. If you don't ask for what you really want, how will you know when you find it?

[X] [X]
[X] [X]

If you put two X marks on the left side in any issue to indicate that you expect the applicant to have both attributes, sorry -- Superman and Superwoman have other jobs. Be specific. Which characteristic is more important for the job? Perhaps the job needs to be split and done by two people!

If you checked both boxes on the right side, you are getting "mixed messages" from the applicant, who professes to be "a jack of all trades" and can adapt to any job. The applicant wants you to believe that he or she has both attributes. Serious consideration must be given to whether the applicant is emotionally grounded, or has enough specific information about the job.

Look closely into exactly what the job entails and relate the applicant's previous job experiences to it. Ask for specific incidences. Don't be afraid to probe! Are you willing to gamble now and pay later for issues that are not clear or defined? You'll only say later, "I knew it all the time."

3. THE CAREER ANALYZER™

*How to tell if what you're doing now
is what you really want to be doing*

I WANT TO: THE REALITY IS:

Part A   Part B

I

Create things to sell   [ ]   [ ]   I create things to sell
Sell what already exists   [ ]   [ ]   I sell what already exists

II

Call on people   [ ]   [ ]   I call on people
Have people come to me   [ ]   [ ]   People come to me

III

Make money   [ ]   [ ]   I make money
Express my talents   [ ]   [ ]   I express my talents

IV

Work with people   [ ]   [ ]   Work with people
Work with things   [ ]   [ ]   Work with things

V

Be my own boss   [ ]   [ ]   I am my own boss
Work for someone else   [ ]   [ ]   I Work for someone else

VI

Work under deadlines   [ ]   [ ]   I work under deadlines
Work at my own pace   [ ]   [ ]   I work at my own pace

VII

Work on an incentive basis   [ ]   [ ]   I work on an incentive basis
Work for a salary   [ ]   [ ]   I work for a salary

The Career Analyzer™

Directions:

Copy the analyzer or cut out the Career Analyzer™ form at the back of the book with the meaning of the issues at hand. Fold the analyzer form lengthwise exposing only Part A showing only the 'I Want To' side.

Put an X in one of each of the seven pairs of statements. Turn the form over and do the same with 'The Reality Is' side, then open the form and connect each pair of X's across the page. Open the form and connect a line to each 'X' in each pair of statements. The lines may be parallel across the top, parallel across the bottom, diagonal in each direction, or there may be blank boxes on either side of the form.

Applied to the Career Analyzer™, you will be comparing what you want to do -- your expectation -- with what you are actually doing now -- the reality. If what you are doing is not what you want to be doing, you will see, graphically, in which one or more of seven expectation areas you are out of alignment.

In matching skills and careers, decisions are often based on an expectation of what we think we would like to be doing according to qualities we have or think we have. Expectations may be unrealistic, or well grounded.

Most of us don't know all of the things we like or want in a career. We almost always know what we don't like to be doing. We'll call our predilections, our work preferences for what we do want to be doing, a 'calling'.

The Benefits

The Career Analyzer™ lets you see very quickly if your 'calling' – in 7 specific areas -- is in alignment with what you are doing … or not. There will be a far greater chance of being successful in your career and satisfied with your choice, if what you want to do is matched with what you are doing now.

When you work for someone else, you are a 'Supplier' to your employer. You become a 'Consumer' on payday or when you decide to work for yourself.

Consumers initiate requests
- Nothing is put into motion unless a request is made
- If you don't ask for something, nobody knows you want it
- If you don't know what you want, you can only get what's given to you
- If you ask for something, you may or may not get it
- If you don't get it, ask for it somewhere else
- If you can't get it anywhere, forget it and ask for something else

Suppliers fulfill requests

- If you are asked for something, you don't have to give it
- If you offer something, it doesn't have to be accepted
- If what you have to offer someone isn't accepted, offer it to someone else
- If what you have to give isn't accepted by anyone, offer something else
- If nobody asks you for anything, create a need you can fill

Understanding the connections

There are seven different connection patterns that are possible in each of the seven sets of statements.

1. Upper left to upper right
2. Upper left to lower right
3. Lower left to upper right
4. Lower left to lower right
5. Left side only blank
6. Right side only blank
7. Both sides blank

When you understand the meaning of each connection you will understand your relationship with your job. Now with the completed form in hand, check your connections.

$$[\,X\,] \text{--} [\,X\,]$$
$$[\quad] \quad [\quad]$$

A parallel line across the top shows that what you want to do is matched with what you are doing. You're probably successful and have lots of drive and ambition. Congratulations! This condition of satisfaction is very important to you. You have actualized what you have wanted in this area. If you have five or more parallel connections, you are probably very satisfied in your work.

Now that you know what the optimum connection is, don't try to force this connection. If the Career Analyzer™ form shows seven matches across the top, you'd better believe that it's perhaps too good to be true – or that you really have it made!

$$[\,X\,] \quad [\quad]$$
$$\backslash$$
$$[\quad] \quad [X]$$

This diagonal line indicates that what you want is not in line with what you are doing. Your expectations are high and you've sold yourself short. What are you afraid of? It appears that you're confident in what you want to do, but you've settled for less. What are you going to do about it? You knew what the job entailed. Why did you take it? It seems like something got in the way of your goals. Do you know what it is?

```
[   ]   [ X ]
       /
[ X ]   [   ]
```

This diagonal line also indicates that what you want is not in alignment with what you are doing, but in this case you've chosen a job that doesn't express your personality and work habits. You're sure of your basic preferences and yet you've chosen to move in the fast lane, perhaps you're over your head. Maybe money was the carrot that was dangled in front of you. Is it worth it? You're the only one that can answer that.

```
[   ]   [   ]
[ X ] -- [ X ]
```

This parallel line indicates that there is a match between what you want to do and what you are doing. You recognize that you are not an extrovert and you are aware of your limitations and do not want to put undue pressure or stress on yourself. You are better at task oriented projects rather than in a sales environment. Congratulations! Satisfaction with your job and with yourself is your reward.

```
[   ] [   ]
[ X ] [   ]
```

This incomplete connection is regarded as a diagonal line. You know what you want to do but you don't know exactly what you are doing. The reality of your job seems to have gotten away from you. Perhaps you are bored, disinterested, or feel that you're in a rut. What are going to do about it? To make any change is to force you to look at where you are and how you got there. Now what?

```
[   ] [   ]
[   ] [ X ]
```

This incomplete connection is also regarded as a diagonal line. You have no personal preference for your job yet you know exactly what you are doing. Is it that you don't care what you do, or if you looked at what you truly want to do, you would become upset with yourself or consider yourself to be selfish? The definition of selfish in the real world is, not doing what someone else wants you to do. Which is worse? Not doing what you want to do, or not asking for what you want?

Blanks on both sides indicate that this issue is not relevant to your job. It may also indicate that this issue is the most important one to address. If you feel that your expectations – what you want to do – may never be fulfilled, you wouldn't want to have them. You are avoiding getting

```
```

upset. Are you hiding something? If you don't express what you want as a Consumer, there's no Supplier to hear you and give you what you want. What do you have to lose?

Conclusion

The more diagonals you have, the more you need to reassess your relationship with your job.

If you have three or more diagonals, it's clear you're in the wrong job!

If you are unhappy doing your job and you do nothing, you will continue to be stressed and upset. How long do you wish this to continue? A month … a year … the rest of your working life?

If you are unhappy with your job, you now know why. You have not found your 'calling' and you don't like what you're doing. You have three alternatives:

1. Change what you want to do – your expectation
2. Change what you're doing – the reality
3. Quit the job – leave the relationship

To quit the job means to find one that matches your 'calling', what you want to be doing. Everyone makes his or her job. That is to say, a person molds the job so that it fits the person who is doing it. Perhaps you can ask for a job within the company that better suits your talents and still utilizes the experience you gained with the company.

You may never find a job that fills seven 'calling' preferences. If you matched at least five preferences, that's pretty good! Chances are when you're in a job that offers you the opportunity to express your talents the money will be there. Do you want to be doing something you don't like because of the money? Or do you want to be doing something you do like, and be the best Supplier you can be to your employer?

If you are happy with your job and have at least five parallel connections – congratulations! You've found your 'calling' and you are doing what you want to be doing.

The X-ray of your relationship with your job and your 'calling' may help you to get off your position and move forward – or recognize that you are indeed suited to what you are doing. Now give yourself some time, say a week, to consider what you are going to do or not do. How do you feel? Do you now have tools that you didn't have before that will help you make better decisions that you couldn't make before?

4. THE HOUSE BUYER'S ANALYZER™

Seven steps to finding your dream house

I WANT: I SAW:

PART A   PART B

1. AGE

A NEW HOUSE	[ ]	[ ]	A NEW HOUSE
AN OLD HOUSE	[ ]	[ ]	AN OLD HOUSE

2. PRIVACY

PRIVACY/ACREAGE	[ ]	[ ]	PRIVACY /ACREAGE
DEVELOPMENT/COMMUNITY	[ ]	[ ]	DEVELOPMENT/COMMUNITY

3. STYLE

CUSTOM/INDIVIDUALITY	[ ]	[ ]	CUSTOM /INDIVIDUALITY
A BASIC DESIGN HOUSE	[ ]	[ ]	A BASIC DESIGN HOUSE

4. CONDITION

MOVE-IN CONDITION	[ ]	[ ]	MOVE-IN CONDITION
HANDYMAN/REMODELING	[ ]	[ ]	HANDYMAN/REMODELING

5. SPACE

OPEN INTERIOR SPACE	[ ]	[ ]	OPEN INTERIOR SPACE
WELL DEFINED ROOMS	[ ]	[ ]	WELL DEFINED ROOMS

6.TYPE

A MODERN HOUSE	[ ]	[ ]	A MODERN HOUSE
A TRADITIONAL HOUSE	[ ]	[ ]	A TRADITIONAL HOUSE

7. PRICE

AMENITIES & LUXURY	[ ]	[ ]	AMENITIES & LUXURY
PRICE AND/OR INVESTMENT	[ ]	[ ]	PRICE AND/OR INVESTMENT

Date_____   MLS Listing number _____   Agent _____ _____

House address_____ Town_____

THE SEVEN STEPS TO FINDING YOUR DREAM HOUSE

Copy the analyzer or cut out the House Buyer's analyzer™ form at the back of the book with the meaning of the issues at hand.

Step One: Fold the form in half and fill out Part A "I WANT" on the House Buyer's Analyzer™

Step Two: Give the agent the form and discuss your needs

Step Three: Look at houses with the agent, fill out Part B; "I SAW"

Step Four: Discuss the connections with the agent

Step Five: Revisit the house; check out each content issue of concern

Step Six: Go for it; put in a bid!

Step Seven: Get your mortgage

Follow each step, and use your broker to help you bring a difficult and emotionally draining decision-making task down to an enjoyable and perhaps a financially enriching experience.

Let's take the first step.

Fill out Part A: I WANT, on the House Buyer's Analyzer™

First, make extra copies of the Buyer's Analyzer™. You'll need a form to fill out for each house that the agent shows you and each member of your family who has a say in the matter. The agent will be happy to supply you with forms too.

You will be comparing what you want, what your expectations are for a house on Part A, with the reality of what you see, after the agent shows you a house in Part B.

Read each pair of sentences under Part A, "I WANT", and put an X in the box that expresses what you want. If you're undecided as to what you want, leave that issue blank and go back to it when you've made a decision. The meanings of each of the issues are explained on the page after The House Buyer's Analyzer™.

OVERVIEW
For most of us, buying a house is the most important financial decision of our lives. The assistance of a professional realtor is invaluable; they're trained in every aspect of the process from locating to closing on the house you want. Plus, as professionals, they are also experts on your local area.

But who helps us with the emotional side of the decision? Regardless of where we're presently living, many of us walk around with a picture of the dream house we'd really like to live in. Then when we go out looking for a house, we'll measure everything we see up against that picture -- whether it's realistic or not. In this area we have little to go on -- or measure -- other than our feelings.

The House Buyer's Analyzer™ was designed to help you -- and help the broker help you -- find and put a bid on a house that's as close to the ideal you have in mind as is realistically possible. (Of course if you dream about a mansion on acres and acres of land and all your budget will bear is a one-bedroom condominium, it won't work.)

The House Buyer's Analyzer™ deals with basic attributes -- from an emotional point of view -- and allows you to define and express your considerations in an objective manner. There are seven steps outlined in this booklet to help you and the agent find the house you want. At each step, you need to tell the truth about what
you want to make it work best for you -- and to help the agent find what you're looking for.

Of the seven pairs of questions on the House Buyer's Analyzer™, six intangible or emotional considerations and one issue relates to the price of the house. If the buying decision is going to be made by more than one person, everyone involved needs to fill out his or her form and compare answers -- ideally, before the agent shows you houses.

When the House Buyer's Analyzer™ is filled out, comparing your expectations of what you want with the reality of the house you're looking at, it provides an X-ray, a definitive comparison, for you to see whether or not you've found a close match. It also gives the agent the ability to find and show you houses that closely match your expectations.

The seven buying issues address your wants from a basic starting point -- the foundation. We'll call these issues the context considerations for buying; they quantify your emotional considerations in a qualitative approach and formal procedure.

The practical considerations, we'll call these the content considerations, can be considered next. This is the house construction. These include the number of rooms, including the number of bedrooms and bathrooms, the square footage, the type of heating, the number of amps, amenities like a fireplace, attached garage, proximity to shopping, etc.

THE MEANING OF THE ISSUES

1. AGE:

Deciding on whether to live in an old house or a new house is like sorting apples. Where do you draw the line? Is it the year it was built, the condition of the outside of the house, the interior design, the age of the appliances? Decide on what you want and tell your broker what you feel.

· 2. PRIVACY:

What does privacy mean to you? It can go from not having a neighbor within 250 feet to not having a neighboring house within view from anywhere on your property. How much open space and acreage do you really need and want? Can you afford to pay for raw land that you'll never cultivate or commercially use and the additional taxes? You can have privacy even within a planned community or development association. How far away or close to community services, activities, public transportation, schools, etc. do you want to be?

3. STYLE:

This buying issue takes into consideration your personality. Do you want a one-of-a-kind house, a house that doesn't look like any other house in the neighborhood area? Do you want a house that expresses your own individuality? If so, choose custom/individuality.

On the other hand, if it doesn't make a difference if your house is not drastically different than other houses in the area and you're not personally attached to a particular "look", you'll choose a basic design house that can be any style from modern to a remodeled barn.

4. CONDITION:

We all have a tendency to put on rose-colored glasses when we're evaluating this issue. If you fall in love with a house and don't thoroughly inspect it, you may overlook some problems that might cost you a bundle to repair after you've bought the house. Of course you'll hire an engineer to inspect the house for any structural or hazardous conditions and to make sure everything is in working order.

If you don't want to do any work whatsoever and just want to move in and begin living in it from day one, then you'll choose move-in condition.

On the other hand, if you're creative and handy with tools and look at remodeling and fixing up as a challenge, you won't mind making repairs and cosmetic fix-up. This can include painting, landscaping, patching, and perhaps hire tradesmen to do wallpapering, refinish cabinets, lay carpeting, etc, especially if the price of the house is low enough to induce you to put in some sweat equity to increase its value.

There's a small gap between move-in condition and making minor repairs. There's a big chasm between minor repairs and making major repairs, characterized as a "handyman special." These major repairs may include architectural changes such as moving walls, you're putting up new walls, boiler repairs, roof replacement, new heating systems, new wiring, adding-on rooms, etc. -- no job for a week-end warrior unless you have the time and patience.

Don't make an offer to purchase a house unless you're absolutely sure of its condition and how much you have to shell out in repairs. If you're handy with tools and you can do some or all of the work yourself, that's great. Can you manage a contractor or group of tradesmen who will be doing the work?

5. SPACE:

This issue deals with the amount of space in the house and how it is used and allocated. Do you want open interior space with large great rooms? Do you want picture windows, open staircases and balconies, an island kitchen? If so, you'll choose
open-interior space.

On the other hand, do you like well-defined rooms with a door to each room and a traditional use, such as a dining room next to the kitchen? Do you want to see rooms that you can easily identify as to their use, such as a playroom, a den, a workshop, or a children's bedroom?

If so, you'll choose well-defined rooms.

6. TYPE:

This issue deals with the look of the house and how it relates to its interior layout and design. How do you picture your dream house?

Its modern or new fixtures and appliances as well as the layout may characterize a modern house. Does the kitchen have ceramic tiles? Are the appliances "built-in" as opposed to "old fashioned" looking? Is there track lighting and high-hats in the ceiling as opposed to ornamental tulip bulbs? Modern houses have dens and playrooms. Is there a Jacuzzi in the bathroom or the bedroom as opposed to a freestanding bathtub with claw feet in the bathroom? Do you want a fireplace with a heat-saving blower or an open hearth?

If you want a house with up-to-date features, you'll choose a modern house. Many buyers have the image of a traditional house with a screened-in porch, a second floor balcony, high ceilings, a fireplace in the bedroom, a pantry, even a detached garage, or any one of a number of features that they remember of a house from their childhood. The dictionary defines tradition as the handing down of beliefs and/or customs from generation to generation. If these are important issues, you'll choose a traditional house. A traditional house includes Colonial, Victorian, etc.

7. PRICE:

The issue here is what is your goal? Are you looking for a house that has amenities and luxury such as a hot tub, a sauna, decks all around, spaciousness with state-of-the-art appliances because you can afford it and you're not overly concerned with the monthly mortgage payment? If so, you'll choose amenities & luxury.

You'll consider price if you have a limited amount of money to put down and your earnings are not expected to increase dramatically over the next 5 years. What can you afford to pay? Are you a handyman? You'll consider the price if you're going to buy the house as a fixer-upper and plan to turn it over and resell it at a profit. If so, you'll choose price and/or investment.

When considering price, ask your agent for comparable house values … what other houses have sold for that compare with the house you are considering. It's wonderful to get a bargain, and you don't want to overpay either.

When you fill out the form, notice if there are any inconsistencies in what you want. For example, wanting a new house is incompatible with wanting a house to remodel or a handyman special. Wanting an old house is incompatible with wanting open interior space unless you want a barn, because older houses were built with rooms laid out in a traditional manner.

Wanting open interior space is difficult to reconcile with wanting price and/or investment, because usually only newer more expensive houses have great rooms or cathedral ceilings.

A desire for custom/individuality is not compatible with price and/or investment because a custom built house costs more to build than a conventionally built house.

The clearer you are as to what you want, the better your chances of finding just what you're looking for. If you're not sure in certain areas, it's best to discuss this with your agent who can present options and opportunities for you to consider.

STEP TWO: Give the agent the form and discuss your needs

With Part A "I WANT" filled out, discuss your needs in each of the seven issues with the agent. In effect, you'll be asking the agent to have the same vision that you have. For this to happen, you need to be as clear as possible on each of the emotional issues.

The content issues may be easier to deal with. The agent will ask you questions such as, how many children you have, how much you're willing to spend, where you work, the type of house you want, and any other question that will help reveal your preferences. The agent will also ask what you've seen, in what areas, how long you have been looking, if you've worked with any other agency, if you have to sell your present house before you buy, when you can close, and other questions that will inform the agent of your particular circumstances.

STEP THREE: Look at houses with the agent; Fill out Part B; "I SAW"

While you're looking at a house, put an X in the most appropriate box in Part B, "I SAW", in each of the seven statements. This is the reality side. This is what you see in a house from your point of view.

After you've finished, connect the X's in each issue in Part A with the X's in Part B, forming lines which will be parallel or diagonal. You will now be looking at an X-ray of what your expectations are, compared to the reality of what you saw. The more parallel lines you show, the more your expectations match with the reality and the more confident you can be that your basic house buying considerations are being met.

THE MEANING OF THE CONNECTIONS

[X]---[X]

Parallel lines connected top to top or bottom to bottom from Part A to Part B in each sentence pair shows that what you want in a house is consistent with what you saw in a house. A condition of satisfaction has been met.

```
[X] [ ]     [ ] [X]
   \   or   /
[ ] [X]     [X] [ ]
```

Diagonal lines in either direction indicate a mismatch between what you want and what you saw.

```
[ ] [ ]
[ ] [X]
```

A blank box on the left indicates that you are not sure of what you want. If you don't know what you want, you have no way of knowing if what you saw is what you want.

```
[ ] [ ]
[X] [ ]
```

A blank box on the right indicates that you know what you want but you are not sure of what you saw. Perhaps you don't want to find what you want because you don't want to make a decision to buy yet.

```
[X] [X]
[X] [ ]
```

If you've marked both boxes in some issues within the pair in Part A, you may be ambivalent as to what you really want, or you may want both attributes, such as a certain degree of privacy, but still want to live in a community setting.

You may also have emotional considerations not expressed that need to be looked into.

```
[X] [X]
[ ] [X]
```

If both boxes are marked within the pair in Part B, you know what you want, but you don't want to be locked in to making the decision as to what you saw. To do so may require a commitment on your part that you're not ready to make.

Now that you know the meaning of the connections, don't force a parallel line to be agreeable with what someone else likes or how the agent sees it. Call it like it is. It's your money and nobody gets to spend it for you or tell you what you like or don't like. This is a very important point.

STEP FOUR: Discuss the results with the agent.

If the agent isn't showing you exactly the kind of house you want to see, the mismatch (a diagonal line) will show up in that issue. If a condition of satisfaction has been met, that is, your expectation of what you want in a house matches the reality of what you saw (a parallel line), you will know you and the agent are on target.

As the buyer, it is your job to tell the agent when there isn't a match in an issue and when there is. Help the agent help you make your dream house a reality. If the agent isn't showing you enough houses that match most, if not all, of your requirements, perhaps you need to change either your expectations or the reality of what is available in the area at that time.

Leave a copy of the filled out House Buyer's Analyzer™ with the agent. The agent can then refer to it and call you when new listings appear that match your requirements.

In a month's time, or even sooner, you may see upwards of 10 or 25 or more houses. The House Buyer's Analyzer™ will help you to keep track of what you've seen, what you don't like, what comes close to what you do like, and offers you the opportunity to make comparisons of houses and allow you to change or fine tune your wants should you have to make compromises.

If you're not able to find what you're looking for, don't get discouraged. If you've seen over a dozen houses and none of them come close to what you want, you have three choices. You can:

> 1. CHANGE YOUR EXPECTATION
> 2. CHANGE THE REALITY
> 3. LEAVE THE RELATIONSHIP

To change your expectation means to change what you want in some of the issues in Part A, because you can't find exactly what you want. Start with those issues that are the most important ones to you, those that you'll never change...not even if it means not buying a house. Circle them in order of importance, 1-2-3 and so forth.

The issues not circled are the ones about which you can change your expectation. Read each statement in that issue. Are they both acceptable to you? Can you live with either choice? If so, you've shown that you can change your expectation. If you can't change your expectation about any of your buying issues, then you have to consider changing the reality.

To change the reality means that you have to find the house that will match what you want. You have to keep on looking until you find it, or in some way find a common ground where your expectation is able to live with the reality. If you can't change your expectation and you can't change the reality, then you have one other choice, and that is to leave the relationship.

Leaving the relationship can mean two things. You can find another agent who will show you the type of house you want to see, one that is comparable to your expectations or, you can stop looking for a house. You can decide to stay where you are and do some remodeling and/or add-on to your house, or build a house that will fit your pictures.

Let's say you find a house that matches 5 or more of the attributes that you want. You've also inspected the house to your full satisfaction and there's nothing about the house with which you can find fault. Under these circumstances, there's nothing to stop you from putting a bid on it; right? And yet, you don't want to! What's the problem? You may have underlying considerations that you're withholding that you need to talk about and discuss with your spouse, associate, or with the agent.

There are no hard and fast rules to go by to let you know when to put a bid on a house. It's an emotional process that everyone needs to go through. However, the closer you match your basic needs with the reality of what the house can provide for you, the faster and more confident you will be about putting in a bid.

Most of us know when we see a house we don't want. That is important because it can lead us to what we do want. There's an old proverb that says, "be careful what you wish for, you may get it!" If we wish for the house of our dreams, we have to be careful that the dream doesn't turn out to be a nightmare!

O.K. So you've filled out both sides of the House Buyer's Analyzer™ and you've got a match in most if not all of the seven issues and the physical features of the house are what you want. What do you do now?

STEP FIVE: Revisit the house; check out each issue of concern.

The Content Questionnaire Checklist poses many questions about the house. Your agent can probably answer some and get the rest for you. The items are not in any particular order. You may have considerations that are not on this list, and if so, be sure to write them down and make sure you get your questions answered!

After you buy the house, you'll have to find out for yourself how everything works, or who to call when something goes wrong, or where to get what part, and a hundred other things about the house that you could have gotten answers to if you had a checklist at the beginning.

CONTENT QUESTIONNAIRE CHECKLIST

1. Time travel to work?
2. Driveway condition?
3. Attached garage?
4. Quality of school district?
5. Bussing to school?
6. Distance to school?
7. Recreational areas?
8. Septic System location?
9. Deed Restrictions?
10. Attic storage space?
11. Fireplaces?
12. Any negotiable items?
13. Noises from street?
14. Type of heating?
15. Additional acres available?
16. Commercial use?
17. Privacy front & back?
18. Waterfront rights?
19. Cable/TV reception?
20. Rental income?
21. Enough closet space?
22. No. telephone outlets?
23. Direction house faces?
24.
25. Ability to add-on/build?
26. How far to shopping?
27. Children in area?
28. House square footage?
29. Ethnic neighborhood?
30. Depth/water output per min.?
31. Zoning?
32. Property taxes?
33. Gas or electric stove?
34. Assumable mortgage?
35. Outside items included?
36. Garage capacity?
37. Yearly heating cost?
38. Yearly electricity cost?
39. Ability to subdivide?
40. Items not included?
41. Reason for selling?
42. Landscaping costs?
43. Work at home space?
44. Riparian (water) rights?
45. Room for guests?
46. Full basement?
47. Hot water capacity?
48. Churches or Temples nearby?

Other considerations:_____

_____

Circle the numbers to check out. Get your questions answered!

STEP SIX: Go for it; put in a bid!

It's at this point that you may get cold feet. How much should you offer the seller? Are you sure it's the house you REALLY want? If you've done your homework and matched what you want with what you saw, had the house re-inspected and found that you got the same good feelings about it, and also got all your questions asked and answered to your satisfaction, now's the time to go for it.

If you put in a realistic bid, the seller may counter-offer or accept your asking price. If you make an offer to purchase a house, you usually deposit 1% of the bid price (not a requirement in all states) with the broker to hold in escrow. If your bid is rejected, your check is returned to you. Which will upset you more, not putting a bid on the house based on what you can afford or not having your bid accepted?

Don't be afraid to put in a bid on what you can afford -- on any house. The agent by law must submit every bid to the seller -- no matter what it is.

Almost every buyer considers the price of the house as being the most important issue. It isn't! It's your and your family's enjoyment of it. The issue is, how much down payment can you make to reduce the mortgage and, how much a month can you afford? You're going to be living in that house for a very long time and the cost is going to be amortized over a long period of time.

Listed below are various mortgage interest rates with the corresponding monthly mortgage payment for each $1,000 in the price of the house based upon a 30-year fixed mortgage:

MORTGAGE RATES

INTEREST RATE	MORTGAGE PER $1,000	INTEREST RATE	MORTGAGE PER $1,000
5.5%	$5.68	8.0%	$7.34
6.0%	6.00	8.5%	7.69
6.5%	6.32	9.0%	8.05
7.0%	6.65	9.5%	8.41
7.5%	6.99	10.0%	8.78

Let's use an example of what the monthly mortgage P+I payment would be. P+I stands for principal and interest. A variable rate or a 15-year mortgage will alter the mortgage payment amount per $1,000.

The purchase price of the house is $150,000 and you put down 10%, $15,000, and carry a $135,000 mortgage. If your interest rate is 7%, you would multiply $135,000 by $6.65, the amount shown next to the 7% rate. Your monthly mortgage would be $897.75. The mortgage rates have been rounded to the nearest penny, so there will be a slight difference in the actual amount. Accurately calculated, the exact mortgage amount is $898.16.

Suppose the seller wants $150,000, a good value for the house. You offer $130,000 and the seller won't budge. If you multiply the $20,000 by $6.65, you'll see that your mortgage will increase by $133.00 a month to $1,030.75. The $20,000 is being spread over 30 years. Is it worth it? You decide.

Another example:

You can afford to pay $475 a month and you have $7,000 for a down payment. How much can you afford to pay for a house? You find one that you can buy for $75,000. Let's figure it out.

Selling price	$75,000
Down payment	7,000
Mortgage	68,000

The mortgage company's interest rate is 7.5%, 30-year fixed. The mortgage rate per $1,000 is $6.99. Multiplying $68,000 x $6.99 shows $475.32 as your monthly mortgage. The actual monthly payment computed on a calculator is $475.47 per month. Pretty close! You're on target.

Can you come up with a little more down payment to reduce your monthly payment? Don't forget that you have to add the monthly escrow amounts for taxes and insurance. The mortgage company may also charge you "points" or interest paid up front to get the loan. If the mortgage company quotes you a rate of 7.5%, 30-year fixed, with 2 points, that means that you have to pay 2% (2 points) of the mortgage amount of $68,000, which would be $1,360, at the time of closing.

Always figure the total amount of money you will need to buy a house:

     A. Down payment
     B. Closing costs including attorney's fee
     C. Mortgage application fee
     D. Mortgage points
     E. Moving costs
     F. House inspection charge
     G. Water test (if applicable)
     H. Environmental tests

Look at what your monthly payments will be at any given interest rate and cost per thousand dollars to buy a house. Don't just consider the selling price. To dicker over say, $5,000, and lose the house that you really want is not your goal unless the increase of $33.25 a month ($5,000 x 6.65) will strap you.

To find out what you can afford to pay for a house, use these guidelines. Better yet, get pre-approved from a bank or a mortgage company. They have rigid guidelines to follow based upon your income and expenses. They use the 28/36 ratios. Here's how it works.

28% RATIO: Divide the PITI (that's the monthly Principle + Interest + Taxes + Insurance that you'll pay, by your monthly gross income. It usually cannot exceed 28%.

36% RATIO: Divide the PITI PLUS your monthly payments (car, credit cards, loans, etc.) by your monthly gross income. It usually cannot exceed 36%.

These are the formulas. Use them to figure out your ratios using your income and monthly expenses. Conventional lenders also require that your down payment must come from your own resources. You can't borrow the money from your parents or from a friend - and you have to show where it came from.

You would also add the real estate, school, and other taxes and insurance that the mortgage company would add to your monthly mortgage payment. They would keep this money in escrow and pay the bills on your behalf when they come due. The seller can tell you what his monthly escrow amount is to give you an indication of what the additional monthly payment will cost you.

STEP SEVEN: Get your mortgage

It's usually better to get pre-approved for a mortgage before you go house hunting. By being pre-approved, you will know exactly what you can afford to pay for a house and how high you can bid. You don't want to put a bid on a house, have it accepted by the buyer, and then find out that you're income can't support the mortgage.

Once the seller accepts your bid, do shop around for the best mortgage rate, and I do mean shop! Every bank and mortgage company that offers mortgages has different rates and programs. The broker will be happy to tell you who they've worked with before.

There are a number of brochures on house financing under the heading of Consumer Economics & Housing Topics, put out by Media Services Distribution Center, 7-8 Research Park, Cornell University, Ithaca, NY 14850. You can write to them for individual title name and series prices. Topics in the H.O.M.E. series (Home Ownership Made Easier) include:

WAYS TO SAVE ON YOUR MORTGAGE
MORTGAGE CHOICES
HOUSING COSTS: HOW MUCH CAN YOU AFFORD
MORTGAGE BASICS
MORTGAGE CHOICES
GOVERNMENT-ASSISTED MORTGAGES: FHA, FmHA,
VA, and SONYMA
CLOSING COSTS

CHOOSING A MORTGAGE WORKSHEET and: Definition of Terms used in Real Estate transactions

The U.S. Department of Housing and Urban Development (HUD) 451 Seventh Street, S.W. Washington, D.C. 20410 puts out booklets on buying a home. Two are: Settlement Costs, A HUD Guide Revised Edition (this is mandatory for mortgage brokers to give you) and, Homeowner's Glossary of Building Terms. Both of these booklets are available for sale, as is a booklet put out by the U.S. Department of Agriculture, Program Aid Number 1034 called, Simple Home Repairs...Inside. Even if you're all thumbs, it's a good booklet to have around.

To order the above booklets, write: Superintendent of Documents, U.S. Government Printing Office, Washington, D.C. 20402, and ask for the costs.

This brings us to the end of the seven-step guide to buying a house. All you have to do is take the first step. Call your agent. He or she will help you find your dream house.

5. A COMPETITIVE ADVANTAGE™

What is your business known for?

Part A			Part B
I WANT THE COMPANY TO BE KNOWN FOR:			**CUSTOMERS BUY FROM US BECAUSE WE OFFER:**

1

| the fastest delivery | [ ] | [ ] | the fastest delivery |
| competitive delivery | [ ] | [ ] | competitive delivery |

2

| the lowest prices | [ ] | [ ] | the lowest prices |
| competitive prices | [ ] | [ ] | competitive prices |

3

| the widest variety | [ ] | [ ] | the widest variety |
| competitive variety | [ ] | [ ] | competitive variety |

4

| the most specialization | [ ] | [ ] | the most specialization |
| competitive specialization | [ ] | [ ] | competitive specialization |

5

| the best quality | [ ] | [ ] | the best quality |
| competitive quality | [ ] | [ ] | competitive quality |

6

| most innovation | [ ] | [ ] | most innovation |
| competitive innovation | [ ] | [ ] | competitive innovation |

7

| the best service | [ ] | [ ] | the best service |
| competitive service | [ ] | [ ] | competitive service |

What are you Known For?

Copy or cut out A Competitive Edge Analyzer™ at the back of the book and fold it lengthwise along the center vertical lines with only the 'I WANT' side showing. Put an 'X' in the appropriate box in each of the seven pairs of statements.

Then turn the form over and again put an 'X' in the appropriate box in each of the seven pairs of statements. Then open the form and connect each 'X' across the form.

> **You are looking at an X-ray of your expectation matched to the reality of what your business is known for!**

Helpful Hints

#1 and # 7 are incompatible. You cannot offer innovation, which takes time, and also offer the best delivery.

#2 and #5 are incompatible. The best quality produces more waste, increasing the price of the product.

#3 and #4 are incompatible. You cannot be a specialist offering the most variety.

#5 and #7 are incompatible. Innovations have high R &D costs; price cannot be the lowest.

#1 and #5 are incompatible. Delivery is a value added cost that adds to the selling price.

#3 and #7 are incompatible. Being the innovator takes time to develop on a product-by-product basis. There's not enough time to also offer the most variety.

#4 and #5 are incompatible. Being the specialist requires quality control that is costly to develop. Price cannot be a 'known for' feature.

A COMPETITIVE ADVANTAGE™

As applied to a competitive advantage for a business, the methodology is used to compare the expectations of what CEO's, presidents, operating officers, and managers want their company and /or divisions to be known for, and the reality of why their customers buy their products. We'll call competitive advantages the 'KF' (known for) qualities.

In picturing his company, a businessman will emphasize those attributes that exemplify his expectations of what his company's products, including its image, is known for. That is, your customers buy from you because your business has perceived benefits. They believe that what you supply is better than what your competitors supply. This is your competitive edge. Lose it, and you lose your customers.

Your competitive edge is derived from the "known for" characteristics of your business. These 'KF' characteristics are derived from the 'Key Business Resources' that you use to fill your customers orders.

The key business resources (KBR's) are the glue that holds the organization together. The kinds of resources needed to produce the deliverable create the "known for" factors that give the business its competitive edge.

How you use the KBR's determine the way you run your business and sell your products. Some KBR's are: Objectives and Measures, Business Plan, System and Procedures, Equity, Working Capital, Skills, Facilities, Capital Equipment, Deliverable Specifications, Orders, Customer Master Record, Materials and Supplies, and Customers.

Knowing exactly what your competitive edge is, what your business is known for, or how to maximize your KBR's is not always easy to do, especially if a company is in more than one business.

Key Business Resources

KBR's are the things you care about and keep an inventory of and manage – in your head, on a piece of paper, in a computer, anywhere!

Generic KBR's common to all types of businesses are listed by organizational function. Go to pages 4 and 5 and print them out. Identify all the KBR's and check all those that apply to your organization. If you don't know if you're using a particular key business resource, ask yourself this question:

Am I keeping track of the activities required to maintain this resource?

Activities are the life cycle steps that are necessary to maintain a resource. There are 16 generic steps for every activity. These are listed on the "16 Life Cycle Steps" form. If your answer is 'no', you do not keep track of the activities, and you do not consider it a key business resource. If you do consider it to be a key business resource, then you need to keep track of it and manage it.

Next to each checked KBR, enter the name of the individual on the form responsible for managing that KBR in the space provided. Identify all of the key business resources and enter the name of the person who is responsible for managing it. If you call a resource by a different name in your business, change it to that name. The next step, with report in hand, is to name the person responsible for managing that resource. This may take some time if you have a large organization.

If you do not have a person responsible for a key business resource -- you have a problem!
If you have more than one person responsible for the same key business resource – you have a problem!
If you have one person responsible for too many key business resources within the same business function – you have a problem!

Make changes for responsibility on the form. You now have a T/O, table of organization to work with and update as your business expands and changes.

If you don't consider something a resource, then you don't keep an inventory of it and don't need people to manage it and track the activities associated with it.

Print out as many copies of the "16 Life Cycle Steps" forms as the number of KBR's that you have – one for each. At the top of each form enter the name of that KBR.

If you do not have a person responsible for each activity for each resource -- you have a problem!

If you have more than one person responsible for the same activity for a resource – you have a problem!

If you have one person responsible for too many activities for the same resource – you have a problem!

KEY BUSINESS RESOURCES BY BUSINESS FUNCTION   **Person Responsible**

O **General management** _____

O Business plan _____

ADMINISTRATION

O **Administration Management** _____

O Personnel Management _____

O Information Systems _____

O Systems & Procedures _____

O Objectives & Measures _____

O Working Capital _____

O Equity _____

O Skills _____

O Facilities _____

O Standards & Methods _____

O Capital Equipment _____

O Deliverable Definition for Specifications _____

O Image _____

O Education _____

O Benefits Administration _____

O Legal _____

O Medical _____

O Safety _____

O Security _____

FINANCE

O Financial Management _____

O Accounting _____

O Bookkeeping _____

O Accounts Payable _____

O Accounts Receivable _____

O Credit & Collections _____

OPERATIONS

- O Materials Management _____
- O Procurement _____
- O Buying _____
- O Receiving _____
- O Distribution _____
- O Shipping _____
- O Warehouse Management _____
- O Stock Keeping _____
- O Raw Materials Management _____
- O Facilities Management _____
- O Facilities Maintenance _____
- O Capital Equipment Management _____
- O Capital Equipment Maintenance _____
- O Tool Control Administration _____
- O Rental Operations _____
- O Rentals Maintenance _____
- O Product Control _____
- O Production _____
- O Quality Control _____
- O Manufacturing Engineering _____
- O Development Engineering _____
- O Production Engineering _____
- O R & D Engineering _____
- O Materials & Supplies _____
- O Production Capacity _____
- O In-process Goods _____
- O Raw Materials _____
- O Technology _____
- O Vendors _____
- O Product Locator Record _____
- O Production Specifications _____
- O Warehousing _____
- O Distribution _____
- O Prices _____

CUSTOMER INTERFACE

- O Customer Relations _____
  - O Marketing _____
  - O Sales _____
  - O Service & Maintenance _____
  - O Customer Services _____
  - O Reservations Administration _____
  - O Rental Customer Services _____

- ⭘ Warranty Administration   _____
- ⭘ Customer Master Records   _____
- ⭘ Items Available For Rent   _____
- ⭘ Items On Rental   _____
- ⭘ Rental Item Specifications   _____
- ⭘ Competitive Information Resource   _____
- ⭘ Market Information Resource   _____
- ⭘ Reservations   _____
- ⭘ Orders   _____
- ⭘ Items Available For Sale   _____

LIFE CYCLE STEPS

A Life Cycle Step in information handling terms is an activity performed in the continuous management of a resource, in a sequence of steps from inception to consummation.

Every KBR in a business needs to be managed, otherwise there would be no discipline and the business would soon be out of control. The next step is to have the people responsible for each KBR to assign people who are responsible foro each of the 16 life cycle steps in each KBR. n small organizations it is not unusual to have one person responsible for many KBR's and also be responsible for many activities.

Here are the 16 life cycle steps and a form to keep track of them follows. Print one out for each KBR that applies to your organization and fill it out. A description and objective is given for each activity.

When you have finished entering responsibility assignments, you will have a table of organization (T/O) for your entire organization: assignments of resources and activities. You will see exactly where a step is being omitted and who is responsible. As your business expands, and resources are added, use the 16 life cycle steps as a template for each new resource, adding to your table of organization ... manage your business as it grows!

Next to each activity is the responsible business function for that life cycle step: P=Planning; O=Operations; C=Control.

1. Set Requirements = P
    - forecast the demands and future needs
    - reduce the risk of being surprised by unexpected events, internal and external

2. Specify = P
    - establish inventory rules
    - specify the nature of the item to be received or supplied
    - reduce the risk of procuring or producing incorrect and/or resource wasting KBR's.

3. Select Source = P
- choose the most appropriate vendor
- reduce the risk of being stuck with one or more wrong vendors or customers

4. Decide when to order = O
- minimize cash outflow
- anticipate price fluctuations

5. Place the order = O
- authorize resources to be expended to initiate or procure the inventory
- reduce the risk of getting or doing something wrong

6. Accept quality = O
- insure that the new inventory is acceptable before it moves into or out of the business
- reduce the risk of getting or supplying bad products

7, Integrate = O
- add the accepted item to the present set of items in inventory
- reduce the risk of losing or not being able to find inventory

8. Respond to requests = O
- respond timely to requests from customers, inter/intra-departments for item
- reduce the risk of not supplying to requests for products

9. Measure inventory statistics = C
- maintain accurate records of the resource
- reduce the risk of having too much or too little

10. Monitor performance = C
- make sure the inventory remains acceptable throughout its life
- reduce the risk of products going bad and no one finding out about it

11. Upgrade = O
- upgrade the inventory performance if requirements change
- reduce the risk of not having the ability to perform future tasks

12. Maintain = O
- keep the inventory in good operating condition
- reduce the risk of not having inventory available due to malfunction

13. Account for = C
- keep track of the cost of the inventory and from what account
- reduce the risk of not amortizing and depreciating inventory

14. Dispose of or transfer = C
   - move the inventory as required
   - reduce the risk of keeping inventory around too long

15. Charging others for = O
   - invoice customers or cost center for item or services
   - reduce the risk of not charging for funds expended

16. Pay for = O
   - keep track of where and how the money is spent
   - reduce the risk of spending funds improperly
   - reduce the risk of paying for inventory more than once

THE 16 LIFE CYCLE STEPS
RESPONSIBILITY ASSIGNMENT

[Print out one for each KBR in your organization]

KBR NAME_____

ACTIVIITES   **RESPONSIBLE PERSON**

1. Set Requirements = P   _____
    - forecast the demands and future needs
    - reduce the risk of being surprised by unexpected events, internal and external

2. Specify = P   _____
    - establish inventory rules
    - specify the nature of the item to be received or supplied
    - reduce the risk of procuring or producing incorrect and/or resource wasting KBR's.

3. Select Source = P   _____
    - choose the most appropriate vendor
    - reduce the risk of being stuck with one or more wrong vendors or customers

4. Decide when to order = O   _____
    - minimize cash outflow
    - anticipate price fluctuations

5. Place the order = O   _____
    - authorize resources to be expended to initiate or procure the inventory
    - reduce the risk of getting or doing something wrong

6. Accept quality = O   _____
    - insure that the new inventory is acceptable before it moves into or out of the business
    - reduce the risk of getting or supplying bad products

7, Integrate = O   _____
    - add the accepted item to the present set of items in inventory
    - reduce the risk of losing or not being able to find products

8. Respond to requests = O   _____
    - respond timely to requests from customers, inter/intra-departments for item
    - reduce the risk of not supplying to requests

9. Measure inventory statistics = C   _____
    - maintain accurate records of the resource
    - reduce the risk of having too much or too little

10. Monitor performance = C _____
    - make sure the inventory remains acceptable throughout its life
    - reduce the risk of inventory going bad and no one finding out

11. Upgrade = O _____
    - upgrade the inventory performance if requirements change
    - reduce the risk of not having the ability to perform future tasks

12. Maintain = O _____
    - keep the inventory in good operating condition
    - reduce the risk of not having inventory available due to malfunction

13. Account for = C _____
    - keep track of the cost of the inventory and from what account
    - reduce the risk of not amortizing and depreciating inventory

14. Dispose of or transfer = C _____
    - move the inventory as required
    - reduce the risk of keeping it around too long

15. Charging others for = O _____
    - invoice customers or cost center for item or services
    - reduce the risk of not charging for funds expended

16. Pay for = O _____
    - keep track of where and how the money is spent
    - reduce the risk of spending funds improperly
    - reduce the risk of paying for inventory more than once

Establishing a Competitive Edge

What is the deliverable that you supply to your customers? It can be one or more of the following depending upon what your customers ask you for.

1. A Product
2. A service
3. Space

A business may receive different types of orders from its customers, dealing with the same deliverable. If you are in the washing machine business, you may receive the following different types of orders from customers:

1. Send me a truckload of washing machines – a wholesaler
2. Send me the following replacement parts – a distributor
3. Make a new kind of washing machine for me - manufacturer
4. Fix my broken washer – a service company
5. Deliver a washing machine to my house – a retailer

If each of these order requests requires different resources to fill the order, then the business is really in more than one business. If the business could fill each of the above order requests, that business would really be in five different businesses: a manufacturer, a distributor, a wholesaler, a service company, and a retailer. Or the business could be in only one business if only one order request could be filled.

Let's look at each order request to determine the resources needed to fill the orders and create the 'known for' qualities for that organization.

#1
The fastest delivery is the 'known for' objective for #1 and #2, requiring a large warehouse to stock washing machines and parts with inventory control.

#2
This calls for being 'known for' carrying the widest selection of parts, and the resources needed are a large inventory with inventory control, and perhaps delivery vehicles as needed to deliver auto parts to automobile repair shops.

#3
To be 'known for' innovations, you need machine tool, dies, and skilled labor as your resources.

#4
The ability to provide the best service is most important for #4 and resources required: are trained technicians and vehicles.

If your expectations for wanting your company to be "known for" are not in alignment with the "reality" of what your business is actually known for, your marketing strategy will be misdirected.

It is important for the success of any business to reconcile what may be three separate user views of your business.

1. What you expect your business to be "known for"
2. What your employees think your business is "known for"
3. What your customers think your business is "known for"

If you are in more than one business, as most businesses are, you must identify your business type and choose the major deliverable for which you want to establish your 'known for' attributes.

You may also want to go back and segregate the KBR's, responsibility assignments, and activity assignments if you are in more than one business and offer more than one type of deliverable.

Each different order request from your customers requires a different mix of competitive qualities and must be treated as a different business otherwise your business strategy and tactics will be ineffective. Expectations that are unfulfilled usually result in misdiagnosing the reason for not succeeding. Often heard is, "we planned it this way", (the expectation) and, "it didn't work" (the reality).

The reality was that:

- **It worked the way the resources of the business were used**
- **The way they were used determined the company's competitive edge**

THE MEANING OF THE CONNECTIONS

There are eight different connection patterns that are possible in each of the seven sets of questions.

1. Upper left to upper right
2. Upper left to lower right
3. Lower left to upper right
4. Lower left to lower right
5. X marks on the left side only
6. X marks on the right side only
7. No marks on either side
8. Marks in every box on each side

Each connection that creates a diagonal line indicates that your expectation for wanting your company to be known for a particular quality is not in line with the reality of what your company is really know for. Any incomplete connection is also considered a diagonal line. The more diagonal lines you have, the more your expectations do not match the reality – and a cause for concern.

I

[X] - [X]

[ ]   [ ]

A parallel line across the top indicates that the 'KF' qualities are in alignment with the reality of why the customers buy from the company. You are focused on where you want to go and how to get there using the company's resources to their best advantage Now that you know what the optimum connection is, don't try to force it. Allow your vision to be guided by your pulse of where the company is going; be responsive when you see deviations from its course.

II

[X]   [ ]

\

[ ]   [X]

An upper left to lower right diagonal line indicates that you have an expectation about this KF that is not being met and the reality is, this factor may not be one of the company's true strengths.

There is a desire to change the image of the company, and consideration must be given to the fact that you may never be able to change the way you are doing business, such as become the high quality producer where price has always been the predominant factor -- what you have always been known for.

Perhaps better utilization of your key business resources will help you establish a strategy to realize your goal.

III

[ ]   [X]

/

[X]   [ ]

A lower left to upper right diagonal line indicates that your expectation of the company's resources are not in alignment with the reality of of the company's true strengths. Your organization is using the key business resources to achieve a competitive advantage in this area – but you don't think so! Your company's image is different than what you think. Perhaps a revaluation of your resources, a new marketing and advertising plan, or a combination is in order. Discuss this with your key personnel as to what they think. They're closest to the firing line. There's a real benefit in pursuing this further.

Your choices are to change your expectation or to change the reality. Which choice do you think will result in developing a strategy for success in this area at the lowest cost?

IV

[ ]   [ ]
[X] - **[X]**

This parallel line indicates that the company responds and reacts to competition's strategy, meeting changes as they arise. The resources of the company are not being utilized to their fullest to achieve a competitive edge, or this 'known for' is not an issue in keeping customers or getting new ones. You decide.

What would it take to develop this 'known for' into a competitive advantage? Bring in new technology, new machinery, hire outside specialists. Could you justify the cost in relationship to the additional profit, if any, that would be generated. Who do have to talk this over with in your organization? Could that be the problem?

V

[ ]   [ ]
[X]   [ ]

This incomplete connection is considered a diagonal line. There is a clear expectation of what you want the company to be known for without knowing if the company is known for in this area. You have to know where you are now in order to get to where you want to be. You need to do some R & D and go ask your customers, your employees, what they think your company is known for, with the form in hand. It appears that you have lost control and the pulse of the business, or you never devised a marketing strategy, and let the business grow by default. You'll find it difficult taking the business to another level unless you devise a strategy that fits your personality and – the resources you have available to you.

If you don't know what competitive advantage you're offering, how can you measure the effectiveness of any strategy you put into practice? The same holds true if the 'X' were in the top box, except in that case, a specific known for is advantage is desired, without the knowledge of what the business is really known for. Equally dangerous!

VI

[ ]   [ ]
[ ]   **[X]**

This incomplete connection is also considered a diagonal line. There is a clear expectation to be just competitive without a specific strategy and no knowledge of what the company is known for. The same holds true if the 'X' were in the top box, except there would be no planned strategy to capitalize on the company's strengths – only to maintain the status quo of the company's operations.

There is no 'drive' to be known for anything. The entrepreneurial spirit seems to have faded. Why? There is no predominant quality and reason for customers to buy the company's products. Without a formulated strategy, and use of resources, it is almost impossible to develop a competitive advantage – only competitive reactions. Perhaps it's time to turn the reins over to a younger more energetic person.

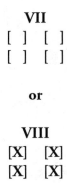

VII

[ ]   [ ]
[ ]   [ ]

or

VIII

[X]   [X]
[X]   [X]

No marks in #7 and marks in all the boxes in #8 indicate that you have either lost the ability to plan any strategy for your company or you did not read the directions on how to fill out the form. Which is it?

You now have additional communication tools to either redesign your business plan based on your diagonal connections in each area, and congratulate yourself if your expectations are in line with the reality of what your business is known for, as shown by parallel lines in each area.

Why people buy anything

There are 7 basic reasons why people buy anything.

1. The product is purchased for resell
2. It satisfies an emotional need
3. It has healing properties
4. It satisfies a self or corporate image:
5. It fulfills a physical need
6. It is used as a tool or part to fix or complete something
7. It satisfies a utilitarian requirement

Identify the major KBR's that you checked off that give your company its competitive edge. Now match a reason above with a 'known for': why people buy your products.

If some of your products aren't selling well, consider that you haven't identified or established the company's KF characteristics with those specific products. What resources don't you have that will allow you to change the marketing strategy for those products? Are they people skills? Capital improvements? Increased production capacity?

Where can you get them? Would the cost justify the increased revenue that you think you would get in return? What would be the competitive advantage you would now have in marketing these products? Have you considered dropping some lines and concentrating only on what you do best?

The 7 reasons for waste
You may want to take a closer look at the seven reasons what your problems are in your business and do some cleaning to add to your bottom line.

1. Overproduction, making too much
2. Transportation, too much movement
3. Motion, people moving about or searching too much for things
4. Waiting, idle time, waiting for information
5. Processing, too much effort, no value added
6. Inventory, too much
7. Defects, too many errors/rework

SECTION V

THE BEGINNING

This is the beginning because in reality it is the beginning – of the rest of your life. You cannot undo anything in the past. It's over, finished. So where do you begin?

The first thing you might do is clean, if you can't think of something to create. You have the tools to help you, especially in your relationships with people in your life. That's a good place to start; make phone calls, send emails, or write letters to reweave the fibers of relationships that have unraveled. It makes no difference when it happened or with whom. You make the overture.

There are lots of things to clean up in your life that don't involve relationships. Here's a short list of simple things to do and I'm sure you can add a page or two.

1 Clean your room or your apartment or your house; wash the windows too.
2. Take all your soiled clothes to the dry cleaners; keep the clothes basket in your bedroom so you don't throw your clothes on the floor every night.
3. Throw out or give away all the clothes you know you're not going to wear
4. Write a check for $10 to your favorite charity
5. Balance your checkbook or learn how to do it
6. Call your parents and your children every week
7. Get a haircut every month and wash your hair regularly
8. Brush your teeth every night and floss! If you're not true to your teeth, they'll be false to you.
9. Clean out your car including the trunk.
10. Carry a notepad or one of those computer gizmos around with you and make to-do notes so you won't forget what your wife tells you to bring home.
11. Make sure that before you go to bed at night, the sink is clean!
12. Always say to the most important person in your life, 'I love you.'

You now have new communication tools to help you build and/or rebuild your life as you want it to be. Remember, 'want' is the role of a Consumer, and no matter how much you want something, nothing will happen unless a Supplier gives it to you or you give it to yourself.

I don't see anyone else around willing to be a paladin and come to your rescue, so you're going to have to switch roles and play the part of the Supplier, and be the Supplier to yourself. Always ask yourself, 'What am I building? The answer will come to you and then use the appropriate tools to build it. If the answer doesn't come to you, stop doing what you're doing and go build what you want.

Which reminds me of the story....

...it's very hard to get a book published by an unknown author, let alone get an agent to represent you so I went to New York to see the McGraw Hill publishing company in their own building. I told the receptionist I wanted to see Mr. McGraw and she said he didn't see anybody and I had to submit my draft by mail or email it. I got upset and raised my voice to her and Mr. McGraw Jr. came out of his office when he heard me.

I told him my story and asked, would he read it? He told me to go to Hill!

I hope this journey in learning how to use new tools has been educational and empowering for you. It's been the most exciting project I've undertaken and I thank you for traveling with me all the way through the book.

> If I told you everything there was to know about me, till there was nothing left for me to say, and you told me everything there was to say about you, with nothing left to say, there would still be one thing left to say to each other:
>
> I love you!
>
> *The magnitude of mans knowledge is his capacity for love*

P.S. The forms for each of the six programs as well as mini Upset Analyzer™ forms are reproduced in triplicate on the following pages.

1a. CONSUMER PAST UPSET ANALYZER™

I am upset because you_____

I EXPECTED: **IN REALITY I GOT:**

Part A   **Part B**

1. Response

An unusual response   [ ]   [ ]   An unusual response
A usual response   [ ]   [ ]   A usual response

I1. Agreement

A changed agreement   [ ]   [ ]   A changed agreement
The old agreement   [ ]   [ ]   The old agreement

111. Alternatives

Alternatives   [ ]   [ ]   Alternatives
No alternatives   [ ]   [ ]   No alternatives

IV. Understanding

Your understanding   [ ]   [ ]   Your understanding
No understanding   [ ]   [ ]   No understanding

V. Control

T not blame you   [ ]   [ ]   To not blame you
To blame you   [ ]   [ ]   To blame you

VI. Initiate

To initiate   [ ]   [ ]   To initiate
To not initiate   [ ]   [ ]   To not initiate

VII. Feedback

To give feedback   [ ]   [ ]   To give feedback
Not to give feedback   [ ]   [ ]   Not to give feedback

1a. CONSUMER PAST UPSET ANALYZER™

I am upset because you_____

I EXPECTED:		IN REALITY I GOT:
Part A		**Part B**

1. Response

| An unusual response | [ ] [ ] | An unusual response |
| A usual response | [ ] [ ] | A usual response |

I1. Agreement

| A changed agreement | [ ] [ ] | A changed agreement |
| The old agreement | [ ] [ ] | The old agreement |

111. Alternatives

| Alternatives | [ ] [ ] | Alternatives |
| No alternatives | [ ] [ ] | No alternatives |

IV. Understanding

| Your understanding | [ ] [ ] | Your understanding |
| No understanding | [ ] [ ] | No understanding |

V. Control

| T not blame you | [ ] [ ] | To not blame you |
| To blame you | [ ] [ ] | To blame you |

VI. Initiate

| To initiate | [ ] [ ] | To initiate |
| To not initiate | [ ] [ ] | To not initiate |

VII. Feedback

| To give feedback | [ ] [ ] | To give feedback |
| Not to give feedback | [ ] [ ] | Not to give feedback |

1a. CONSUMER PAST UPSET ANALYZER™

I am upset because you_____

I EXPECTED: **IN REALITY I GOT:**

Part A	**1. Response**			**Part B**
An unusual response	[ ]	[ ]		An unusual response
A usual response	[ ]	[ ]		A usual response

I1. Agreement

A changed agreement	[ ]	[ ]		A changed agreement
The old agreement	[ ]	[ ]		The old agreement

111. Alternatives

Alternatives	[ ]	[ ]		Alternatives
No alternatives	[ ]	[ ]		No alternatives

IV. Understanding

Your understanding	[ ]	[ ]		Your understanding
No understanding	[ ]	[ ]		No understanding

V. Control

T not blame you	[ ]	[ ]		To not blame you
To blame you	[ ]	[ ]		To blame you

VI. Initiate

To initiate	[ ]	[ ]		To initiate
To not initiate	[ ]	[ ]		To not initiate

VII. Feedback

To give feedback	[ ]	[ ]		To give feedback
Not to give feedback	[ ]	[ ]		Not to give feedback

1b. CONSUMER FUTURE UPSET ANALYZER™

I am upset because you_____

I WANT:		I WILL REALLY GET:
Part A		**Part B**

I. Response

| An unusual response | [ ]   [ ] | An unusual response |
| A usual response | [ ]   [ ] | A usual response |

II. Agreements

| A changed agreement | [ ]   [ ] | A changed agreement |
| The old agreement | [ ]   [ ] | The old agreement |

III. Alternatives

| Alternatives | [ ]   [ ] | Alternatives |
| No alternatives | [ ]   [ ] | No alternatives |

IV. Understanding

| Your understanding | [ ]   [ ] | Your understanding |
| No understanding | [ ]   [ ] | No understanding |

V. Control

| To not blame you | [ ]   [ ] | To not blame you |
| To blame you | [ ]   [ ] | To blame you |

VI. Initiate

| To initiate | [ ]   [ ] | To initiate |
| To not initiate | [ ]   [ ] | To not initiate |

VII. Feedback

| To give feedback | [ ]   [ ] | To give feedback |
| Not to give feedback | [ ]   [ ] | Not to give feedback |

1b. CONSUMER FUTURE UPSET ANALYZER™

I am upset because you_____

I WANT:			I WILL REALLY GET:
Part A			**Part B**

I. Response

An unusual response	[ ]	[ ]	An unusual response
A usual response	[ ]	[ ]	A usual response

II. Agreements

A changed agreement	[ ]	[ ]	A changed agreement
The old agreement	[ ]	[ ]	The old agreement

III. Alternatives

Alternatives	[ ]	[ ]	Alternatives
No alternatives	[ ]	[ ]	No alternatives

IV. Understanding

Your understanding	[ ]	[ ]	Your understanding
No understanding	[ ]	[ ]	No understanding

V. Control

To not blame you	[ ]	[ ]	To not blame you
To blame you	[ ]	[ ]	To blame you

VI. Initiate

To initiate	[ ]	[ ]	To initiate
To not initiate	[ ]	[ ]	To not initiate

VII. Feedback

To give feedback	[ ]	[ ]	To give feedback
Not to give feedback	[ ]	[ ]	Not to give feedback

1b. CONSUMER FUTURE UPSET ANALYZER™

I am upset because you_____

I WANT: **I WILL REALLY GET:**

Part A   ### Part B

I. Response

| An unusual response | [ ]   [ ] | An unusual response |
| A usual response | [ ]   [ ] | A usual response |

II. Agreements

| A changed agreement | [ ]   [ ] | A changed agreement |
| The old agreement | [ ]   [ ] | The old agreement |

III. Alternatives

| Alternatives | [ ]   [ ] | Alternatives |
| No alternatives | [ ]   [ ] | No alternatives |

IV. Understanding

| Your understanding | [ ]   [ ] | Your understanding |
| No understanding | [ ]   [ ] | No understanding |

V. Control

| To not blame you | [ ]   [ ] | To not blame you |
| To blame you | [ ]   [ ] | To blame you |

VI. Initiate

| To initiate | [ ]   [ ] | To initiate |
| To not initiate | [ ]   [ ] | To not initiate |

VII. Feedback

| To give feedback | [ ]   [ ] | To give feedback |
| Not to give feedback | [ ]   [ ] | Not to give feedback |

1c. SUPPLIER PAST UPSET ANALYZER™

I am upset because you_____

I EXPECTED TO: **IN REALITY:**

Part A   **Part B**

I. Response

Give an unusual response   [ ]   [ ]   You wanted an unusual response
Give my usual response   [ ]   [ ]   You wanted my usual response

II. Agreement

Change our agreement   [ ]   [ ]   You wanted changes
Not change our agreement   [ ]   [ ]   You didn't want changes

III. Alternatives

Explore alternatives   [ ]   [ ]   You wanted alternatives
Not explore alternatives   [ ]   [ ]   You didn't want alternatives

IV. Understanding

Understand your side   [ ]   [ ]   You wanted understanding
Not understand your side   [ ]   [ ]   You didn't want understanding

V. Control

Not control   [ ]   [ ]   I didn't control
Control   [ ]   [ ]   I did control

VI. Initiate

Be the initiator   [ ]   [ ]   I was the initiator
Not be the initiator   [ ]   [ ]   You were the initiator

VII. Feedback

Get feedback   [ ]   [ ]   You gave feedback
Not get feedback   [ ]   [ ]   You didn't give feedback

1c. SUPPLIER PAST UPSET ANALYZER™

I am upset because you_____

I EXPECTED TO:		IN REALITY:

Part A			**Part B**

I. Response

Give an unusual response	[ ]	[ ]	You wanted an unusual response
Give my usual response	[ ]	[ ]	You wanted my usual response

II. Agreement

Change our agreement	[ ]	[ ]	You wanted changes
Not change our agreement	[ ]	[ ]	You didn't want changes

III. Alternatives

Explore alternatives	[ ]	[ ]	You wanted alternatives
Not explore alternatives	[ ]	[ ]	You didn't want alternatives

IV. Understanding

Understand your side	[ ]	[ ]	You wanted understanding
Not understand your side	[ ]	[ ]	You didn't want understanding

V. Control

Not control	[ ]	[ ]	I didn't control
Control	[ ]	[ ]	I did control

VI. Initiate

Be the initiator	[ ]	[ ]	I was the initiator
Not be the initiator	[ ]	[ ]	You were the initiator

VII. Feedback

Get feedback	[ ]	[ ]	You gave feedback
Not get feedback	[ ]	[ ]	You didn't give feedback

1c. SUPPLIER PAST UPSET ANALYZER™

I am upset because you_____

I EXPECTED TO: **IN REALITY:**

Part A   **Part B**

I. Response

Give an unusual response   [ ]   [ ]   You wanted an unusual response
Give my usual response   [ ]   [ ]   You wanted my usual response

II. Agreement

Change our agreement   [ ]   [ ]   You wanted changes
Not change our agreement   [ ]   [ ]   You didn't want changes

III. Alternatives

Explore alternatives   [ ]   [ ]   You wanted alternatives
Not explore alternatives   [ ]   [ ]   You didn't want alternatives

IV. Understanding

Understand your side   [ ]   [ ]   You wanted understanding
Not understand your side   [ ]   [ ]   You didn't want understanding

V. Control

Not control   [ ]   [ ]   I didn't control
Control   [ ]   [ ]   I did control

VI. Initiate

Be the initiator   [ ]   [ ]   I was the initiator
Not be the initiator   [ ]   [ ]   You were the initiator

VII. Feedback

Get feedback   [ ]   [ ]   You gave feedback
Not get feedback   [ ]   [ ]   You didn't give feedback

1d. SUPPLIER FUTURE UPSET ANALYZER™

I am upset because you_____

I WANT TO: **I KNOW YOU WILL:**

Part A   ### Part B

I. Response

Give an unusual response   [ ]   [ ]   Want an unusual response
Give my usual response   [ ]   [ ]   Not want my usual response

II. Agreement

Change our agreement   [ ]   [ ]   Want changes
Not change our agreement   [ ]   [ ]   Not want changes

III. Alternatives

Explore alternatives   [ ]   [ ]   Want alternatives
Not explore alternatives   [ ]   [ ]   Not want alternatives

IV. Understanding

Understand your side   [ ]   [ ]   Want understanding
Not understand your side   [ ]   [ ]   Not want understanding

V. Control

Not control   [ ]   [ ]   Not be controlled
Control   [ ]   [ ]   Be controlled

VI. Initiate

Be the initiator   [ ]   [ ]   Not be the initiator
Not be the initiator   [ ]   [ ]   Be the initiator

VII. Feedback

Get feedback   [ ]   [ ]   Give feedback
Not get feedback   [ ]   [ ]   Not give feedback

1d. SUPPLIER FUTURE UPSET ANALYZER™

I am upset because you_____

I WANT TO: **I KNOW YOU WILL:**

Part A   ### Part B

I. Response

Give an unusual response   [ ]   [ ]   Want an unusual response
Give my usual response   [ ]   [ ]   Not want my usual response

II. Agreement

Change our agreement   [ ]   [ ]   Want changes
Not change our agreement   [ ]   [ ]   Not want changes

III. Alternatives

Explore alternatives   [ ]   [ ]   Want alternatives
Not explore alternatives   [ ]   [ ]   Not want alternatives

IV. Understanding

Understand your side   [ ]   [ ]   Want understanding
Not understand your side   [ ]   [ ]   Not want understanding

V. Control

Not control   [ ]   [ ]   Not be controlled
Control   [ ]   [ ]   Be controlled

VI. Initiate

Be the initiator   [ ]   [ ]   Not be the initiator
Not be the initiator   [ ]   [ ]   Be the initiator

VII. Feedback

Get feedback   [ ]   [ ]   Give feedback
Not get feedback   [ ]   [ ]   Not give feedback

1d. SUPPLIER FUTURE UPSET ANALYZER™

I am upset because you_____

I WANT TO:			I KNOW YOU WILL:

Part A			**Part B**

I. Response

Give an unusual response	[ ]	[ ]	Want an unusual response
Give my usual response	[ ]	[ ]	Not want my usual response

II. Agreement

Change our agreement	[ ]	[ ]	Want changes
Not change our agreement	[ ]	[ ]	Not want changes

III. Alternatives

Explore alternatives	[ ]	[ ]	Want alternatives
Not explore alternatives	[ ]	[ ]	Not want alternatives

IV. Understanding

Understand your side	[ ]	[ ]	Want understanding
Not understand your side	[ ]	[ ]	Not want understanding

V. Control

Not control	[ ]	[ ]	Not be controlled
Control	[ ]	[ ]	Be controlled

VI. Initiate

Be the initiator	[ ]	[ ]	Not be the initiator
Not be the initiator	[ ]	[ ]	Be the initiator

VII. Feedback

Get feedback	[ ]	[ ]	Give feedback
Not get feedback	[ ]	[ ]	Not give feedback

CONSUMER PAST UPSET ANALYZER™

I am upset because you_____

I EXPECTED:			IN REALITY I GOT:
Part A	**I**		**Part B**
An unusual response	[ ]	[ ]	An unusual response
A usual response	[ ]	[ ]	A usual response
	II		
A changed agreement	[ ]	[ ]	A changed agreement
The old agreement	[ ]	[ ]	The old agreement
	III		
Alternatives	[ ]	[ ]	Alternatives
No alternatives	[ ]	[ ]	No alternatives
	IV		
Your understanding	[ ]	[ ]	Your understanding
No understanding	[ ]	[ ]	No understanding
	V		
To not blame you	[ ]	[ ]	To not blame you
To blame you	[ ]	[ ]	To blame you
	VI		
To initiate	[ ]	[ ]	To initiate
To not initiate	[ ]	[ ]	To not initiate
	VII		
To give feedback	[ ]	[ ]	To give feedback
Not to give feedback	[ ]	[ ]	Not to give feedback

CONSUMER FUTURE UPSET ANALYZER™

I am upset because you_____

I WANT:			I WILL REALLY GET:
Part A	**I**		**Part B**
An unusual response	[ ]	[ ]	An unusual response
A usual response	[ ]	[ ]	A usual response
	II		
A changed agreement	[ ]	[ ]	A changed agreement
The old agreement	[ ]	[ ]	The old agreement
	III		
Alternatives	[ ]	[ ]	Alternatives
No alternatives	[ ]	[ ]	No alternatives
	IV		
Your understanding	[ ]	[ ]	Your understanding
No understanding	[ ]	[ ]	No understanding
	V		
To not blame you	[ ]	[ ]	To not blame you
To blame you	[ ]	[ ]	To blame you
	VI		
To initiate	[ ]	[ ]	To initiate
To not initiate	[ ]	[ ]	To not initiate
	VII		
To give feedback	[ ]	[ ]	To give feedback
Not to give feedback	[ ]	[ ]	Not to give feedback

SUPPLIER PAST UPSET ANALYZER™

I am upset because you_____

I EXPECTED TO:			IN REALITY:
Part A	**I**		**Part B**
Give an unusual response	[ ]	[ ]	You wanted an unusual response
Give my usual response	[ ]	[ ]	You wanted my usual response
	II		
Change our agreement	[ ]	[ ]	You wanted changes
Not change our agreement	[ ]	[ ]	You didn't want changes
	III		
Explore alternatives	[ ]	[ ]	You wanted alternatives
Not explore alternatives	[ ]	[ ]	You didn't want alternatives
	IV		
Understand your side	[ ]	[ ]	You wanted understanding
Not understand your side	[ ]	[ ]	You didn't want understanding
	V		
Not control	[ ]	[ ]	I didn't control
Control	[ ]	[ ]	I did control
	VI		
Be the initiator	[ ]	[ ]	I was the initiator
Not be the initiator	[ ]	[ ]	You were the initiator
	VII		
Get feedback	[ ]	[ ]	You gave feedback
not get feedback	[ ]	[ ]	You didn't give feedback

SUPPLIER FUTURE UPSET ANALYZER™

I am upset because you_____

I WANT TO:			I KNOW YOU WILL:
Part A	**I**		**Part B**
Give an unusual response	[ ]	[ ]	Want an unusual response
Give my usual response	[ ]	[ ]	Not want my usual response
	II		
Change our agreement	[ ]	[ ]	Want changes
Not change our agreement	[ ]	[ ]	Not want changes
	III		
Explore alternatives	[ ]	[ ]	Want alternatives
Not explore alternatives	[ ]	[ ]	Not want alternatives
	IV		
Understand your side	[ ]	[ ]	Want understanding
Not understand your side	[ ]	[ ]	Not want understanding
	V		
Not control	[ ]	[ ]	Not be controlled
Control	[ ]	[ ]	Be controlled
	VI		
Be the initiator	[ ]	[ ]	Not be the initiator
Not be the initiator	[ ]	[ ]	Be the initiator
	VII		
Get feedback	[ ]	[ ]	Give feedback
Not get feedback	[ ]	[ ]	Not give feedback

CONSUMER PAST UPSET ANALYZER™

I am upset because you_____

I EXPECTED:			IN REALITY I GOT:
Part A	**I**		**Part B**
An unusual response	[ ]	[ ]	An unusual response
A usual response	[ ]	[ ]	A usual response
	II		
A changed agreement	[ ]	[ ]	A changed agreement
The old agreement	[ ]	[ ]	The old agreement
	III		
Alternatives	[ ]	[ ]	Alternatives
No alternatives	[ ]	[ ]	No alternatives
	IV		
Your understanding	[ ]	[ ]	Your understanding
No understanding	[ ]	[ ]	No understanding
	V		
To not blame you	[ ]	[ ]	To not blame you
To blame you	[ ]	[ ]	To blame you
	VI		
To initiate	[ ]	[ ]	To initiate
To not initiate	[ ]	[ ]	To not initiate
	VII		
To give feedback	[ ]	[ ]	To give feedback
Not to give feedback	[ ]	[ ]	Not to give feedback

CONSUMER FUTURE UPSET ANALYZER™

I am upset because you_____

I WANT:			I WILL REALLY GET:
Part A	**I**		**Part B**
An unusual response	[ ]	[ ]	An unusual response
A usual response	[ ]	[ ]	A usual response
	II		
A changed agreement	[ ]	[ ]	A changed agreement
The old agreement	[ ]	[ ]	The old agreement
	III		
Alternatives	[ ]	[ ]	Alternatives
No alternatives	[ ]	[ ]	No alternatives
	IV		
Your understanding	[ ]	[ ]	Your understanding
No understanding	[ ]	[ ]	No understanding
	V		
To not blame you	[ ]	[ ]	To not blame you
To blame you	[ ]	[ ]	To blame you
	VI		
To initiate	[ ]	[ ]	To initiate
To not initiate	[ ]	[ ]	To not initiate
	VII		
To give feedback	[ ]	[ ]	To give feedback
Not to give feedback	[ ]	[ ]	Not to give feedback

SUPPLIER PAST UPSET ANALYZER™

I am upset because you_____

I EXPECTED TO:			IN REALITY:
Part A		I	Part B
Give an unusual response	[ ]	[ ]	You wanted an unusual response
Give my usual response	[ ]	[ ]	You wanted my usual response
		II	
Change our agreement	[ ]	[ ]	You wanted changes
Not change our agreement	[ ]	[ ]	You didn't want changes
		III	
Explore alternatives	[ ]	[ ]	You wanted alternatives
Not explore alternatives	[ ]	[ ]	You didn't want alternatives
		IV	
Understand your side	[ ]	[ ]	You wanted understanding
Not understand your side	[ ]	[ ]	You didn't want understanding
		V	
Not control	[ ]	[ ]	I didn't control
Control	[ ]	[ ]	I did control
		VI	
Be the initiator	[ ]	[ ]	I was the initiator
Not be the initiator	[ ]	[ ]	You were the initiator
		VII	
Get feedback	[ ]	[ ]	You gave feedback
not get feedback	[ ]	[ ]	You didn't give feedback

SUPPLIER FUTURE UPSET ANALYZER™

I am upset because you_____

I WANT TO:			I KNOW YOU WILL:
Part A		I	Part B
Give an unusual response	[ ]	[ ]	Want an unusual response
Give my usual response	[ ]	[ ]	Not want my usual response
		II	
Change our agreement	[ ]	[ ]	Want changes
Not change our agreement	[ ]	[ ]	Not want changes
		III	
Explore alternatives	[ ]	[ ]	Want alternatives
Not explore alternatives	[ ]	[ ]	Not want alternatives
		IV	
Understand your side	[ ]	[ ]	Want understanding
Not understand your side	[ ]	[ ]	Not want understanding
		V	
Not control	[ ]	[ ]	Not be controlled
Control	[ ]	[ ]	Be controlled
		VI	
Be the initiator	[ ]	[ ]	Not be the initiator
Not be the initiator	[ ]	[ ]	Be the initiator
		VII	
Get feedback	[ ]	[ ]	Give feedback
Not get feedback	[ ]	[ ]	Not give feedback

CONSUMER PAST UPSET ANALYZER™

I am upset because you_____

I EXPECTED:		IN REALITY I GOT:

Part A	I	Part B
An unusual response	[ ] [ ]	An unusual response
A usual response	[ ] [ ]	A usual response
	II	
A changed agreement	[ ] [ ]	A changed agreement
The old agreement	[ ] [ ]	The old agreement
	III	
Alternatives	[ ] [ ]	Alternatives
No alternatives	[ ] [ ]	No alternatives
	IV	
Your understanding	[ ] [ ]	Your understanding
No understanding	[ ] [ ]	No understanding
	V	
To not blame you	[ ] [ ]	To not blame you
To blame you	[ ] [ ]	To blame you
	VI	
To initiate	[ ] [ ]	To initiate
To not initiate	[ ] [ ]	To not initiate
	VII	
To give feedback	[ ] [ ]	To give feedback
Not to give feedback	[ ] [ ]	Not to give feedback

CONSUMER FUTURE UPSET ANALYZER™

I am upset because you_____

I WANT:		I WILL REALLY GET:

Part A	I	Part B
An unusual response	[ ] [ ]	An unusual response
A usual response	[ ] [ ]	A usual response
	II	
A changed agreement	[ ] [ ]	A changed agreement
The old agreement	[ ] [ ]	The old agreement
	III	
Alternatives	[ ] [ ]	Alternatives
No alternatives	[ ] [ ]	No alternatives
	IV	
Your understanding	[ ] [ ]	Your understanding
No understanding	[ ] [ ]	No understanding
	V	
To not blame you	[ ] [ ]	To not blame you
To blame you	[ ] [ ]	To blame you
	VI	
To initiate	[ ] [ ]	To initiate
To not initiate	[ ] [ ]	To not initiate
	VII	
To give feedback	[ ] [ ]	To give feedback
Not to give feedback	[ ] [ ]	Not to give feedback

SUPPLIER PAST UPSET ANALYZER™

I am upset because you_____

I EXPECTED TO:			IN REALITY:
Part A	**I**		**Part B**
Give an unusual response	[ ]	[ ]	You wanted an unusual response
Give my usual response	[ ]	[ ]	You wanted my usual response
	II		
Change our agreement	[ ]	[ ]	You wanted changes
Not change our agreement	[ ]	[ ]	You didn't want changes
	III		
Explore alternatives	[ ]	[ ]	You wanted alternatives
Not explore alternatives	[ ]	[ ]	You didn't want alternatives
	IV		
Understand your side	[ ]	[ ]	You wanted understanding
Not understand your side	[ ]	[ ]	You didn't want understanding
	V		
Not control	[ ]	[ ]	I didn't control
Control	[ ]	[ ]	I did control
	VI		
Be the initiator	[ ]	[ ]	I was the initiator
Not be the initiator	[ ]	[ ]	You were the initiator
	VII		
Get feedback	[ ]	[ ]	You gave feedback
not get feedback	[ ]	[ ]	You didn't give feedback

SUPPLIER FUTURE UPSET ANALYZER™

I am upset because you_____

I WANT TO:			I KNOW YOU WILL:
Part A	**I**		**Part B**
Give an unusual response	[ ]	[ ]	Want an unusual response
Give my usual response	[ ]	[ ]	Not want my usual response
	II		
Change our agreement	[ ]	[ ]	Want changes
Not change our agreement	[ ]	[ ]	Not want changes
	III		
Explore alternatives	[ ]	[ ]	Want alternatives
Not explore alternatives	[ ]	[ ]	Not want alternatives
	IV		
Understand your side	[ ]	[ ]	Want understanding
Not understand your side	[ ]	[ ]	Not want understanding
	V		
Not control	[ ]	[ ]	Not be controlled
Control	[ ]	[ ]	Be controlled
	VI		
Be the initiator	[ ]	[ ]	Not be the initiator
Not be the initiator	[ ]	[ ]	Be the initiator
	VII		
Get feedback	[ ]	[ ]	Give feedback
Not get feedback	[ ]	[ ]	Not give feedback

THE CAREER ANALYZER™

*How to tell if what you're doing now
is what you really want to be doing*

I WANT TO:				THE REALITY IS:
Part A				**Part B**
		1		
Create things to sell	[ ]		[ ]	I create things to sell
Sell what already exists	[ ]		[ ]	I sell what already exists
		2		
Call on people	[ ]		[ ]	I call on people
Have people come to me	[ ]		[ ]	People come to me
		3		
Make money	[ ]		[ ]	I make money
Express my talents	[ ]		[ ]	I express my talents
		4		
Work with people	[ ]		[ ]	Work with people
Work with things	[ ]		[ ]	Work with things
		5		
Be my own boss	[ ]		[ ]	I am my own boss
Work for someone else	[ ]		[ ]	I Work for someone else
		6		
Work under deadlines	[ ]		[ ]	I work under deadlines
Work at my own pace	[ ]		[ ]	I work at my own pace
		7		
Work on an incentive basis	[ ]		[ ]	I work on an incentive basis
Work for a salary	[ ]		[ ]	I work for a salary

THE CAREER ANALYZER™

How to tell if what you're doing now
is what you really want to be doing

<u>**I WANT TO:**</u>   <u>**THE REALITY IS:**</u>

Part A   **Part B**

1

Create things to sell   [ ]   [ ]   I create things to sell
Sell what already exists   [ ]   [ ]   I sell what already exists

2

Call on people   [ ]   [ ]   I call on people
Have people come to me   [ ]   [ ]   People come to me

3

Make money   [ ]   [ ]   I make money
Express my talents   [ ]   [ ]   I express my talents

4

Work with people   [ ]   [ ]   Work with people
Work with things   [ ]   [ ]   Work with things

5

Be my own boss   [ ]   [ ]   I am my own boss
Work for someone else   [ ]   [ ]   I Work for someone else

6

Work under deadlines   [ ]   [ ]   I work under deadlines
Work at my own pace   [ ]   [ ]   I work at my own pace

7

Work on an incentive basis   [ ]   [ ]   I work on an incentive basis
Work for a salary   [ ]   [ ]   I work for a salary

THE CAREER ANALYZER™

How to tell if what you're doing now
is what you really want to be doing

<table>
<tr><td colspan="2"><u>__I WANT TO:__</u></td><td></td><td></td><td colspan="2"><u>__THE REALITY IS:__</u></td></tr>
<tr><td colspan="2">**Part A**</td><td></td><td></td><td colspan="2">**Part B**</td></tr>
<tr><td></td><td></td><td colspan="2" align="center">**1**</td><td></td><td></td></tr>
<tr><td colspan="2">Create things to sell</td><td>[ ]</td><td>[ ]</td><td colspan="2">I create things to sell</td></tr>
<tr><td colspan="2">Sell what already exists</td><td>[ ]</td><td>[ ]</td><td colspan="2">I sell what already exists</td></tr>
<tr><td></td><td></td><td colspan="2" align="center">**2**</td><td></td><td></td></tr>
<tr><td colspan="2">Call on people</td><td>[ ]</td><td>[ ]</td><td colspan="2">I call on people</td></tr>
<tr><td colspan="2">Have people come to me</td><td>[ ]</td><td>[ ]</td><td colspan="2">People come to me</td></tr>
<tr><td></td><td></td><td colspan="2" align="center">**3**</td><td></td><td></td></tr>
<tr><td colspan="2">Make money</td><td>[ ]</td><td>[ ]</td><td colspan="2">I make money</td></tr>
<tr><td colspan="2">Express my talents</td><td>[ ]</td><td>[ ]</td><td colspan="2">I express my talents</td></tr>
<tr><td></td><td></td><td colspan="2" align="center">**4**</td><td></td><td></td></tr>
<tr><td colspan="2">Work with people</td><td>[ ]</td><td>[ ]</td><td colspan="2">Work with people</td></tr>
<tr><td colspan="2">Work with things</td><td>[ ]</td><td>[ ]</td><td colspan="2">Work with things</td></tr>
<tr><td></td><td></td><td colspan="2" align="center">**5**</td><td></td><td></td></tr>
<tr><td colspan="2">Be my own boss</td><td>[ ]</td><td>[ ]</td><td colspan="2">I am my own boss</td></tr>
<tr><td colspan="2">Work for someone else</td><td>[ ]</td><td>[ ]</td><td colspan="2">I Work for someone else</td></tr>
<tr><td></td><td></td><td colspan="2" align="center">**6**</td><td></td><td></td></tr>
<tr><td colspan="2">Work under deadlines</td><td>[ ]</td><td>[ ]</td><td colspan="2">I work under deadlines</td></tr>
<tr><td colspan="2">Work at my own pace</td><td>[ ]</td><td>[ ]</td><td colspan="2">I work at my own pace</td></tr>
<tr><td></td><td></td><td colspan="2" align="center">**7**</td><td></td><td></td></tr>
<tr><td colspan="2">Work on an incentive basis</td><td>[ ]</td><td>[ ]</td><td colspan="2">I work on an incentive basis</td></tr>
<tr><td colspan="2">Work for a salary</td><td>[ ]</td><td>[ ]</td><td colspan="2">I work for a salary</td></tr>
</table>

THE HOUSE BUYER'S ANALYZER™

PART A   **PART B**

I WANT: **I SAW:**

1. AGE

A NEW HOUSE	[ ]	[ ]	A NEW HOUSE
AN OLD HOUSE	[ ]	[ ]	AN OLD HOUSE

2. PRIVACY

PRIVACY/ACREAGE	[ ]	[ ]	PRIVACY/ACREAGE
DEVELOPMENT/COMMUNITY	[ ]	[ ]	DEVELOPMENT/COMMUNITY

3. STYLE

CUSTOM/INDIVIDUALITY	[ ]	[ ]	CUSTOM/INDIVIDUALITY
A BASIC DESIGN HOUSE	[ ]	[ ]	A BASIC DESIGN HOUSE

4. CONDITION

MOVE-IN CONDITION	[ ]	[ ]	MOVE-IN CONDITION
HANDYMAN/REMODELING	[ ]	[ ]	HANDYMAN/REMODELING

5. SPACE

OPEN INTERIOR SPACE	[ ]	[ ]	OPEN INTERIOR SPACE
WELL DEFINED ROOMS	[ ]	[ ]	WELL DEFINED ROOMS

6. TYPE

A MODERN HOUSE	[ ]	[ ]	A MODERN HOUSE
A TRADITIONAL HOUSE	[ ]	[ ]	A TRADITIONAL HOUSE

7. PRICE

AMENITIES & LUXURY	[ ]	[ ]	AMENITIES & LUXURY
PRICE AND/OR INVESTMENT	[ ]	[ ]	RICE AND/OR INVESTMENT

Date_____   MLS Listing number _____   Real estate agent _____

House address_____ Town _____

THE HOUSE BUYER'S ANALYZER™

PART A   **PART B**

I WANT: **I SAW:**

1. AGE

A NEW HOUSE   [ ]   [ ]   A NEW HOUSE
AN OLD HOUSE   [ ]   [ ]   AN OLD HOUSE

2. PRIVACY

PRIVACY/ACREAGE   [ ]   [ ]   PRIVACY/ACREAGE
DEVELOPMENT/COMMUNITY [ ]   [ ]   DEVELOPMENT/COMMUNITY

3. STYLE

CUSTOM/INDIVIDUALITY   [ ]   [ ]   CUSTOM/INDIVIDUALITY
A BASIC DESIGN HOUSE   [ ]   [ ]   A BASIC DESIGN HOUSE

4. CONDITION

MOVE-IN CONDITION   [ ]   [ ]   MOVE-IN CONDITION
HANDYMAN/REMODELING   [ ]   [ ]   HANDYMAN/REMODELING

5. SPACE

OPEN INTERIOR SPACE   [ ]   [ ]   OPEN INTERIOR SPACE
WELL DEFINED ROOMS   [ ]   [ ]   WELL DEFINED ROOMS

6. TYPE

A MODERN HOUSE   [ ]   [ ]   A MODERN HOUSE
A TRADITIONAL HOUSE   [ ]   [ ]   A TRADITIONAL HOUSE

7. PRICE

AMENITIES & LUXURY   [ ]   [ ]   AMENITIES & LUXURY
PRICE AND/OR INVESTMENT [ ]   [ ]   RICE AND/OR INVESTMENT

Date_____   **MLS Listing number** _____   **Real estate agent** _____

House address_____ **Town** _____

THE HOUSE BUYER'S ANALYZER™

PART A   **PART B**

I WANT: **I SAW:**

1. AGE

A NEW HOUSE   [ ]   [ ]   A NEW HOUSE
AN OLD HOUSE   [ ]   [ ]   AN OLD HOUSE

2. PRIVACY

PRIVACY/ACREAGE   [ ]   [ ]   PRIVACY/ACREAGE
DEVELOPMENT/COMMUNITY   [ ]   [ ]   DEVELOPMENT/COMMUNITY

3. STYLE

CUSTOM/INDIVIDUALITY   [ ]   [ ]   CUSTOM/INDIVIDUALITY
A BASIC DESIGN HOUSE   [ ]   [ ]   A BASIC DESIGN HOUSE

4. CONDITION

MOVE-IN CONDITION   [ ]   [ ]   MOVE-IN CONDITION
HANDYMAN/REMODELING   [ ]   [ ]   HANDYMAN/REMODELING

5. SPACE

OPEN INTERIOR SPACE   [ ]   [ ]   OPEN INTERIOR SPACE
WELL DEFINED ROOMS   [ ]   [ ]   WELL DEFINED ROOMS

6. TYPE

A MODERN HOUSE   [ ]   [ ]   A MODERN HOUSE
A TRADITIONAL HOUSE   [ ]   [ ]   A TRADITIONAL HOUSE

7. PRICE

AMENITIES & LUXURY   [ ]   [ ]   AMENITIES & LUXURY
PRICE AND/OR INVESTMENT [ ]   [ ]   RICE AND/OR INVESTMENT

Date_____   **MLS Listing number** _____   **Real estate agent** _____

House address_____ **Town** _____

THE INTERVIEW ANALYZER™

I want someone who: **In reality this person:**

Part A   **Part B**

1

Responds in an unusual manner   [ ]   [ ]   Responds in an unusual manner
Responds in a usual manner   [ ]   [ ]   Responds in a usual manner

2

Adapts to changes   [ ]   [ ]   Adapts to changes
Sticks to the rules   [ ]   [ ]   Sticks to the rules

3

Looks for alternatives   [ ]   [ ]   Looks for alternatives
Follows instructions   [ ]   [ ]   Follows instructions

4

Is people oriented   [ ]   [ ]   Is people oriented
Is task oriented   [ ]   [ ]   Is task oriented

5

Lets the results speak for itself [ ]   [ ]   Lets the results speak for itself
Proves each point   [ ]   [ ]   Proves each point

6

Sets own priorities   [ ]   [ ]   Sets own priorities
Follows the schedules   [ ]   [ ]   Follows the schedules

7

Discusses issues   [ ]   [ ]   Discusses issues
Accepts conditions   [ ]   [ ]   Accepts conditions

Applicant's name_____ **Date**_____

Brief job description_____

Comments_____

Interviewer's name_____

THE INTERVIEW ANALYZER™

I want someone who: **In reality this person:**

Part A   **Part B**

1

Responds in an unusual manner   [   ]   [   ]   Responds in an unusual manner
Responds in a usual manner   [   ]   [   ]   Responds in a usual manner

2

Adapts to changes   [   ]   [   ]   Adapts to changes
Sticks to the rules   [   ]   [   ]   Sticks to the rules

3

Looks for alternatives   [   ]   [   ]   Looks for alternatives
Follows instructions   [   ]   [   ]   Follows instructions

4

Is people oriented   [   ]   [   ]   Is people oriented
Is task oriented   [   ]   [   ]   Is task oriented

5

Lets the results speak for itself [   ]   [   ]   Lets the results speak for itself
Proves each point   [   ]   [   ]   Proves each point

6

Sets own priorities   [   ]   [   ]   Sets own priorities
Follows the schedules   [   ]   [   ]   Follows the schedules

7

Discusses issues   [   ]   [   ]   Discusses issues
Accepts conditions   [   ]   [   ]   Accepts conditions

Applicant's name_____   **Date**_____

Brief job description_____

Comments_____

Interviewer's name_____

THE INTERVIEW ANALYZER™

I want someone who: **In reality this person:**

Part A   **Part B**

1

Responds in an unusual manner   [ ]   [ ]   Responds in an unusual manner
Responds in a usual manner   [ ]   [ ]   Responds in a usual manner

2

Adapts to changes   [ ]   [ ]   Adapts to changes
Sticks to the rules   [ ]   [ ]   Sticks to the rules

3

Looks for alternatives   [ ]   [ ]   Looks for alternatives
Follows instructions   [ ]   [ ]   Follows instructions

4

Is people oriented   [ ]   [ ]   Is people oriented
Is task oriented   [ ]   [ ]   Is task oriented

5

Lets the results speak for itself [ ] [ ]   Lets the results speak for itself
Proves each point   [ ]   [ ]   Proves each point

6

Sets own priorities   [ ]   [ ]   Sets own priorities
Follows the schedules   [ ]   [ ]   Follows the schedules

7

Discusses issues   [ ]   [ ]   Discusses issues
Accepts conditions   [ ]   [ ]   Accepts conditions

Applicant's name_____ **Date**_____

Brief job description_____

Comments_____

Interviewer's name_____

A COMPETITIVE ADVANTAGE™
What is your business known for?

I want the company to be known for:					Customers buy from us because we offer:

Part A   **Part B**

1

the fastest delivery   [ ]   [ ]   the fastest delivery
competitive delivery   [ ]   [ ]   competitive delivery

2

the lowest prices   [ ]   [ ]   the lowest prices
competitive prices   [ ]   [ ]   competitive prices

3

the widest variety   [ ]   [ ]   the widest variety
competitive variety   [ ]   [ ]   competitive variety

4

the most specialization   [ ]   [ ]   the most specialization
competitive specialization   [ ]   [ ]   competitive specialization

5

the best quality   [ ]   [ ]   the best quality
competitive quality   [ ]   ]]   competitive quality

6

most innovation   [ ]   [ ]   most innovation
competitive innovation   [ ]   [ ]   competitive innovation

7

the best service   [ ]   [ ]   the best service
competitive service   [ ]   ]]   competitive service

A COMPETITIVE ADVANTAGE™
What is your business known for?

I want the company to be known for:					Customers buy from us because we offer:
Part A					**Part B**

1

the fastest delivery	[ ]	[ ]	the fastest delivery
competitive delivery	[ ]	[ ]	competitive delivery

2

the lowest prices	[ ]	[ ]	the lowest prices
competitive prices	[ ]	[ ]	competitive prices

3

the widest variety	[ ]	[ ]	the widest variety
competitive variety	[ ]	[ ]	competitive variety

4

the most specialization	[ ]	[ ]	the most specialization
competitive specialization	[ ]	[ ]	competitive specialization

5

the best quality	[ ]	[ ]	the best quality
competitive quality	[ ]	]]	competitive quality

6

most innovation	[ ]	[ ]	most innovation
competitive innovation	[ ]	[ ]	competitive innovation

7

the best service	[ ]	[ ]	the best service
competitive service	[ ]	]]	competitive service

A COMPETITIVE ADVANTAGE™
What is your business known for?

I want the company to be known for:					Customers buy from us because we offer:
Part A					**Part B**

1

the fastest delivery	[ ]	[ ]	the fastest delivery
competitive delivery	[ ]	[ ]	competitive delivery

2

the lowest prices	[ ]	[ ]	the lowest prices
competitive prices	[ ]	[ ]	competitive prices

3

the widest variety	[ ]	[ ]	the widest variety
competitive variety	[ ]	[ ]	competitive variety

4

the most specialization	[ ]	[ ]	the most specialization
competitive specialization	[ ]	[ ]	competitive specialization

5

the best quality	[ ]	[ ]	the best quality
competitive quality	[ ]	]]	competitive quality

6

most innovation	[ ]	[ ]	most innovation
competitive innovation	[ ]	[ ]	competitive innovation

7

the best service	[ ]	[ ]	the best service
competitive service	[ ]	]]	competitive service

THE RELATIONSHIP ANALYZER™
A guide to improving your relationships

PART A

PART B

I need someone who:

This person:

1. Wisdom

Part A			Part B
Is spontaneous	[ ]	[ ]	Is spontaneous
Is predictable	[ ]	[ ]	Is predictable

2. Perception

Always keeps agreements	[ ]	[ ]	Always keeps agreements
Allows agreements to change	[ ]	[ ]	Allows agreements to change

3. Communication

Offers alternatives	[ ]	[ ]	Offers alternatives
Does not offer alternatives	[ ]	[ ]	Does not offer alternatives

4. Heart

Is understanding	[ ]	[ ]	Is understanding
Is objective	[ ]	[ ]	Is objective

5. Power

Does not control	[ ]	[ ]	Does not control
Controls	[ ]	[ ]	Controls

6. Pleasure

Initiates	[ ]	[ ]	Initiates
Does not initiate	[ ]	[ ]	Does not initiate

7. Security

Gives feedback	[ ]	[ ]	Gives feedback
Does not give feedback	[ ]	[ ]	Does not give feedback

THE RELATIONSHIP ANALYZER™
A guide to improving your relationships

PART A				**PART B**
I need someone who:				**This person:**

1. Wisdom

Is spontaneous	[ ]		[ ]	Is spontaneous
Is predictable	[ ]		[ ]	Is predictable

2. Perception

Always keeps agreements	[ ]		[ ]	Always keeps agreements
Allows agreements to change	[ ]		[ ]	Allows agreements to change

3. Communication

Offers alternatives	[ ]		[ ]	Offers alternatives
Does not offer alternatives	[ ]		[ ]	Does not offer alternatives

4. Heart

Is understanding	[ ]		[ ]	Is understanding
Is objective	[ ]		[ ]	Is objective

5. Power

Does not control	[ ]		[ ]	Does not control
Controls	[ ]		[ ]	Controls

6. Pleasure

Initiates	[ ]		[ ]	Initiates
Does not initiate	[ ]		[ ]	Does not initiate

7. Security

Gives feedback	[ ]		[ ]	Gives feedback
Does not give feedback	[ ]		[ ]	Does not give feedback

THE RELATIONSHIP ANALYZER™
A guide to improving your relationships

PART A   **PART B**

I need someone who: **This person:**

1. Wisdom

| Is spontaneous | [ ] | [ ] | Is spontaneous |
| Is predictable | [ ] | [ ] | Is predictable |

2. Perception

| Always keeps agreements | [ ] | [ ] | Always keeps agreements |
| Allows agreements to change | [ ] | [ ] | Allows agreements to change |

3. Communication

| Offers alternatives | [ ] | [ ] | Offers alternatives |
| Does not offer alternatives | [ ] | [ ] | Does not offer alternatives |

4. Heart

| Is understanding | [ ] | [ ] | Is understanding |
| Is objective | [ ] | [ ] | Is objective |

5. Power

| Does not control | [ ] | [ ] | Does not control |
| Controls | [ ] | [ ] | Controls |

6. Pleasure

| Initiates | [ ] | [ ] | Initiates |
| Does not initiate | [ ] | [ ] | Does not initiate |

7. Security

| Gives feedback | [ ] | [ ] | Gives feedback |
| Does not give feedback | [ ] | [ ] | Does not give feedback |

Printed in the United States
by Baker & Taylor Publisher Services